LACEY SILKS

To my first sexy boss who will never read this: you gave me the
idea for this book.

"I watched her beautiful body give into my need. On my bed. In my home. And it was everything I never expected."
~ Tristan Silver, Silver's Pawn

FROM THE AUTHOR

I originally wrote Layers Deep in 2013. While the novel was one of my bestselling novels, the story needed improvement and soon enough evolved into a new story line with a male point of view and deeper connections. Thus came the birth of Silver's Pawn. I hope you enjoy Allie and Tristan's suspenseful adventure. The Silver Family Saga guarantees laughter, love and sexy times ;) (because Tristan and Allie can't get their hands off each other).

She's the pawn I break and the strength I never expected.

Allie Green, rookie cop, held the key to solving my case. My dangerously irresistible employee harbored no fear of the mafia, drank like a fish, and swore like a sailor, as she fought the demons from her troubled past. So I crossed the line a boss should never cross. Multiple times.
And I held no regrets until I used Allie as a pawn—and the woman I hadn't expected to love fell into enemy hands.

He has the information I need and the body I crave.
Tristan Silver knew what he wanted when he hired me. Or so he thought. I yielded to his desires because my billionaire boss had the resources I needed and the distractions I couldn't resist. As vengeance boiled in my veins, heat throbbed everywhere else.
So I used him. Multiple times.
Until I failed at the job he'd hired me to do, and our scorching romance spilled its secrets like blood.

Silver's Pawn is the third novel in the *Silver Brothers Securities Family Saga*. Intended for mature audiences.

I stood in the middle of 5th Avenue as the city's nightlife and all its thugs awakened. The intersection lights changed, and cars passed me on both sides. Spotlights lit up the sky on my right, where luxury cars were parked along the curb in front of Kendra's thriving nightclub. The crowd in line shuffled forward. If she had been here, my client would have been happy, and Silver Securities would have had no problems. The problem was, she wasn't here.

On my left, the charred ruins of Club Forever lent a burned stench to the air. Obviously, nothing lasted forever. We'd intended for the abandoned property to solve our problems; instead, the purchase magnified them. A flashlight beam cut through the darkness in a broken window, and my focus shifted to the front door of an adjacent hotel, where a girl stepped out onto the sidewalk. A john followed her. The couple slipped into a black SUV, and my insides twisted. If it hadn't been for the failed bust and the fire, we would have shut down the cartel. But we didn't. Hartley had his security change names and locations. On top of that, they had kidnapped our client.

The flashlight shone again on the lower floor. I waited for a clearing on the road and hurried across the street. I pushed open the side door and stepped into the shadows. Inside, a distant echo of noises carried through. I followed the sound down the stairs to the basement, where the fire hadn't damaged the building.

I reached the lowest step. I followed a shared stairwell to the basement, which connected to the hotel. The voices became clearer, except they weren't really talking. The deep moans, heavy sighs, and uncontrolled breathing could only mean one thing around here: an orgy. I moved from beyond the shadows. The handful of naked people in the middle of a candlelit room completed a jigsaw puzzle I had no intention of solving.

What the fuck?

They lay on scattered blankets across the old couches and floor, all somehow connected. I opened my mouth to get the crowd moving, but closed it just as quick when I saw her. Dressed in a cop's uniform, she was standing across the room, staring at the act. Her drawn gun rested at the side of her strong thigh as she watched them in wonder. She licked her parted lips. Her breaths deepened and became heavier as she took a step forward.

What the hell are you doing? I shook my head in disbelief.

She bit that lower lip and leaned her shoulder against a wall. She switched her crossed legs in the process and adjusted her crotch.

My mouth curved. She looked too young to be a cop from a distance. And she was definitely too small. Too vulnerable.

Further back, something was creeping in the shadows. Yet she remained still, unaware of the approaching danger, leaving me with no choice.

"Behind you!" I stepped out into the faint light, pointing her way.

Startled, her head flew up and her eyes grew wide. She whipped her body around on instinct, but the creep in the shadows had disappeared.

"This party is over! Get dressed and get out!" I called out.

The cop spun around once more and paced forward with her gun held forward, pointing the weapon in random directions.

"This is the police. Nobody move!"

The orgy scattered. They all grabbed whatever clothes they could find within reach and ran.

"Don't move!" she yelled out.

As expected, no one listened, and I wasn't about to stop them, either. I needed the place to clear. Scar Wagner was starting renovations next week. The posh club would be the perfect lure for perverted predators.

"Get out of here!" I yelled, heading across the room to the cop.

"Hey, you!" She pointed the gun at me. "What do you think you're doing?"

"I'm saving you from embarrassment."

"They're getting away!"

She hurried after the last one, but I was there, so her attention turned my way. I grabbed her arm, disarmed her, and drew her to my body, then spun around before I pushed her face forward, right against that wall. She yelped out in the process. I pressed my body hard against hers, constricting her.

"Let me go." She writhed in my grip.

I had to hand it to her; she was definitely strong and feisty.

"I'm gonna have you arrested for this!"

Her lips parted, and she looked back over her shoulder, catching my gaze. The patch of moonlight that snuck in between burned boards from above reflected in her cat-like eyes. It was then that I noticed her true beauty – her caring eyes, pointy nose, and freckles. She was the most gorgeous woman I'd seen in a long time. I inhaled her scent. She must have had wrapped her auburn hair in a hurry, before it dried, which resulted in a magnified aroma of lavender and straw-berries.

"Your dick is against my ass," she growled. Little did she know, to my dick, her noises translated as an invitation. The challenge in her tone added an extra spice to the mix, and my mind flew straight to the gutter. It had been a while since someone this young had held my attention for longer than a blink. As much as the idea of having her fight her way out of my grip turned me on right now, consent wasn't up for negoti-ation. I tightened my grip around her and shrugged. "So? You're messing up my game."

Scar Wagner had called earlier and told me we had visitors across the street. While it was unlikely Martinez would show up, I couldn't chance he would.

"Fuck your game! You've just assaulted a police officer! Step away so I can do my fucking job and make an arrest!" Her anger vibrated through my body, and I liked it. "Unless you're in on this?"

I laughed, and since everyone else had left, I let her go. Another outburst of hers and I'd be the one bursting.

"The only person who should be arrested right now is you," I said.

"Wait – let me guess. Because I'm absolutely sinful?" She rolled her eyes.

"I was going to say because you're trespassing."

The certainty on her face faded. She looked me over, swal-lowed hard, and laughed back in a challenge, pretending she didn't recognize me. I liked her keeping some cards to herself even more. I had to hand it to her; she did a decent job.

"Is my uniform not enough for you to notice who I am? Oh, wait, of course not. It's because I'm a woman, isn't it? Why would you notice anything else about me?"

"That's sarcasm, right? It's cute, but you really are trespassing. Check the records. This is private property, and I presume you don't have a warrant."

She frowned. "If that's so, you're trespassing as well."

I held my stance.

"Am I supposed to let these... these..." Her cheeks flushed red as she pointed to the spot where an orgy had played out moments earlier. "... these scoundrels run?"

"They looked more like swingers to me."

"Argh... that's even grosser."

"For what it's worth, this place will be undergoing renovations soon."

"Wonderful. Another club on the same street. More places to sell drugs and bodies." She paused, scanned me over, and froze. "I can't believe you let them get away. Did you know they used to run a swingers' club down here?"

Unfortunately, that wasn't the only club they ran.

"You would have gotten nothing out of those kids," I told her. "They were acting out fantasies they heard about the brothel, and they're not the people you should be looking for."

Her forehead creased. "Where's your ID? What are you doing here?"

She slid the gun back inside its holster and crossed her arms over her chest. She'd interrupted my scouting; that was what I was doing here. Silvers used to own the building in partnership with the Hartley's. This place had given birth to a lifelong lie, and we'd worked for years to lure all the wrong people into our trap. Scar Wagner planned to clean up the place and the fire on the one night he closed was a warning.

I looked around the dark room. Flipped cushions, torn fabric, broken lights, and cigarette butts littered the ground. Cuffs, whips, chains, and dildos hung on a sectioned wall spared by the fire.

"Sex-trafficking, slavery, blackmail, and auctions. Bodies

sold like chattel," I said under my breath. "That's what went on here. Girls like you used to meet their hell in this basement."

"Girls like me?"

"You know – pretty, young, and delicate. Are you even old enough to be a cop?" I leaned in closer to her face. In hindsight, that was a mistake because her scent made my head spin. "You look too young to be a police officer."

"I have good genes. What do you know about the auctions?" she asked.

She definitely had good genes, but did she seriously not know who I was?

Impossible.

Maybe it was better this way? My name came with too many caveats and broken bridges.

"I know everything about them and not enough." I lowered my shoulders. "My name is Tristan Silver. My buddy takes care of this place. I saw flashlights in the windows. We've had reports of loitering, so I came to check it out."

She stilled, which told me she definitely knew who I was. I didn't partake in name-dropping often, but the stunned yet relieved look on her face was worth it. I had yet to determine the reason for her relief, but the last thing I wanted was to be seen here, standing with a cop.

"Of Silver Securities?" She stepped closer for a better look.

"Yeah, that one."

"I've heard of you." She swallowed hard and shifted from one foot to the other. "It looks like the… scoundrels left."

I chuckled… *scoundrels.* If scoundrels were my only problem, I'd be a free man. If they were the issue, Kendra would be here, and I wouldn't have a missing client.

"Sorry." I cleared my throat. "That wasn't funny."

"If you're Silver, then you know something more about this place."

"A cartel kidnapped my friend last week," I said. "She owns

the place across the street, and they'll sell her at an auction if I don't find her. "

"An auction? Like sex-trafficking? How do you even find out about those?" Her voice quivered.

"Years of intel. Connections."

"I've heard about Silver. I mean, everyone's heard. I'm sorry about your friend. Have you filed a missing person's report?"

I shook my head.

"You should call the police. They have resources."

I laughed. "The police?"

She was right about one thing: the police had a resource all right, and their best resource was me.

"You don't think we can do our job?" Her brows lifted.

I looked her over from the bottom up. Her muscled thighs and wider shoulders showed strength underneath the uniform. Combined with her delicate lips and doe eyes, the officer could definitely do her job.

"That's not what I'm saying."

"But you won't report a missing person?"

I wouldn't waste any more time in this dump. Scar would clean up the mess tomorrow, and I was nowhere near finding Kendra.

"The police can't help." I glanced at her badge. "Stay away from this place, officer... Green."

Green... Green... Green... Why does that name sound familiar?

Her brows narrowed. I turned to leave, but she grasped my wrist.

"Why stay away?"

I spun back around to face her and lowered my voice. "You shouldn't hang around dark basements because evil men come here to do bad things to girls who don't listen."

She appeared unfazed and tilted her head to the side. "Sounds to me like this is exactly where I should be. You know, because I'm a fucking cop and all!"

She was undoubtedly… something.

"Your name wouldn't be Allie, would it?" I swallowed hard and felt my dick react to the realization. She wasn't supposed to be this delicate and perfect.

"Yes. I'm Allie Green. How did you know?"

Well, well… what were the chances?

Tristan Silver walked into the auditorium, and the hum of whispers faded into silence. I focused my gaze on the man who stole all attention and stopped myself mid-breath. He crossed the room in slow motion, and my knees softened. It had been three days since we'd stood face to face, breath to breath, counting down the time temptation would win. When he held me at the club that night, I knew I was in trouble. Big trouble. And from the few minutes I'd spent with the bodyguard billionaire, I knew he was the one I'd been looking for. could help me. But I hadn't expected Mr. Tristan Silver to flip my life upside down. Not that fast. Those things only happened in fairy tales, and my life was certainly not that.

"Well, well, well. Look who Satan dragged in." Laura, my best friend and partner in most crimes, stared at the podium where our Sergeant was struggling to raise the mike to suit Mr. Silver's height.

The three long days and two sleepless nights since I'd run into the billionaire mogul at the burned club dragged as I waited to visit my mother. She'd likely look for a new place this time because it had been a while since her last move. To top off my great luck, my best friend's baby was switching to solids, and, well… it wasn't easy living with a one-year-old and a stubborn single mother.

"Any chance you're visiting your parents this weekend?"

"Hath hell frozen over?" she snorted.

A few colleagues chuckled as the top part of the microphone rod slipped out of the bottom and the Sergeant became a baton-twirling prelude to today's weird day. Sergeant Dwayne regained his balance and held out the mike to our guest speaker, who lifted his hand in a tactful rejection.

Of course Tristan Silver didn't need a mike to command the room.

"You're going to have to tell them soon that they're grandparents."

"I managed this long, I can make it until Foxy graduates."

I chuckled.

"Why are you asking?" Her head flew to the front, then back to me again.

"Sleep. I need sleep." I rubbed my eyes.

Laura's baby hadn't exactly been planned, but now that Fox was here, he was the best godson I could imagine. He was the best surprise Laura had ever received. My best friend made the perfect mom. Foxy's cute giggles and dimpled cheeks made the sleepless nights worth it.

Laura's attention remained on Mr. Silver. "You're going to nail him, aren't you?"

"Who? Him? What? No, it's not like that."

It was totally like that. While I recognized Tristan Silver as a potential employer with access to secretive records, I also knew that he wasn't the traditional employer. So if an opportunity to get the information I sought presented itself, who was I to challenge it?

"Right. The toilet clogged again. Fox tried to flush a duck."

"Eww, why didn't you get it out?"

She twirled a pen between her fingers and looked out into

space. "I have this problem called *time management with a one-year-old.* I tried the plunger, but it didn't work. Thought I should let you know before the weekend."

"Thanks. Hopefully we can find a plumber before Monday."

Tristan Silver removed his suit jacket and hung it over the back of a chair. He rolled the sleeves of his white crisp shirt, and an image of me pulling the fabric apart to reveal his chest flashed in my mind.

"How are we supposed to concentrate now?" Laura whispered.

"I don't know."

"I didn't know you went for older men."

"Only the ones who age like fine wine. Close your mouth." My gaze remained on the GQ cover-worthy stud. He crossed the floor in his sleek, tailor-made suit, minus the jacket, like Adonis. Yeah, I'd done my homework. Mister *You shouldn't hang around in dark basements* was one of the most important billionaires in the country. Not that google was any help when I cross-referenced the SS logo on his cuffs. Silver Securities ensured the family's private lives remained protected.

A giggle echoed through the room, and his cheek brightened, complementing his tan. A group of officers in the front row covered their mouths.

Silver's calculated steps lengthened with confidence. He stopped by the Sergeant's desk, pulled his hands behind his back, and spread his legs ever so slightly apart, facing the fully seated lecture hall. I swallowed hard. As he shifted his feet, the inseam of his pants touched a curve underneath his zipper.

Oh my.

"I don't think that's a gun in his pocket," Laura whispered from the side.

It sure wasn't. I squeezed my knees together as warmth swooshed through my stomach. A memory of his arms around me, pressing me against that basement wall, slipped through my mind.

Stop it!

I pushed the hormones back into their cave. The opportunity mother always talked about was here, and it was time to take the bull's horn. Or was it take the bull by his horn? It didn't matter. I'd seen plenty bulls at our farm, and I would never go near one; but my mother was one of the smartest women in the world, so the least I could do was concentrate on Tristan Silver.

"This is Mr. Silver from Silver Securities." Sergeant Dwayne cleared his voice to camouflage his nerves. It was a rare sight to see him tense up like that. I'd thought about this moment for a long time, but now that it was here, I too didn't know how to act, so I joined the rest of the squad in a long stare at the life-sized Ken doll as Silver slowly began scanning the seats, starting at the front row.

Sergeant Dwayne took Mr. Silver's indifference as an invitation to continue. "If you live in New York, you've heard of Silver Securities. The application on your desk is for a vacant position at this company, who rarely hires outside of the family. This is an opportunity to put your skills to the test, people."

Dwayne's lifted tone didn't phase Silver. In fact, the man appeared displeased, but he continued scanning the seats, from one officer to another, as if he were looking for someone in particular.

Papers ruffled, and everyone's heads lowered to the application. I kept my attention on Silver.

Of course I had heard of Silver Securities. Everyone had heard of Silver Securities. The family-owned leading investigations and private security firm could be my ticket to freedom. A job at Silver Securities would give me the intelligence I'd been looking for. All access to supposedly deleted government data, which contained locations of fucking ex-cops who ruined mothers, daughters, and families. This job could bring my mother the justice she'd never received.

But I'd always pictured the owner as a man in his sixties with gray hair, or at least sporting a respectable toupee. Tristan Silver's hair had its own personality, lifting lightly to the air-conditioning breeze. The family kept out of the spotlight, and their rare appearances at fundraisers without cameras allowed for almost unheard-of privacy. With tools and the power of influence at their disposal, secrets could disappear forever.

Silver lifted his gaze to the next row, the second below me. I took in his tense posture. The outlines underneath his suit suggested a yummy physique. By which I meant, strong. He definitely worked out, likely with a personal trainer who catered to every beautiful muscle sculpting his body, hugged by that tailored suit.

"Drool, Allie. Wipe the drool off your face," Laura elbowed me in the ribcage for the third time.

I pulled my sleeve across my mouth just as his gaze reached the row below me. A sharp inhale from nerves stung my lungs. Most in the room were still busy with the application: heads down and pens gripped. They scribbled, while I kept still. Silver kept me still. What the hell was happening to me? My breath locked in my lungs and then released at the same time he exhaled. His gaze held steady as he scanned across the rows, crossing from one seat to another. A slight twitch pulsed on the side of his neck. He slid a finger between his throat and the tight shirt, releasing the top button. The sleek suit couldn't be the attire of his choice. As comfortable as Silver wanted to appear, he stood out like a drop of black oil in white milk.

Unexpected heat flowed up my body as I pictured him in shorts, perhaps jeans, and a T-shirt. The corner of my mouth twitched as one by one, his clothes came off while I undressed him in my mind. Silver's skin boasted a natural tan tone. Though summer had passed a few weeks ago, a fresh layer of sun-kissed glow complemented his piercing hazel eyes. I thought it would be easier to look at him if I imagined he was naked, but it wasn't. His toned physique screamed *private trainer* and *spare time*. The further my thoughts drifted away from reality, the harder my stomach tightened into a double knot, and my heart was beating like it was midnight and I was about to book a thief. I heaved in a breath and joined Silver's unbroken stare over each person, awaiting my turn and counting down the seconds before my Christmas morning came on a Monday night in September.

A voice of reason mumbled somewhere in the back of my head. My best friend was sitting beside me, but I couldn't hear a word she'd said. Everyone else focused on the applications, while I just stared. They scribbled and embellished accomplishments in a quest for a job which Silver likely had already filled.

His eyes finally came to rest on mine. He paused and held my gaze. For a moment, I thought I'd let my imagination go wild, but as his stare bore deeper into mine, I realized Silver was here for a different reason. Me.

Shit. Shit. Shit!

I lowered my head as he pointed me out to the Sergeant. Everyone turned around at the same time, and I quickly lowered my head like a panicked kid caught stealing gum. The one offense I'd racked up before following in my father's footsteps as a cop would haunt me to my grave.

Laura's elbow in my ribs brought me back, and I looked up again. The moment between us had already passed. Silver turned his back to the class, whispered something to the Sergeant, and left.

"Aren't you going to apply?" My roommate and the bestie I more often had a reason to kill than live with elbowed me again.

"Stop that. You know I bruise easily."

Silver didn't strike me as the pen and paper or application type of guy. From my research, he was more hands on, and I would not waste an opportunity by filling out paperwork.

"There's not a woman or man in this room who wouldn't like to work for that piece of meat."

Silver was a distraction I couldn't afford, yet he had the information I couldn't get elsewhere.

"Was my gawk that obvious?" Laura's instinct made her a brilliant partner. Sometimes she was too smart for her own good, and the same instincts that made her a great cop and a mother made her a stubborn ass. For instance, I'd tried to persuade her to tell the baby's father about Foxy, but Laura was convinced he didn't want children.

"Do you think it's a coincidence that you ran into his cousin a few weeks back? At that insurance company?" Laura's voice hitched and her cheeks flushed red.

"What's the matter?" I asked.

"Nothing." She shook her head.

"Liar."

"Well, nothing of importance for now. So? What do you think?"

"I don't believe in coincidences," I whispered. I knew why I needed him, but I didn't know why he needed me. I hadn't stopped thinking about him since the night we met at the burned club.

His hazel eyes gave nothing away. Most of our lecture hall drooled at the opportunity to work with Silver. I drooled to work with *him*, underneath *him* and over *him*.

All over him.

"Earth to Allie." Laura elbowed me for the third time. At least the nudge was gentler, but that was probably because my rib ached so much already I stopped telling the difference three jabs ago. Either that or the acetaminophen I took earlier had begun working.

My head flew up as Silver stepped back inside the auditorium. My pen slipped out of my grip and bounced on the edge of my desk. The echo was enough to draw his attention, and our gazes locked. His secretive stare held mine as he removed his jacket from a chair and put it back on.

I tilted my head.

Why me? What position is he hiring for?

He turned around and headed for the door again. An officer caught Silver in the doorway. They shook hands and took their conversation out into the hall.

I grabbed the application, crumpled the paper, and stuffed it in a pocket.

"You're not applying?" Laura asked.

I would, but not yet. I wasn't ready. I'd make the move once I knew my mother was safe.

Frustration played with my head and heart for the rest of that day and the day after. Silver haunted me until he found me drowning in a delicious bottle of tequila. That was the night I realized this man could pawn my heart, and I'd let him, because I needed his help more than he needed mine.

Chapter 3

Tristan

"**I**s Silver Securities not good enough for you?" I leaned against the bar. Allie Green froze in her seat and shut her eyes tight like I had caught her breaking the law. Her neck shrank like a turtle's before she composed herself.

She threw her head back, downing a shot of tequila like she wanted to drown. She looked even hotter in civilian clothes.

Just... perfect.

Silver Securities' tactic to pawn women wasn't my favorite, but it worked. It was our best chance to get our foot in the door and save Kendra.

"Why do you say that?" She turned on her stool toward me. Her knee bumped against mine and ended up between my legs. A coy smile lifted the corner of her mouth. Her balance was off; her body swaying from side to side.

"You haven't applied yet. I hope you're not driving." I removed my leather jacket and set it over the chair.

"And you care because?" The bravado flowed out on her tequila breath. The half-empty bottle waited on the bar beside her.

"Because accidents happen when you least expect them, and drunk drivers kill people."

She stilled and tried reading my face. But years of practice had taught me to hide my scars well.

"Are you my next mistake?" she asked, without missing a beat. She could definitely hold her liquor. Hiring Allie Green wasn't supposed to be this difficult. She wasn't supposed be this intriguing and playful. Young blood ran through her like a vibrant mountain spring. I'd expected... well, definitely someone not this: mouthy, strong, and beautiful. But if I played my cards right, she could be the right mistake.

She waved her hand and nearly fell off her seat. "Don't worry, Silver. I'll call a cab."

"Well, at least you know who I am."

She chuckled and poured herself another shot. I swallowed hard as she threw back the liquor, then pressed her lips against a lemon slice.

"Do you swallow all your shots in one gulp?" I closed the gap between my knees, trapping her leg, and leaned in.

She smirked, like she'd been preparing to play my game her entire life, but didn't know how to get to the finish line.

What if I were her finish line?

I shook off the unexpected thought. Her witty mouth brought my attention back to her liquor-swollen lips when she replied, "Yes, I always swallow well."

Like I hoped—mouthy and confident. Maybe she knew how to get to that finish line after all. I may have pre-judged the petite brunette who'd booked Gabriel Silver a few weeks back. She didn't recognize him either, which meant Allie lived under a rock or we were that good. Security and intelligence had its advantages. Staying clear of social media and everything this world had forgotten about; civility and humanity flowed in the Silver blood.

"Why didn't you apply for the position at Silver Securities?" I asked.

She bit her lip and fluttered her lashes, turning on every

charm in the book. Her cheeks tinted with a rosy shade, and I nodded to the barman to remove the bottle.

"You want me to be honest or give you a crappy answer? Actually, my honest answer is crappy." She swayed from side to side. "I'm damaged."

I opened my mouth to object, but she continued. "I'm a strike. You know, like in baseball."

"You like baseball?"

"No, but I know the rules. I played in grade school, but I remember rules. Rules are in my blood."

"Okay," I laughed. Patience wasn't my strength, but somehow I found all of it when I listened to her.

"My first strike was arresting Gabriel Silver. You know—your cousin and partner at Silver Securities?"

I held my poker face, which wasn't easy when listening to her.

"How would he feel if I worked for you?"

"Gabriel Silver is the one who gave me your name," I told her.

"What?"

"He won't be an issue. We work from different continents. And once you hear my arguments—"

"The second strike was when I broke every rule the night we met—you know, in that basement. I should have arrested you, but I didn't. Why would you want to hire a rookie cop who'd failed?"

She reminded me of the scene of naked bodies and the fact that she'd stood beyond the group, mesmerized. Sexy. Hot and wanton. But that group wasn't who we were after.

"Is that what you think the teenagers were doing in that basement? Because all I saw was a consensual orgy, and young adults doing what they do best: party."

She lifted her hand, holding two fingers up. I had a feeling nothing I said had registered with Allie.

"Number three." She changed the fingers she was holding up from two to four and finally settled on the right number. "You're too attractive. I mean, seriously. How do women go around not thinking '*Whoa*' when they look at all that?"

I coughed into my fist, clearing my throat. "Allie, believe it or not, you are the only woman who has had me this intrigued in a long time.

A very long time.

"I'm sure we can work together. I need you." She went to grab the tequila bottle and noticed it missing. "You cut me off? Seriously? Is that how you want to play?"

I growled, "I definitely want to play, Allie."

Shit. Had I lost my touch? "Allie, I need you sober. Fast."

"Aha! You need me sober to consent you to me and you."

"I need you sober because I want to hire you."

"But if you're my boss"—she scanned me from the bottom up and smiled in that drunken-gooey way—"my hot, older, and mature boss, that would be incest."

I cleared my throat to get rid of the snicker.

"Incest involves family members. If I'm your boss, you're my employee."

"Correct!" She made a chiming game noise looked around for the bottle again.

I sighed. "Why are you drinking, Allie?"

"It's a sad anniversary, and I don't like being sad," she pouted. Jesus, she looked even more innocent when she pouted. Her freckles popped and her eyes welled. She quickly brushed aside the threatening tear and shook off something horrid.

"Can I take you home?"

She shook her head. "Nope. Not home. I definitely can't go home. It's Thursday."

"Okay?"

"My roommate has this thing on Thursday nights with her

secret boyfriend, and the baby is with the sitter, which means I need to stay away until the sock comes off the doorknob, and with Laura, well, let's just say the sock never comes off the doorknob. At least, it used to be that way. Now it's just crying and crying and crying… all the time crying."

"You have a baby?"

"Not me, silly. My bestie. The sock now tells me to tiptoe because it's rare he sleeps through the night."

"Ah, the baby is away, and she's having a… sleepover? Is that the right way to put it?"

"I guess. Are you following me?" she asked out of nowhere.

I leaned against the back of the stool, having a better look at her petite frame. Could she really do this job?

"Observant. I did follow you."

"Why?"

"Because you didn't apply for the job. I need you Allie."

She mellowed in her seat and bit her lip. "Sorry. It's… my life is complicated."

"Everyone's life is complicated. Now are you going to apply, or do I have to beg you?"

A coy smile lifted the corner of her mouth. "I like begging. Not me begging. You begging."

Of course she would like that.

I pictured her on her knees, begging me. The image didn't sit well, so I shook it off. Begging would never work for a cop. Allie commanded and demanded, not begged.

When she motioned with her hand for the tequila bottle, I nodded to the barman to pour two shots.

"Let's do this the right way." She dragged a lemon wedge over her left hand, sprinkled salt on top, and waited for mine. I held out my hand. She pulled a trail of lemon juice over my hand and added the salt.

"Ready?" Her brows rose and slowly lowered. "To great partnerships?"

I lifted my shot to hers and clinked it. "I'll drink to that."

She drew my salty hand to her mouth and licked it. I got hard in an instant. I took her small head into mine and drew my tongue over her skin. She shivered. I tilted the glass at my lips, and the smooth liquor eased down my throat. I bit on the lemon to cut through the alcohol and then set the shot glass aside. When my gaze returned to her face, a stray drop lingered in the corner of her mouth. I wiped it away with my thumb and sucked it off my finger while she stared at me with her mouth half open. Her pursed lips compelled me to go to the place my dick already fantasized about, and it took all my strength not to crush my mouth to hers.

Instead, I cleared my throat and, like a coward, changed the subject to hiring her at Silver Securities. "There are better places to drink than this."

"Are you referring to your club Kissed?" She tilted her head to the side.

Right. Kissed. The epitome of my nightmares.

"No, but I see you've done your homework."

The family had agreed we'd all handle the club until we found Kendra. She was everyone's responsibility.

"I'm just that good at *everything* I do."

Allie's drunk flirting gave the conversation a genuine essence. It had been a long time since a woman had intrigued me as much as she did. Her youthful laughter took me back in time to when Simone had smiled like her and laughed like her. Except Simone was gone. While Silver Securities held a low profile to serve those in high places, our work came with plenty of dating obstacles and dangers. It was much easier to work than date.

"So, Green. Are you going to come work for me or not?"

"What position are you hiring for? I can't imagine Silver Securities lacking… you know… security."

The chances she would remember this conversation fell

with every count of tequila, and she'd had a lot, so I joked with partial truth, "I'm looking for a hooker."

Allie coughed and covered her mouth, mumbling, "A what?"

"I need a girl who attracts all the wrong guys. You seem like a perfect fit."

After all, she'd caught *my* attention.

"If that's a compliment, then it's a bad one. And for your information, I've never dated."

"Never?"

She shook her head. "Nope. No time. We moved a lot, and when you date, it's hard to hide. I mean… it's hard to hide when you date." She waved her hand in dismissal. "You know what I mean, right?"

"Right. And why do you need to hide?"

It hit me then I might not have done all the background research on Allie Green that I should have. But I would. After she booked Gabriel Silver and he recommended her, I knew she had to be special. Besides, she was one of the few who knew what Martinez looked like, and she definitely fit the part of the strong, beautiful, and conniving cutie I needed her to play. Maybe we'd need to change the conniving to submissive, but she was our best chance.

"You have a way with words, Mr. Silver." She giggled. "But if you work for me—"

"You mean if *you* work for *me*?"

"That's what I said. If you work for me, we can't have sex."

I closed in for the kill. "We should get the sex out of the way then before you work for me."

Except she was dunker than a sailor. As much as I wanted to, I preferred my women clearheaded. I sighed.

She slipped off her stool and leaned into my body with a drunken-sounding whisper. "That would work."

My hard dick pushed against her soft belly. Moments later, her knees buckled underneath her, and I caught her before she hit the floor. I thanked my boxing reflexes for the aid.

"Thanks. I'm not feeling too well."

No shit, Einstein.

"You're welcome. Come on. Let's get you home." I left a few bills on the bar, draped her arm over my shoulder, and held her around the waist for support, focusing on the front door.

"You're strong, Mr. Silver."

I caught the elastic slipping off her side braid just as she fluttered her naturally long lashes. The freckles sprinkled over her face and her eyes held me still. She had beautiful eyes: bright, full of wonder, and captivating, like a panther's.

"Thanks. You're... very... very..."

"Drunk?" she asked.

"I was going to say intriguing."

"You've already said that tonight."

For someone who mixed words in sentences and drank more than an average man, Allie's memory remained intact.

"I failed the interview, didn't I?" she asked out of nowhere.

"You failed nothing, Allie."

"So I'm hired?"

"Not yet. You'll quickly see that paperwork at Silver Securities is everything."

"I hate paperwork," she mumbled.

Not until she sobered and understood what she was signing. Not before I found control around her, like a proper boss. Breaking rules before then was one thing, but once she was one of the team, that was a line I wouldn't cross. Not as her boss.

I secured my arm around her waist and led her out the front door. A fall breeze swept by. It held a hint of frost and sobered the lungs. In the distance, lighting flew across the sky, illuminating Manhattan's skyscraper silhouette. A thundering roar followed. The ground shook underneath our soles, and

Allie looked up to the sky, eyes wide and mouth open. "I don't like thunder."

"Neither do I."

"But I like rain."

Me too.

It was easy to be around her unfiltered personality. I stepped towards my Bentley, parked at the curb, and secured her in the back seat. She grabbed my wrist before I closed the door. "I rarely do rides with strangers, but you're not a stranger."

"No, I'm not, Allie. I'm a friend."

She let go of my wrist. "Good."

I kept just under the speed limit all the way to her apartment. I parked and helped her to the front door.

"Good night, Allie." I leaned in and kissed her on the cheek. Her face tinted with a pinkish shade as I whispered, "Are you going to be okay?'

"Yes, thank you for the ride. I appreciate it."

"Anytime."

"Good night, Mr. Silver."

She lifted on her toes and placed a soft peck near the corner of my mouth, teasing me like the provocateur I needed her to be. The first drops of rain fell as soon as she stepped inside. I waited for the lock to click and hurried to my car. Once inside, the rain broke unforgivingly against the roof.

I sat in the car until the answer I didn't want to find appeared on the screen. Donald Wright, the ex-sheriff who'd assaulted Allie's mother, had ties to the Hartleys and Congress. I pressed my thumb to the phone and dialed my brother's line.

"Set up the trade. I've got Green."

Two days had passed since Tristan Silver drove me home. While my memory of the night he'd found me at a bar drowning my self-pity in a bottle of tequila was foggy, the approaching anniversary of the day a monster had changed my life was as clear as if it had happened yesterday. Halloween was just around the corner, and I was due for a trip to visit my mother. Not only that, I needed her blessing before I found Wright.

I stretched my arms out wide on my way to the bathroom and yawned. Foxy's toy squeaked underneath my foot, and I jumped up.

The moon shone through a slit in the curtains. While I regretted wasting a weekend on sobering up, the tequila had dulled the pain. The liquor drowned out the past, and for at least a moment I could pretend to be normal and happy and lost to Silver's hypnotizing… everything. From the sinking dimple to the crooked smile that twisted through a scar, he was definitely easy on the eye. His carefree hair at the bar, let loose after an uptight day. The white line over his upper lip was as sexy and dangerous as the rest of him. Keeping my mind sharp around him wouldn't be easy.

I shuffled my feet to the couch and pulled a blanket over my body. Laura returned from her night shift at four in the morning. I flicked on the lamp by the sofa as she was halfway crawling out of her pants.

"What the hell?" She tipped over to the floor. "What are you doing up?"

"I thought you had someone upstairs. You were working?"

"I pulled an extra shift. Saving money for Fox's third birthday."

"That's ten months from now."

"It's a big gift."

I was about to tell her how the greatest gift she could give the boy was to tell her parents they had become grandparents, but Laura was on a roll of keeping Fox all to herself. She was a wonderful mother, and her level of responsibility had skyrocketed since she'd had him. And she had the best babysitter in the world. Mrs. Brewer lived across the street and loved Foxy like a grandmother.

Her gaze flew to the half-empty bottle of tequila.

"Oh, for goodness' sake, I told you we should get more lemons. You ran out."

"I'm sure lemons are the least of my problems." I sighed. "You can't drink. Foxy needs breakfast."

"I have milk in the freezer, and I'll pump this out. I should start weaning him anyways."

She removed the elastic from her hair, and dampened locks fell down to her shoulders. The wet hair meant she'd had a rough night and had to use the showers at headquarters. Neither of us really enjoyed showering at work.

She plopped on the couch beside me and sank in. I covered her with a blanket.

"All right. What's your problem?" she asked. "Because I'm sure it can't beat mine."

"Wanna bet?"

She laughed. "Yeah. I do."

I turned my head towards her. "Oh, my God. You're serious."

This shouldn't have surprised me. She'd had an identical look of determination in her eyes when she told me she was pregnant and refused to tell the baby's daddy. In her defense, he wanted nothing to do with her.

"Of course I'm serious." She finally looked at me from the side. "There's this guy—"

"There's a guy? Oh, my God, what does that mean? I mean—"

"I don't know. It's so fucking complicated, I don't even know where to start."

"Start at the beginning." After a moment of silence, she finally looked up. Her shoulders lifted and fell in a shrug. "I don't know how I got into this mess. He's... he's just so... foxy. You know?"

"Foxy?"

"He has this silver beard—"

"You mean gray?"

She shook her head. "No. It's silver, and it matches his bright eyes. Holy crap, are those eyes ever piercing!"

"Wait a minute. There's only one man whose eyes got your heart pumping."

And it was the Foxy's daddy. I didn't know his name, but I knew it had to be someone from our trip to Colorado two years ago: someone Laura avoided like the plague, and I couldn't figure out why.

"It wasn't just his eyes that got my heart pumping." She snickered.

Our Christmas gig as nutcrackers at a luxury billionaire resort almost three years ago had ended with a surprise both in our bellies, though I'm not sure it was fair to compare her pregnancy to my food poisoning. I'd gone to the hospital while she had had a fling with a guest.

"Oh, Laura! You found him? You hooked up with the baby daddy?"

"No, not yet. It's… complicated. But I've seen him. I don't think he's looking for anything serious."

"Maybe he would be if you told him about Fox."

Her nostrils flared.

"Okay, I need a name. Any name."

"I think he only wants me for the good blow jobs."

"You gave him a blow job?"

"Not yet, but I'm sure he knows I could. This dude knows everything. He's a walking google machine."

Laura excelled at diverting conversations.

"Are you ever going to tell me what happened?"

She bit her lip. "I will. Not now, but soon. I promise."

My forehead creased. "Wait—it's not Tristan Silver, is it? Because I know he was there."

She tilted her head and looked at me like I was crazy. "It's not Tristan."

A rare moment of awkward silence passed between us. "So have you applied?"

"I wouldn't call spending an evening getting drunk at a bar with Silver applying."

"You what? This is great! It's what you wanted, isn't it?"

"Yes, but I didn't apply. I told you I was drunk. And stupid. I'm pretty sure I referred to him as McBoss."

"But he offered you a position, didn't he?"

"He may have." I squirmed, and she did the same. "You know what that means?"

Her face fell flat and composed. "Allie, your ghosts haunt your present. You need to either forget them or bury them where they belong. In the past."

Bury was exactly what I had in mind. The moment Wright's body settled six feet under, I could move on, and we would finally find justice and peace.

"I'm working on it."

And just as fast, Laura's mood flipped. "You mean to tell me the hottest, richest, sexiest, and most available bachelor in New York drove you home Friday night, and you didn't invite him in?"

"Why do you think he's available? There has to be something wrong with him."

"Girl, all I saw in that auditorium were all the right things."

"Yeah, but he's older. Thirty-seven."

"You did homework."

"A ten-second google search is not homework. I found nothing else."

"Thirty-seven is not old, Allie. Besides, you don't have to deal with immature bullshit. If a man doesn't know who he is by his thirties, and spends his time gaming in his mamma's basement, he'll never grow up."

Tristan Silver definitely had the kind of attractive mature confidence I hadn't considered before.

"I don't think he games. I was drunk, and he was nice. He walked me to the door, made sure I was okay, and told me he'd see me after I came back from Charleston. Apparently I have a big mouth when I drink."

"You're not wrong there."

"Tell me more about your date."

I was guessing it hadn't gone well because Laura was early and left Foxy at the babysitter's.

"My biggest challenge is keeping him away from the boobs. Once they leak, he'll know."

"He doesn't know you have a baby?"

"No, and he's not going to find out. At least, not yet."

"Well, it's going to be hard to keep up the ruse with those jugs." I pointed to her leaky breast.

She stuffed a round nipple pad inside her bra. "I don't know how my mother did it with seven of us. Kids come with a lot of caveats, don't they?"

"I hope that's rhetorical because I don't know. You could always ask her."

She laughed at me like I'd lost my mind.

"Hell hath not frozen over yet. Besides, I'm not ready for all the *I told you so's*." Laura double-checked her bra cup fit in the mirror. "He'd be a brilliant father."

"He doesn't want them?"

"I'm not so sure yet."

"You can start by telling him about Foxy and see how he reacts."

Her gaze skidded across the room. "That's more complicated than you think."

"Who is this guy?"

"Never mind."

I wished I could help Laura with her dating situation, which must have been difficult for a single mother. Heck, it was difficult without any kids.

"Maybe he's not the right guy?"

"No, he's just fine, all right. It's me this time. It's definitely me."

I sighed. What Laura needed was a break and her family's help, which she'd deny, of course. In the meantime, I was her support system and she was mine.

"I found Foxy's rubber fox toy in the toilet when I puked. It's in the garbage. I'll buy him a new one."

"Gross."

"I'm serious Laura. Something's off. I can feel it."

"So, take the job and find out what it is."

"If I take the job, it's to find Wright."

The Eggo Laura had popped into the toaster sprang up.

I yawned. "I'm going to the gym to work off some of this

tequila. I'm leaving for Charleston tomorrow morning. Kiss Foxy for me."

"You kiss Peg for me when you see her. Tell her I miss her."

Laura had become like a second daughter to my mother and the closest thing to a sister I would ever have. We'd met on the first day of police academy and never looked back.

"Of course I will. And Laura, you deserve to be happy. Don't settle for a gray beard and silver hair. Settle for a heart of gold."

"He's got a silver one, so hopefully that'll be enough. As for you, just take the damn job already. You need to do what you need to do. Don't let this opportunity go."

I relaxed back into the couch. "Thanks. I just wish Tristan Silver wasn't my boss, you know? Because the way this ends in my head, he won't be happy with me."

I'd put pen to paper as soon as I returned from Charleston. It was time to move my mom before the next phase of my plan. Laura covered my hand with hers, and I turned my head her way.

"You're a survivor. You do what you gotta do. And if it so happens you break his little heart, we'll go out man-scouting at Kissed, where we'll hang off thick biceps like monkeys. I need to hit the pillow." She pushed off the sofa and weaved between the furniture, heading for her bedroom.

"What time is Mrs. Brewer brining Foxy?"

"Too early. Enjoy your week off. Good night."

"Thanks, babe. Night."

I grabbed a probiotic shake and clicked on my laptop. The position for Silver Securities remained on the website, and I wondered whether Silver was serious about hiring me. I bit on the lightly burned waffle Laura had left. It tasted perfect and reminded me of what had to be done. Every morning, the stupid Eggo refocused my goals. Its charred aroma rekindled memories of that day thirteen years ago when David Wright had destroyed my family.

* * *

My mother was washing the dishes by the sink. Her hips swayed from side to side as she hummed under her breath. The last batch of waffle batter baked inside the grill, its aroma filling the house. I kissed Mother's cheek, then her growing belly, and hurried to school.

Mother always made waffles from scratch, but that morning after I returned for a book I'd left in the hallway would be the last time she'd make them. I snuck back inside the house and watched her joyfully continue with the chores. Mother rarely found time to herself, but she could definitely dance. The hard-working woman carried heavily in the front as she moved across the kitchen, her seven-month bump sticking out like she'd swallowed a watermelon. I didn't interrupt her. If I ran fast enough, I'd still make it to school on time. So I just watched her stolen moment of happiness. She put on a brave face for me every day, but failed to hide the worry in her eyes, feeding the ever-growing lines underneath. They weren't wrinkles; they were paths of worry, fine lines that deepened as she struggled to raise one daughter on her own and carry another one to term.

A shadow passed by the kitchen window. My breath hitched, my stomach gurgled, and goose bumps covered my arms. I knew nothing about instinct yet, but I wish I had. The knock on the back door echoed with insistency. Mother dried her hands on the apron, narrowed her brows, and wobbled to the garden opening.

"Hello, Dave. What brings you by this morning?"

Millie, our chocolate Lab, barked outside.

Mr. Wright was the town's chief of police. They'd known each other since grade school. He'd helped Mother sell Father's tools from the garage and back shed. We'd sold a lot of stuff the past few months and Mr. Wright bought most of the stuff. Mother saved enough for a crib and a new stroller for my baby sister-to-be. Still, I didn't like him. Mr. Wright was mean to the kids. He'd yell when we crossed his lawn, his breath always stank of cigars, and his house was the scariest at Halloween. Since Father passed, Wright had weaseled himself into our lives. The way he looked at Mother, like he wanted to grab her and choke her to death, gave me the shivers. I didn't understand it as instinct, but I remembered the feeling clearly. His obsession became weird enough that when he surprised Mother that morning, I stayed and hid.

His brows furrowed and his neck tensed. He tightened his fists and cracked his neck to the side, releasing pressure.

I flattened my back against the wall in the hallway.

Wright closed the back door. The lock's click sent shivers up my spine. I lowered myself to the floor, and lying down, I barely peeked from underneath where they wouldn't expect me. He rolled up his sleeves tauntingly slowly and stepped up to my mother. The sheriff leaned in to kiss her on the cheek, but she backed away. The kitchen island blocked her further, and he grabbed each side of her face so he could kiss her. She finally pulled away and warned him, "I'm expecting company, Dave. You should leave."

I slowly stood up and took a step back as if I were her, needing distance from this man.

"Who?" he asked.

"Barb's joining me for breakfast," she lied. Everyone knew the church secretary attended morning mass.

I opened the storage door under the staircase with care, slower than ever before, and I hid there. The cracks between the wooden boards revealed half the kitchen. My mother and Wright were out of view, but I heard everything. Unfortunately, sound carried through the space. I wish it hadn't, because mother's screams and pleas would haunt my dreams for the rest of my life.

"See, Peg, I just saw Barb go into church for morning mass.

It'll be an hour before she comes out of there. You know Father Fray and his long sermons, don't you?"

"Perhaps you should visit him once in a while and have a listen, Dave. Maybe you'll think better than to scare pregnant widows."

Silence; then her desperate gasp. I pictured his face against hers as he said, "You don't have to be afraid, Peg. We've known each other for a long time. It must be lonely for you without Ray."

"Don't touch me!"

The sound of a skin-to-skin slap made me jump, and I hoped it was Mother showing Wright she meant business.

"I said, don't touch me."

The fear in her voice tightened my stomach as I imagined her pushing his hands away. I should have stepped out at that moment, something I'd feel guilty about for the rest of my life, but I was only ten, and I remained hidden under the staircase. Mother never found out that I'd hidden. She never found out I'd returned for my book to witness the most painful day of her life.

"Such a pretty face. It hurts me to see you sad, Peg. Too bad Ray died in that hunting accident. Well, it's too bad for him, but not so bad for me."

I swear I heard him smirk. Years later, I questioned whether my father's death out in the woods had truly been an accident. I researched the evidence to prove Wright had orchestrated every nightmare my family ever faced.

Mother's sniffles echoed from the kitchen, and my heart stilled.

"You know it should have been us at that prom, Peg. It would have been me standing at the altar with you if Ray hadn't filled in for your date."

My stomach tightened into a knot, and my body trembled. I covered my mouth with my hand to stop the sobs as I remembered father's prom stories. Fate had brought my parents together when Father's date fell ill and Mother's date broke his leg jumping off a wagon.

"And it should have been my child you're carrying, not his."

My eyes welled as I held back the tears. Was that why the sheriff had always assigned the dangerous cases to Father? Because he was jealous?

"Leave, Dave, before we both do something we regret."

The sound of a metal blade sliding sharp against its iron casing slid through my ears as I heard mother pull out a knife from the holder on the kitchen counter. I backed into the storage corner, where my body trembled in the darkness. I should have helped her, and instead I was trapped in a rhythm of constant shaking.

A swoosh and a punch later, the blade crashed to the tile floor. In that one second, I hoped she'd stabbed him. Hell, I hoped she'd killed him.

Millie barked outside in fury.

"You think a knife will help you, Peg?" The sound of a gun loading clicked in my ears. I imagined him pointing the weapon at Mother; worse yet, at her belly.

"If you want to live to see this baby's face, turn around and lift your fucking dress," he ordered.

I covered my ears, but the screaming, the loud thrashing, and my mom's pleas not to push against the stomach for the sake of her baby broke through. I sobbed in my corner, wishing for the sounds to go away. Unfortunately, wishing didn't always bring the wishes true, and the helpless sound of her muffled cries would remain with me for the rest of my life. Their memory would feed the vengeance I sought.

My bladder let go near the end. The snot under my nose dripped to the floor in streaks, but I wouldn't wipe it for fear of what I'd hear when I pulled my hands away.

It didn't take him long to finish, but it felt like forever to me. I hated myself that day. Fear took the best of me, and I failed to help Mother. I froze like the biggest coward in the world.

Before Wright left, he warned, "You tell anyone I came over, Peg, and I'll take that pretty little girl of yours until she bleeds on my cock. And it will be all your fault."

The door shut closed, and I ran into the kitchen where Mother lay unconscious on the floor. Blood had soaked through her apron and skirt. I covered her with a blanket and dialed for an ambulance.

I later told her I'd returned for a book and found her on the kitchen floor. She knew I was lying, though. I saw the pain in her eyes. Mother never mentioned Wright again. She told no one about the attack and didn't press charges. Her days and nights revolved around grief. My little sister was supposed to be the last piece we had of Father, and we lost her too. I crawled into Mother's hospital bed and lay in her arms while she recovered; physically, at least. At moments, she'd coo at me like I was the baby, calling me Emma in her dreams. Her breast milk leaked, and heart shattered.

We buried Emma beside Father. The little square piece of marble looked out of place, but at least he wasn't alone. Neither was she. A wreath made of fresh daisies I'd picked decorated the cross above her tombstone. Mother stood by the grave for hours, holding onto her swollen tummy as if Emma were still in there. As the casket lowered to the ground, she finally collapsed onto her knees. Wright, the righteous man, stood amongst the town's folk, watching us. Little did he know my fear of him passed the minute I vowed to never be afraid of a man again.

Wight robbed my mother of a daughter, and me of a sister. Mother was never the same after the loss. She stopped making waffles from scratch and went through the motions of life. At night, she locked the door and carried a knife to bed.

A few weeks after the funeral, Mother packed up one night, and we walked Millie to a neighbor's house. We left town right after. I missed the dog, but I didn't dare complain. Mother had enough on her mind. A few train rides later, we arrived at what was supposed to be a new beginning — except Wright never truly left. After we moved, she bought a shotgun and slept with the weapon at her side.

Mother lived in constant fear and mourning while I planned my revenge. It was time to give her life back. She feared Wright would find her, so she moved from city to city. The monster was obsessed. He'd found us twice before, but now I had the means to move her quicker. He was searching for her, I had no doubt, but I'd never been able to find him on my own, and Mother would remain bolted under locks and chains with a bottle of tequila on the kitchen table until the day Wright was dead.

"The tequila helps me forget," she told me when I was older. So I bought her a bottle once in a while if she'd promise me she'd only drink with me, so we could both forget. She kept the promise. At one point, I told her I'd make things right, but I wasn't sure whether she had too many shots to remember.

I hated Wright. I despised him with a passion, and I'd strike back. I'd take his life with no evidence, the same way he took my unborn sister's and my father's.

Allie's boobs jiggled in her tight tank top, and her tiny ass bounced with every step. Sweat dripped down her back. Red patches covered her skin. I turned on the treadmill beside hers and stepped up on the machine. She peeled her gaze away from the protein advertisement and looked my way, tripping over her feet. I pulled on her emergency cord to stop the momentum. The machine slowed, and Allie composed herself.

"Hi." I said. "Are you okay?"

"Yeah. Hi. Thank you. Ahem… I'm clumsy. Sometimes."

"What are you doing here so early in the morning?" I asked.

"Apparently showing off all my graceless abilities." She pushed the laugh through her broken voice and cleared her throat. "Ahem… Are you following me?"

"No, it's a public gym."

"I've been coming here for two years, and I've never seen you."

"I choose when I want to be seen, Allie. Good morning, Cole." I waved to the trainer, and Allie's eyes grew wide.

"Thank you for taking me home Friday night. I was going

to call you to thank you, but then I realized I don't have your number."

"We'll have to change that."

"Well, I have the corporate number, but it would be silly to call you at work to thank you."

"You could call me at work to tell me you'll come work for me. After you come back from Charleston, of course. It's tomorrow you're leaving, isn't it?"

"I guess my mouth ran away from me Friday night." Her lips tightened before they relaxed.

"Your mouth was very intriguing and very informative."

She shifted her weight and bit her lip. Her pouty mouth thinned and her eyes rounded. That lip-biting thing would drive me crazy.

"How so?" she asked.

"For one, you told me you're a great pole dancer."

She tripped over her foot, lost her balance, and almost fell off the treadmill.

"You okay?"

She regained her composure and continued. "Yes, ahem… I used to do that."

"We're looking for someone uniquely skilled, and you're perfect for Silver Securities."

Why did it feel like I had to explain everything? Stacks of resumes were waiting on my desk, and I didn't want to look at any because the perfect candidate, though distracted, was standing in front of me.

She looked at me like I was losing my mind. "I trip over my feet and you call me skilled?"

"Trust me. You're perfect for this job." I scanned her over from the bottom up, taking in her figure. With a little makeup and the right outfit, she'd fit perfectly into the perverted world of sex traffickers. She was our in.

She grabbed her towel and water bottle off the machine.

"But you will need training." I added.

"What training?" She lowered her hands to her hips, controlling her breathing. It didn't stop her boobs from lifting higher and wider.

"Self-defense."

"You haven't done your homework, Mr. Silver, have you?" she laughed.

"You mean the fact that you have a black belt in three martial arts?"

Of course I'd done my fucking homework.

"Is there anything you don't know about me?"

"Your bra size." I shamelessly devoured her ample cleavage until the moment I realized I was hard. It seemed this new partnership would be just as hard as my dick. It had been a while since I'd found the time for myself, and full balls were the consequence.

She had no idea what she was getting into with the job... or with me. She was my pawn, and I wouldn't let her down. My treadmill stopped, and I turned her way.

Her focus lowered to my crotch. "Ahem, you have a little predicament," she snickered.

"I know. That happens a lot around you." I snapped my fingers. "Which, once again, makes you perfect for the job."

"I'd like to keep things professional."

Professional is overrated.

"My dick may have a mind of his own, but I promise you—I am your boss and I will act as one."

"Not yet. You're not my boss yet, correct?"

"Fine. But once I am your boss, we'll keep things professional."

She caught my hint, bit her lip, and replied with sass. "36C."

"That's what I thought."

"Cocky a bit?"

"Always. Confidence keeps the door open and makes life easier." I wiggled my brows.

She rolled her eyes, turned on her heel, and left. I switched off my machine and followed her to a workout studio behind a glass wall. Her shoes squeaked over the freshly polished maple floor.

"Have you always been a tease, Allie?"

She whipped her body around and slammed into my chest. "What?"

"You want the job, but you're not in a hurry to apply because I'm the irresistible Tristan Silver. Your words, not mine."

She tilted her head. Her face tinted with yet another refreshing smirk.

"I can clarify—that's not it, Mr. Cocky."

Well, at least she had that confidence and fearlessness she'd need when she faced a group of perverted men. Her freckled face, pouty lips, and pebbled nipples would attract all the wrong kinds of men.

"Then what is it?"

Her right shoulder lifted in a shrug as she glanced back. "Maybe I am a tease after all. I mean, it's not like you're my boss just yet, are you?"

Fuck me.

She loosened her clinging shirt. Patches of sweat stained her armpits and back, making me want to throw her under the shower. Her soaked ponytail clung to the back of her neck.

"Honestly, right now, you're this mysterious bodyguard investigator I have trouble finding information about. But I know you have the resources our line of work needs."

I leaned against the wall by the exercise equipment. She'd sweat much more when I fucked her. *Before* I hired her. So it wouldn't be awkward later, though I couldn't foresee that happening.

She sipped on her water while scanning me from the bottom up, the same way I had done to her a moment ago. I was beginning to question whether self-control would be as much of an issue for her as much as it was for me.

"Your tits bounce when you run."

She spat the water out in a fountain. I passed her a fresh towel to wipe her mouth. She then got down on her knees and cleared the floor.

"You know that's sexual harassment."

She threw the towel into a bin and paced toward the exercise room on the other side of the gym, where Cole taught Pilates and Zumba in the mornings. I followed alongside and close behind, paying extra attention to her swaying derrière.

"Except you're not hired yet," I reminded her.

She swiveled on her foot and walked thee steps back to me. "It's still harassment."

"Not when the receiving party enjoys and wants the attention. Besides, I wouldn't harass you Allie. I like you too much."

She stopped and I stepped up to her as close as I could. She held her stance.

"You like me?"

"Isn't it obvious?"

"You're trying to throw me off my game, aren't you? It's not gonna work, Silver."

"What exactly is your game?"

She lowered her hands to her hips and looked at me like a German shepherd puppy hearing his favorite words.

"I find concentrating difficult around you. What is it exactly that you want from me? Why me?"

The likelihood she wasn't ready for my answer was as high as the fact I would get hard every time I stood in her presence. The delicate matter of pawning this woman to the greatest scum in the world was... well... delicate, and it was becoming more difficult to imagine doing so.

"I need you for this job, Allie. You saw Kendra's kidnapper. He stopped you in a park and fled when Gabriel Silver approached."

My eyes darted to the side before settling on hers. I cleared my throat, grabbed an exercise pad, and laid it out flat.

"Your cousin? I remember."

"Sit." I pointed.

"I'm not a dog."

I let out a frustrated breath and stepped forward until her back was pressed against the wall. I flattened my palms on its surface, right beside her head. Her breaths quickened, and the vein running down her neck and the soft part of her breasts ripened. With inches between us, I lowered my voice. "Allie, this is going to be the hardest job of your life."

I pressed my erection against her hip. Her strawberry scent drove me crazy. The walls closed in, and my appetite for her heightened. But she had work to do. "I have to ensure you're ready. For anything and everything. I do have a question, though. Why become a cop to give it up for this job?" I pulled away, watching her concentrate.

She stood with her mouth half open, completely bewildered. I rolled a pink exercise ball her way.

"Please, Allie. Sit."

She obliged. I bounced another exercise ball in front of me and sat on that one.

"My family drove down to Florida when I was eight. Five car lengths in front of us, a van lost control, flipped over, and rolled to the side of the road. It caught fire. I don't know where she came from, but an officer pulled over her cruiser and jumped out while everyone else was still in shock. She ran down the hill toward the flames. And one by one, she saved the family. An older man was the last one to walk out, and then the van exploded. The officer's back caught the flames from the blast, and she lit up like a dried Christmas tree. My parents told me she survived. It was the bravest thing I'd ever seen in my life."

She told the lie so well; it was almost believable. She hadn't even answered my question. I knew she'd be perfect for the job.

"Interesting. I'd thought it was because you're looking for someone."

"I... I... How—"

"There's nothing Silver Securities cannot find, and something tells me you know that better than anyone."

"Nothing?"

"Almost nothing." I lowered my head. "Kendra's a client, and we can't find her. But you can. The man from the park, the same man who held my cousin's fiancée at gunpoint, has her. It's the first time in my career this has happened. We can't lose Kendra. She's family, and a lot rests on her wellbeing."

Her forehead creased. "I definitely remember him. Scruffy beard, stinky breath, yellow teeth?" Recognition sparked in her eyes. "His name is Martinez. He works for the elite, and he's pretty much untouchable."

"Like the masons?"

"No, but close. The elite with sources, connections, finances, crooked cops, and a political figure bidding for their welfare in every party. They've created a selective society and eventually they became a mafia as well. Money buys power. Lots of power. It buys all kinds of people: those in the legal system, the force, and the government. Nothing's out of reach, so that's where we come in. We make it more difficult for them to reach the one goal every billionaire has: to become untouchable. Kendra is crucial to a case against those men."

Her lips parted and eyes skidded from side to side. It took a moment for the information to sink in, but if there was one thing I could ever count on in life, it was patience.

"So you want me to infiltrate to find Kendra?"

"Martinez will lead you to Kendra, but we need you to be…
promiscuous. Your record on the force, however, is one of the
cleanest I've seen, Allie. So was your father's, which makes me
question whether you can do the job."

"I can do the job."

"You'll be thrown to the wolves."

"I said, I can do the job."

"I have to make sure you can be persuasive. Provocative." I
paused, noting the intensity with which she was listening to
my instructions. "I want to know what makes you tick. Why do
you keep your mother in hiding? Who are you running away
from? Because in my line of work, we can't afford distractions.
They're fatal."

She struggled to keep my gaze, but remained composed.
She squared her shoulders and blinked twice.

"I don't get distracted. In fact, I promise you I can focus like
a hawk when there's a need. Truthfully, right now, I'm just
trying to build the kind of career my father would be proud of."

I couldn't deny her answer was strong, but it sounded
rehearsed.

"Interesting. Your mother is in Charleston, correct?"

She looked me dead in my eyes, and I knew I'd hit that
trigger in the center of her heart.

"How…? I'm the only one who knows where she lives."

"No, you're not, Allie."

I might not had snooped enough yet, but I would after that
reaction. I rolled my ball closer to hers until the round edges
touched and our knees connected. Her nostrils flared and her
face reddened.

"What are your demons, Mr. Silver? You said everyone has
them."

She tilted her head. The corner of her mouth lifted into a
sultry curve. "Is Kendra your demon? Or is it someone else?
Someone…" She watched my face, and I would have sworn she

could read the pain tracing from there right down to my heart. "Someone you lost."

She hit my trigger in the center.

"Not all demons can be fixed," I told her, and waited in what appeared to be a blinking contest. Her blue-green eyes with copper rims and her scattered freckles softened her face. She was too cute to be a cop, but definitely perfect for all my needs. She reminded me of my younger, happy years before the accident.

"Relax, Allie. I didn't snoop, but you just confirmed that I'm right. Why hide your mother? Why does she move along the east coast every few years?"

Her eyes filled with sadness. They clouded over before her determination returned as she held back tears.

"My demons will not affect my work. I promise. It's just something I have to do."

"All right. You'll take my jet." I lifted my finger before she could argue. "It will be quicker."

"It's not a far drive."

"Doesn't matter. If you're going to work for me, I need you to rest. You may as well get used to the perks the company can offer."

"But—"

"No buts. The only thing I ask is that you come to my office as soon as you return from your trip."

"Friday morning?"

"Yes. We'll get the paperwork out of the way before the weekend."

"Wait—so I'm really hired?"

"As soon as you put pen to paper."

She smiled.

"Stand up." I grabbed her hand and kicked the ball from underneath her. She sprang up without hesitation. I parted my legs and lowered my arms to my sides.

"Hit me," I ordered

"What?"

"This is not a request, but it is a test. I need to know you can stand your ground. Pin me to the floor."

"You just want me on top of you." She crossed her arms over her chest.

"Actually, I want you under me, but all good things come to those who wait. Now, hit me."

I didn't wait for her attack. Instead, I went for her waist, lifting her off the ground. Her instincts kicked in, and she freed herself from my grip. After a few kicks, twists, and flips, I was down on the mat as she straddled my hips.

"You know jujitsu?"

"Kickboxing and karate as well. Third-degree black belt. I've been training since I was eleven."

Fucking brilliant.

"That's not on your resume."

"I prefer the element of surprise. Like now." She smiled and tightened her thighs around me, her crotch in my face. I couldn't help the smug look. Her eyes opened wide, and as she tried to get up, I grabbed her wrists and held her on top of me, then used my strength to flip her over to the mat.

She let out a groan. Her mouth gave me all the wrong ideas. It would give all the scum at the auction all the wrong ideas as well, which once again made her the perfect pawn.

I lowered my body to hers, and her muscles went limp. She stopped the struggle and beamed with the kind of vulnerability the elite pervs exploited. Her sultry eyes, flushed cheeks, and willing mouth invited filthy thoughts. I rested my palms on the sides of her shoulders. The front of her shirt clung to her chest, outlining her full breasts. They were the perfect size for her petite body. I lowered myself and whispered, "Are we going to be a problem, Allie? Because once I'm your boss—"

"Are you asking me if I can keep it in my pants? Because if

you are, I'll have to call you a hypocrite." She looked down to my hard dick without missing a beat.

Fuck me.

Her breath flowed over my cheek and her luscious lips drew an inviting line to the corner of her mouth. I closed my eyes, waiting for her to turn lightly to the right. Instead, she grabbed the back of my neck and used her legs as leverage to lift me over her head and flipped me onto my back.

Her little body held a rare kind of comfortable strength.

"Argh!"

My back ribs ached, but it didn't stop her from straddling me like a broken horse. She gripped my wrists, pinned them above my head, and leaned forward.

"We will not have a problem, boss. I promise you that."

I stared at the narrowed valley between her breasts. They weren't too big, weren't too small—just perfect, and fucking too appetizing. "God, you're going to drive me crazy with those, aren't you?" I growled.

"They paid for my school. I mean, if you've got the assets, why not use them against the perverted world? But I'm sure you already know that."

She stripped, and I had the urge to blind every bastard who ever saw her naked.

"They still are one of your best assets, Allie. No disrespect."

"None taken."

Her grip eased off my wrists, and she slid off me, tantalizingly slowly, like she wanted to feel every curve of my throbbing dick, on purpose.

Fucking hell.

"Thank you for the offer to fly me out. I really appreciate it."

"If you need to move her again, I can help."

"Thank you."

"All right. You'll visit your mother, then come to my office on Friday morning. Everything will be ready."

"Okay," she breathed.

I turned to the right where a group of women lined up behind the glass wall, watching us.

"I think we're putting on a show."

"What?" She turned around and her cheeks tinted with pink.

"You look beautiful when you blush."

She held my stare and blushed again. Her freckles popped with vulnerability all the more. She was lethal.

"I'll send a car for seven in the morning."

"Okay," she said.

We split at the locker rooms, and my heart sank.

I should have kissed her.

Regret loomed, and morning couldn't come soon enough.

I peered out my window, awaiting the cab. Laura had left for work and dropped Foxy off at daycare. I yawned, but it wasn't the toddler who'd kept me up. Silver hadn't left my mind since the cold shower I took last night.

A car engine slowed outside. I pulled back the sheers and watched the Bentley park on the street. Tristan Silver stepped out of the vehicle.

"Shit!" I rushed to the front door, straightening my sweater and capris. I hadn't thought he'd drive me to the airport. I opened the door before he knocked.

The light dress pants and the polo shirt underneath a sporty jacket suited him better than casual jeans. His dampened hair released a minty scent. But I had a feeling that, like everything else in his life, Silver had timed this morning's shower to perfection. His grin lifted the scar on his lip and the dimple sank in, distracting me. He looked amazing, but that same chiseled face held a shadow of worry, and I noted his body stiffened as soon as I opened the door. Darker circles underlined his eyes.

"What's—"

"Good morning. All ready for our trip?"

Wait... what?

"Our trip?"

"I have last-minute business in Charleston, so this works out well for the both of us." He lifted my suitcase like a light handbag.

Last minute, my ass!

"Didn't sleep well last night?" I locked the door and followed him to the Bentley.

"It's hard to sleep when your mind is preoccupied."

"I know exactly what you mean," I said, so casually that it surprised me. I paused at the door and waited as he lowered my suitcase inside the trunk, opened the passenger door, and placed his hand on the small of my back.

Next thing I knew, he was at my ear, whispering seductive offers. "Want me to help you inside?"

Where was the heat coming from?

"No, thanks. I got it."

I climbed into the leather seat. The air-conditioned interior felt like I'd just stepped into a fridge. Shivers ran up my arms, and goose bumps covered my thighs. Silver sat in the driver's seat, closed the door, and turned my way. The heat from his gaze penetrated my body. Tristan took a deep breath of courage and exhaled. "I should have done this yesterday, Allie."

I had no time to reply as he muffled my words with his mouth, and everything inside me shut down. My body went limp, melting into the seat. My arms flopped at my sides while his large hands cupped my small face. The pads of his thumbs caressed my cheeks back and forth. His tongue slipped between my lips, parting my willing mouth. The longing in his sensual kiss pulsed through my body, and the strength to resist him evaporated. I opened my mouth wider. A hint of scotch flowed from his breath to mine, forcing a moan from my chest. His determined tongue spun my head just like the tequila. The world faded in and out of focus, and when he finally pulled away, I couldn't believe what had happened and how much his kiss awakened the woman inside me. But what I couldn't believe the most was how much the kiss doused the lingering pain and vengeance.

He leaned his forehead against mine. "You taste even better than I imagined. So worth it."

I finally let out the long-held breath. "Imagined?"

"My imagination kept me awake all night. Now I don't have to wonder anymore."

I swallowed hard. He was messing with my head and my goals, and I'd prefer at least the latter settled before he messed with my heart.

"I'm glad I satisfied your curiosity, Mr. Silver."

"You satisfied only one part of it. I'm curious about the rest of your body too."

Oh, God! Was he playing with me again? Was this a test? While my body tingled with excitement, my overthinking brain worried about his ulterior motive.

"This isn't a honeymoon, Mr. Silver. If you can't keep your hands to yourself, perhaps I should drive after all." My mouth said one thing, but my body thought another. I couldn't think around this man.

His hands flew up, palms toward me. "That won't be necessary. I promise to keep them to myself. Even at night, I'll keep them all to myself."

The image of Silver stroking himself at night as he thought about me curled my toes.

The smug, immoral grin on his face matched all the dirty thoughts running through my mind.

"But I can't promise I won't think about your mouth…. and everything else, to be honest."

I doubted I could keep my hands away from my body while thinking about him, either.

Silver turned the ignition and drove to one of Long Island's small airports for private planes. He said nothing throughout the drive, which was for the better because I was a total mess as I replayed the *what the fuck* moment in my head. What did he mean with that kiss? This was not part of the job, but it definitely confirmed the attraction between us was two-sided. From my side glance, the smile of satisfaction on his face pushed my heart rate into overdrive. The confidence this man carried was intimidating and appealing at the same time. He acted like he accomplished his daily tasks the moment he opened his eyes and everything ahead was downhill. I guessed one needed his level of confidence for his line of work.

The private jet was small but cozy. The flight attendant served Silver a glass of scotch, and he asked me whether I'd like anything to drink. I declined politely.

"We have tequila on board," Tristan offered.

"I'm not dependent on tequila, Silver." I wondered whether he knew about the bottle in my suitcase I'd packed for my mother.

"I never said you were."

"Fair enough."

The short flight gave me enough time to check emails and pretend I wasn't paying attention to the fact that Tristan Silver had swept me away on a private jet to visit my mother. He made it all seem so normal. Like that kiss we'd shared in the car didn't linger on his lips the way it did on mine. Was this part of a test as well? It didn't matter because I was exactly where I needed to be. When Silver went to the back to make a phone call, I typed out a letter of resignation on my phone and saved it to drafts.

In Charleston, another Bentley was waiting on the tarmac.

"How many Bentleys do you own?" I asked.

"This one's a rental. It's a reliable car. Why?"

"Just surprised you don't ride in limos."

"I like the feel of my hands on the wheel. My psychologist

says it's part of my need to… control. I disagree. If I didn't control the wheel, the car would go off-road and crash, right? It's a survival instinct."

I guessed we all had our way of understanding our damaged psyche. This was the most Silver had opened about himself. Why did he feel like he had no control?

"What about the dark-haired woman under your arm?" I asked out of nowhere, and it appeared I hit the bull's eye. I figured since he was answering personal questions, I should ask.

"You googled me?" he asked.

"Any sound-minded woman would. So I did. For what it's worth, there isn't much on the web, but I did find a graduation photo in microfiche."

He stilled, but the tension eased off his shoulders just as fast. "Now if that doesn't tell you my age, then nothing will."

"Why would you hire an escort?" I poked.

"I assure you she wasn't an escort because, for one, I don't do that. And for two, it was a long time ago."

"Oh."

She was his button.

Silver placed my small suitcase into the trunk and then came around to open my door.

"God knows, my parents wish I would date more. At least to get them a grandchild. They eased off since my cousin James had a kid."

"You have nephews?"

"A niece, actually. Her name is Laila."

"That's a beautiful name."

"She's a chick magnet."

"He's a single dad?"

"Unfortunately, he doesn't take advantage of it as much as he should. He's a great dad; just attracts the wrong women."

Maybe I should fix him up with Laura. They'd have their

kids in common. Perhaps she could move past her one-night stand who, according to Laura, didn't deserve to be a daddy. Those were her words about the man who'd fathered Fox, not mine.

Silver drove along the familiar freeways towards my mother's neighborhood. He kept to the speed limit, and eased in and out of traffic with confidence but care.

While I couldn't wait to see her, I also feared what I'd find. Sometimes it was easier to forget my life when I fantasized about the impossible.

"And is there a woman in your life right now, Mr. Silver?"

After my own sleepless night, I was more confused about our partnership than ever. Why did he have to kiss me like I was his and only his? Like his life depended on my breathing.

"If there was, I wouldn't have kissed you, Allie. And you can call me Tristan."

"Mr. Silver sounds more professional."

"Certainly more professional than McBoss."

"That sounds like I said something stupid last time I had tequila."

"It was cute. You can call me Mr. Silver after Friday. Right now, it's Tristan. But a fair warning—when you call me Mr. Silver, it sounds dirty to me."

I fought not to squirm in the seat with the butterflies in my stomach. I never had butterflies. Tristan parked in front of my mother's apartment and turned my way.

"Perfect." I unbuckled my seatbelt.

He shook his head. "I'll be honest, Allie. I'm surprised you're single. You're witty and a knockout. Men should be lining up at your door."

"They don't when you don't want them to. Also, I usually wear a tight vest over my chest and a gun at my side when I'm out and about. The cop ensemble doesn't exactly scream sexy, and the gun scares off men."

"I don't think they know what they're missing."

I heated from my head all the way down to my toes. "Thank you. I really appreciate the ride. I hope your business goes well... as well."

My voice trembled. What the heck was happening to me?

He reached over my seat and removed a business card from its compartment. "You're welcome. You can find me at the Planters Inn if you need anything. And I mean anything, Allie."

I knew exactly what he meant, and worst of all, I immediately considered taking up his offer. I pocketed the card he gave me. Tristan leaned over and kissed me on my cheek. I closed my eyes, inhaling him. There was nothing better than his scent. For the first time since we'd met, I truly wished for his company.

He pulled away, and I hurried upstairs to my mother's apartment. The sound of unlocking metal chains crawled along my skin. I stepped over the threshold and the dreaded past, pain, and fear, overwhelmed me. I hugged her tight—right after she locked up, of course.

"It's been too long," she said.

"I'm sorry. I've been working."

"Just like your father. So committed to your job. I'm proud of you, Allie, and I know your father would have been too."

I pulled away to have a better look at her sunken eyes and new worry lines. The drapes pulled over the windows sported a spider web, which meant she kept them closed during the day as well. And I could tell she hadn't left the apartment for a while; perhaps she had a neighbor shop for her groceries. She'd only leave out of necessity, and that was how she'd lived for the past fourteen years. My mother didn't live—she survived.

"How are you, Mom?" I opened my suitcase and placed the bottle of tequila on the kitchen table. "And I really mean that. How are you?"

My mother took out two glasses from the cupboard and

placed them by the liquor. This was what we did. We drank together to mourn together and to forget.

I poured about an inch deep from the bottom as she sliced the lemons.

"It's better." This was her standard answer.

"I'm going to kill Wright."

My mother sat down as casually as if she'd heard news about the weather. "You won't do anything so foolish, Allie." She pointed to the seat across the table.

"You'll be free of him."

"I was free the moment I left Pinedale. My only regret was not leaving sooner." She threw her head back, downing the first shot. Her face shifted as the alcohol's first burn passed through her throat.

"What if he finds you again? It's been quiet for a while. Too quiet. I have a feeling it may be time to move."

The two previous times Wright found my mother, his bad timing had saved her from another brutal attack. She'd remained at the store where she saw him following and I'd had the police pick her up. I couldn't count on them everywhere, but I could there. Apparently Wright's connections didn't reach everywhere, which gave mother a chance. Hours later, I was driving her to a new location.

"Wright is an obsessed son of a bitch and knows the law too well. He has connections, and he won't stop."

Her brows lifted. "I'm more worried about you, Allie. You need to live a happy life instead of hiding in the shadows of your mother's past."

"Your past is my past. Your pain is my pain." I took her hand.

"But it shouldn't be this way."

"I will kill him, Mom. I will make sure he never threatens you again."

"I would do anything to change things. Improve your life.

Darling"—she smoothed her hand over my cheek, the way she had when I was younger—"you won't do such a stupid thing. Wright will eventually get what's coming his way, and it's called karma."

"Then call me karma."

She laughed. Her rare moment of happiness lifted my spirit.

"I'm also quitting the force."

My mother's face sobered. "Why?"

"For a new job. A better job. And I've met someone who will help me get rid of Wright." My cheeks warmed, and it wasn't from the liquor.

She narrowed her brows. "Allie, do not let Wright distract you from this. Take a chance and enjoy life for a change. You've been alone way too long. If this man means something to you and agrees to help you kill, then he's not worthy of you. At all. Your father lived by protecting life. God punishes those who don't."

I knew my mother was lying through her teeth. She'd shoot Wright between the eyes the moment she had a chance, no matter what Father had said. Father didn't know Wright the way we did.

"It's all to protect you. Once he's gone, he'll be gone forever." I threw back my shot, letting the first gulp burn my throat. It didn't matter how smooth the tequila was, the first one always burned. After the initiation, the liquor passed through more smoothly, and after a few, it was almost like water.

"I'm fine here." She pointed to the corner of the room where a shotgun stood propped in a corner.

"Did you register it?" I asked.

She shook her head.

"Good. He could find you if you had."

"I told you not to worry. If Wright steps anywhere near me, I won't hesitate."

"I know you won't."

Three quarters of a bottle later, we ordered pizza with wings. The day passed in a haze. I told my mother about the mysterious Tristan Silver and his job offer. My motives didn't thrill her, but she was happy I'd be helping a girl in trouble. She said I reminded her of her young self when she went to a prom. Fortunately, the tequila took my wit away, and I didn't over-think it.

When my mother was ready for bed, I took a quick shower and slid into the one black dress in my suitcase. Laura must have had packed it for me. The fabric hugged my curves as if someone had sewn it to my skin. I rarely felt like a woman when I was out of uniform. The hint of natural makeup on my face took me back in time. It was identical to how my mother had worn hers before the assault, when she actually went outside to let the sun bronze her face. My mother was in her nightgown when I kissed her goodnight and told her not to wait up. I left after the last click of the chain lock sounded.

Time dragged as the cabbie drove to the hotel, but at least I'd sobered enough before he pulled up in front of Planters Inn. I paid the cabbie and stepped out.

Deep breaths, Allie. Deep breaths.

The concierge opened the front door. Inside, polished marble glistened underneath the enormous chandelier. The interior screamed money, and I felt out of place. The faint sound of quiet live music drew my gaze toward the bar. I squared my shoulders, lifted my chin, and headed for the low-lit room.

My fingers and toes tingled. I cracked my head to the side. My heels sank into the plush carpeting and I lifted to my toes. The man at the grand piano began a new tune as I scanned the tables. The orange and brown Tiffany lamps from above hardly illuminated anyone, casting protective shadows on people's faces that allowed for intimate and private conversations. My gaze finally rested on the bar and the familiar broad shoulders of a muscular back. They stretched out under a black shirt that could only belong to one person. A fragment of his thorn tattoo showed from underneath the sleeve, and a glass of scotch swirled the ice cubes in his right hand. Tristan Silver looked as sexy from the back as he did from the front.

I took a deep breath in and slowed my steps toward him. The faint bar light shone from the top, lighting the streaks in his tousled dark hair. I stopped just behind him when I felt someone's gaze on my back. I shook off the nerves and slid my hands from behind around Silver's waist.

"Taste me again."

He turned his head in slow motion. I leaned in and closed my eyes, pressing my lips to his. The immediate response sent my pulse racing. The sweet taste of scotch filled my mouth. His tender tongue welcomed me as if it was once again our first semi-deep kiss. My mouth searched for the small scar ripple on his lip, but I couldn't feel it. His hands rested on my hips and I wondered why he was keeping his distance.

"Is it a habit of yours to kiss strange men?" A familiar voice reverberated from my side.

I pulled away from the delicious mouth and whipped my body around where Tristan was standing, watching me kiss… a stranger?

"What the hell?" My mouth opened like a guppy's, and I pushed away from the look-alike Silver.

"It felt more like heaven," the man said.

My gaze darted from him to Tristan and back before my hand flew up to cover my mouth. The unbelievable resemblance stole my breath. From the high cheeks and deep hazel eyes down to the little dimple in his chin, this man was a slightly older version of Tristan Silver. The only missing piece was the small scar on his upper lip.

"Allie Green, meet Julian Silver, my brother." A wicked smile stretched across Tristan's face.

The man I'd just kissed offered his hand.

"Why did you kiss me back?" I tightened my fists.

"Why do we eat, sleep, or walk?" He grinned like a cocky bastard. "And I'm not the one who kissed you. You kissed me first." He held out his hand, waiting for a proper introduction. I noted his thorn tattoo instead.

"You share a tattoo artist too?"

Julian didn't miss a beat scanning me from the bottom up. "It looks like we share good taste as well."

The brothers could have passed for twins. Tristan's older brother had more devilish charm than Tristan, but it was just as potent. I finally took his hand and shook it in a formal greeting. There was something sexy and intimate about their maturity. They captured the beginnings of beautiful future silver foxes.

"You're not the first one to make the mistake, although next time I'd prefer to be on the receiving end." Tristan guided my elbow to sit up on the bar stool. He then leaned in, whispering, "You look ravishing, by the way."

Tristan's warm breath slid from my cheek, over my bare shoulder, and down my body. The room shrank in my peripheral vision, making me acutely aware that almost every inch of him touched me.

"Thank you. I'm sorry about that, Julian. I won't make the mistake again."

I definitely wouldn't.

"I didn't mind," he answered.

"Trust me, she won't make the mistake again." Tristan's tone sharpened. He sat on my other side, making me part of a yummy Silver brother sandwich.

"I didn't mean to interrupt your evening," I said.

"I'm glad you did, and you're not interrupting. We're done for tonight." He looked toward the bartender and called, "Comisario."

"Wait..." I lowered my hand to his. The touch might as well have been a kiss. It weaved like an electric current up my arm to my face and my lips in a series of heated waves and sweet pulses. I locked my gaze with Tristan's, and swallowed hard, saying, "That's too much."

"It's on me, Allie. Enjoy." The bartender poured a shot of one of the most delicious tequilas I'd ever tasted. Silver tapped the bar with his finger, and the bottle remained in its spot.

"Thank you." I swung the first shot back, letting the smooth liquid run down my throat. It didn't burn the way my first ones normally did, and I welcomed the instant relaxation.

"If you excuse me, I have an early morning." Julian stood up, took my hand in his, and kissed the top of my palm. Unavoidable shivers simmered up my arm.

"Good night."

"It's been a pleasure, Allie. Hopefully, I'll get the same greeting next time." He winked.

"Don't count on it, brother."

They shook hands, which I found too formal for siblings, and Julian strode off toward the elevators. The bartender poured another shot.

"It's nice to know I have options."

"Don't get any ideas. He's madly in love with Kendra, the girl we're looking for."

"In love with a client? Isn't that—"

"Complicated? Yes."

"I was going to say unethical, but I guess *complicated* covers it all, doesn't it?"

Like us? Was that how he defined us? Complicated?

"It does with this case. Given the stress and his clouded judgment, I'm responsible for her return."

"You're a good brother."

"I would be a better brother if I'd found her already."

"That guy, Martinez—who does he work for? You said the elite, but do you have names? Details?"

He laughed.

"I knew I made the right decision with you, Allie, but you're not on the job yet. Friday, remember?"

"Right. And here I thought you made a business excuse just to go on a trip with me." I rolled my eyes and swiveled on the bar stool toward him. My knee touched his and stayed there, the way it had when he'd rescued me from another bar on another drunken night. He shifted, and my leg slid in between his thighs. I bit my lip.

"I did." He sipped on scotch. "The beauty of being my own boss is doing business from wherever I want."

"Are you doing business now?" I swung my head back again. The liquor meandered down my throat, coating it with its sweet taste. "This is good. Real good."

"I'm glad you like it. How is your mother?"

"You're avoiding my question."

"All right. No, I'm not doing business now. I'm enjoying your company, Allie. You look beautiful tonight, and I would love to hear more about your visit with your mother." He slid his hand onto my thigh, smoothing over the velvety fabric. A fresh wave of hormones stirred deep in my belly.

"Thank you. My mother's well. She's happy I visited."

"Did she like the tequila?"

"We both did," I chuckled. He knew me better than I thought.

"I'm glad you came here, Allie." He removed his palm from my thigh and lowered it to the top of mine. "I get little time to relax these days. This is... perfect."

I wasn't too sure what the moment meant and why I'd truly come here, but it felt right. Amazingly perfect, in fact, which frightened me. I wasn't expecting this... trust and personal attention from Tristan Silver. I wasn't sure how it had happened, but I was glad to be here with him. Or perhaps it was the smooth Comisario conspicuously working its way through my body?

"Me too. Any other siblings?" I asked.

"We have a younger sister. She's fourteen and lives with my parents in New Jersey. She was a surprise late in their life. A miracle, you could say. My mom has her hands full with Emma, and our father keeps us busy with work. My grandfather founded our company, and Father has been prepping us to take over ever since I can remember."

I heard nothing more after he said he had a sister. My insides crushed into a tight ball. A rush of sorrow flew through my body, as if it were the day I'd lost my sister all over again. An image of her tiny grave with the wreath of daisies flashed through my mind. My Emma would have been fourteen by now, and I probably would not have been sitting with Silver at a bar.

I shook off the nostalgia. "Your father's still working?"

His subtle laugh was full of happiness and distant memories. "He'll never retire. He says he will, but he won't. And I don't blame him. Our work gets pretty addictive when we win. It saves lives."

"What you do sounds dangerous. I mean, undercover operations, government bodyguards, secret surveillance… I bet you have enemies who'd like your head on a platter."

"Likely, but you have nothing to fear. I work behind the scenes and mostly stay clear of operations. Except for this one. This one's—"

"Personal?"

"Yeah, it sort of is. I realize I'm not twenty-five anymore. I'll be retiring from the field after we get Kendra."

Retiring? He couldn't be over thirty, though the maturity added a couple of years.

"You can't be much older than thirty."

"Thanks. I wish that were true. I'm thirty-seven. I actually share a birthday with my cousin Gabe."

"What? That's impossible." My mouth dropped open.

That's impossible.

"They call it good genes."

"No kidding. How do you keep your face off the internet?"

"Gabe is responsible for the surveillance team, and James hires the right muscle. You'll be working with him at the auction."

James, James, James...

"I met James briefly at your resort in Colorado. He got me to the hospital."

He looked at me bewildered. "And how did I not see you in Colorado?"

"I was the nutcracker holding the door. You think I can do this job with James?"

"It doesn't matter what I think. It matters what *you* think—because the moment they uncover our ruse is the moment we fail."

"I'm the right person for the job," I stated.

"Good."

I took another shot. The buzz worked its way into my head. I knew I should slow down, but this perfect feeling of a simple life and comfortable conversation was too much to resist. It was nice to feel somewhat normal. He squeezed my hand, reminding me it was still there, holding it with reassurance. The question was, would he give me everything I needed?

The likelihood he knew my father was dead was high. Public information was easy to find. I missed my father and often pictured what life would have been like with him. Those imaginary moments fueled my pursuit after Wright.

Tristan continued, "I live in Manhattan, but I'd prefer my parents' home in Oyster's Cove. The city's a convenient place to keep clients' needs and the business balanced."

"I'd pictured you as a country boy."

"You read me well. It's always been my dream to live in the country. It's where I see Emma one day, but she's determined to live in Manhattan."

"What's stopping you from moving?"

"Everything." Darkness covered his eyes. An uneasy vibe passed between us, and I got the feeling Tristan's job impeded his life more than he admitted.

"I love what I do, but I have a big mess to clean up before I commit to anything else in my life."

"A work mess?"

"Work and personal. It's a deadly combination."

"Makes me rethink that kiss this—"

"Don't. Don't rethink it. That was real, or as close to real as it has been for me for a while."

My cheeks flushed with heat. "The job you need me for is personal?"

He shook his head. "Not tonight, Allie. Tonight, I enjoy your company."

His lack of answer gave me my answer, and this time it was me squeezing his hand. I had a few more shots, laughed, talked, and leaned into Tristan more than I intended. I wasn't sure how I ended up in a luxurious hotel room, but the pillow was so comfortable and fluffy and smelled of fresh lavender, I couldn't resist resting my head. My last sight before I closed my eyes was of Tristan as his intoxicating scent lulled me to sleep.

The sun streamed through the window and shone into Allie's eyes. She shot up to a sitting position, gripped the sheets, and held them tight against her breasts. As she scanned the room in panic, her body flushed with pink heat, scattering in delightful patches over her cheeks and arms.

"Where am I?"

"Planters Inn. My room," I said from across the room.

Her head flew my way as she'd realized she wasn't alone.

"Crap."

Last night, the five-minute nap had given her enough energy for another half hour. That energy turned the flirty Allie into a complete tease. I'd sat in a corner armchair watching her sleep off the liquor since the moment she'd slipped her clothes off in front of me.

"Crap," she mumbled again. Her hair held the partial curl from her braid. A strand stuck to her right cheek and mouth. She carefully let go of the sheet with one hand and pulled it away. I glimpsed the bunched nipple underneath the fabric. Sunlight fell across the sheets and over her chest, illuminating her curves.

"I prefer good morning."

I stood up, paced to the other room, and brought a steaming cup of coffee to her bedside. She gripped the mug in the free hand and took a delighted sip. "It's just the way I like it."

"I know." I sat down on the bed's edge.

"Thanks. I needed that."

"I know."

She took another long sip and set the mug aside. A moment of recognition dawned on her face. She lifted the covers, peeked underneath them, and quickly pulled them close to her body again.

"You're naked," I said.

"I know. What the hell happened?" She wrapped the sheet tighter around her petite frame, shut her eyes, and pressed her fingers to her temples, searching through memories.

"Shit!"

And there it was.

"My mother." She met my gaze. "Smooth tequila. Shit, shit, shit! I'm so sorry for this… Whatever happened, I can explain."

I couldn't wait to hear her tell me all about how she'd performed a striptease for me last night, but we had more urgent matters to attend to. Let's just say that a drunk Allie was a fun Allie. She reminded me of my happy, carefree years before Simone died. It still felt like it was only yesterday when we'd flown to Austria, celebrating our engagement, not years ago. I hadn't considered moving on since.

"I have to get home. My mother…"

"Your mother is fine. She knows where you are."

"You spoke with my mother?" she asked. Her face had that *I want to throw up* look.

"She's a beautiful lady, Allie. I can see where you get your charm." I set the newspaper in my hand down on a table.

"You met her?" Her eyes grew wider and her freckles popped.

"She makes the most delicious stack of waffles I've ever tasted."

"She made you waffles? From scratch?"

"They didn't taste like the ones from a box, that's for sure."

"What time is it?" She searched the room for what I assumed was a clock.

Since I knew there was no clock, I replied, "Nine-thirty. I didn't want to wake you."

I stood up and paced to the cushioned seat where her dress and panties were folded into a perfect square. I picked up the black ensemble and passed it to her. Our fingers brushed at the exchange, and she froze.

"Wait. Did we?"

"No," I shook my head. "I don't take advantage of women."

"But you undressed me? I specifically remember your touch…"

Right. That.

"I helped with the zipper. My finger may have skimmed your skin, but that's all. You did the rest."

She grabbed the dress and panties, buried her face in her hands, and slid underneath the covers.

"Allie, why the embarrassment?"

She lowered the covers enough to show her face. "Because I'm stupid. You must think I'm a drunk."

"Not at all. You're human, and you hold on to shit just like everyone else. The alcohol helps with the stress. I've been there. But a fair warning—that road doesn't get you where you should be heading."

She smacked her lips, and I passed her a bottle of water, which she emptied.

"Thank you." She breathed out, relieved. "I'm not sure I'm ready for the metaphors this early in the morning, but I hope I didn't do too much damage last night."

"Other than performing the strip tease?"

"I didn't do that at the bar, did I?"

"No." I laughed. "I got the private version."

I wiggled my eyebrows, and then she laughed. It was cute and riveting how she got me. What wasn't cute was the way she'd ground herself against my groin, right over my hard dick. The intimate lap dance had tested my limits. Innocence covered her skin in a bashful shade of pink. She wore it well. Her youthful face likely distracted criminals. But the chance of her perfectness attracting them was even greater.

I sighed. She was the perfect pawn, and I was getting cold feet. After she fell asleep last night, I covered her and dug into David Wright's records. Allie not only stripped for me last night, but she also talked about a crooked cop. I bought a bottle of tequila and visited Peg Green this morning. It wasn't hard to put two and two together after that, but I had a problem. Wright was a witness in protective custody, related to Donaldson's case. Kendra's life depended on his testimony. Conflict of interest prevented me from touching the bastard, but it wouldn't prevent Allie. And right now, I would give her everything she wanted just so that I'd get the same in return.

I came closer to the bed and deposited a file labeled *Allie Green* on her lap.

"What is that?"

"Everything I need to know about you."

"How?"

I gave her a knowing look. "If you have to ask—"

"No. I got it. You're an investigator. Sorry." She glanced down at the file. "Looks pretty thin to me. You sure you've got everything?"

Was that anger or sarcasm? I couldn't tell, but something told me it was that wall she kept between reality and her fantasy of killing Wright she still held between us.

Fuck! This would be harder than hard.

"May I?"

I nodded.

She flipped through the pages of her past. The stripping days, some photos, where and when she'd moved her mother, how she'd paid for college. Most important, the file showed her resilient nature. She breathed out with relief when she didn't find any mention of Wright. I'd kept those documents for myself.

"I see you know it all." She closed the file.

While I wished she'd trust me enough to tell me about Wright, her trauma was tied around her neck like a fucking permanent noose. But that poker face confirmed she was the right hire. Kendra's life depended on all the skills Allie possessed.

"It's time we put some cards out on the table, Allie. We're taking a trip today."

"But my mother..."

"Your mother is fine. She knows you're safe with me. She threatened not to make me waffles again if I hurt you."

"She did?"

"She loves you and wants to see you happy. And I can't have you distracted when I hire you. I need you to know you're safe and she's safe. Your life will depend on your ability to concentrate."

"How do you know she needs to feel safe?"

"I've seen the locks on the door and the shotgun. The demographics of her safe neighborhoods tell me you've done research before her moves."

She gripped the cup of coffee and sipped between her thoughts. "All right. You're right. Safety is important, so it's likely she needs to move, and I need to get some fresh clothes."

"I brought your suitcase and set out your outfit."

"You picked my clothes?"

"You'd prefer your birthday suit?"

She shook her head.

"I selected something comfortable for you."

Her mouth formed a perfect O, and I decided I needed some distance before we left. A hard-on was distracting enough, and naked Allie, mere feet away from me, was lethal. I'd already used all the control in my reserves this morning.

"Get dressed. Breakfast will be ready in five minutes. I'll be in the dinette."

Her heated stare bore into my back, and it took all my strength not to turn around and take advantage of the situation. Thankfully, Allie didn't keep me waiting long, and she looked as good in jeans and a long fall sweater as in everything else. Her smile grew wider as she spun in a circle.

"You look amazing. I guess I chose the right outfit."

"You got lucky. I don't get to look like this often. The uniform is my life."

"Was your life."

She stilled again, as if she'd just realized what she gave up for Silver Securities. If she thought I'd let her talents go to waste, she was wrong. I'd ensure she flourished.

"Tristan, about last night—"

"You know, I was hoping to get lucky last night, but the tequila won." I leaned in and kissed her cheek. Her semi-dry hair released a fresh essence. It drove me crazy that life couldn't be simpler, where the scent of hair was the highlight of the day. That life would let me take this woman home and relax and find everything that made her tick. Maybe my parents were right. Maybe it was time to start a family, the way James had. Fatherhood suited him more than he'd expected, and he was the best single father I'd ever seen.

Allie cleared her throat, bringing me back to the present. I'd never been stuck so far in the future before. Not since the accident. It had been so long. This year marked the fifteenth year, yet it felt like yesterday. After I lost myself to work, I lost the will to move forward. But my retribution would come when Hartley paid for killing his daughter.

* * *

After breakfast, we drove over an hour west of Charleston. The houses scattered, the distance between them increasing. I steered along a dirt road, weaving up the mountain. The first fall leaves littered the fading grass. A blend of oranges, reds, and yellows decorated the hillside in fall blends. The mountains reminded me of our family ranch.

Allie rolled down the window, and the wind fluttered her hair. The trees grew taller, and the scent of recent rain and fresh moss filled the car. I pulled over to the graveled side near the peak.

"We're here?" she asked, looking around. "It's the middle of nowhere."

"It's exactly where someone would hide, isn't it?" I watched the contours of her face change to interest.

I opened the trunk and removed the rifle.

"Whoa—"

"Don't worry. I'm not the one shooting. You are."

"What exactly am I shooting?"

"Come on." I took her hand and guided her across the wall of shrubs. Beyond, a forest covered the valley below. We walked to the edge of a hill. Allie followed my every step as we crossed to a patch of grass that overlooked the valley.

"Get comfortable."

I unclipped the binoculars from my side belt and lowered myself to the ground. Allie hurried down beside me and immediately searched in the same direction where I was looking. I lifted the binoculars and focused the lens. Moments later, I found the target's house.

"Got it," I whispered, and handed her the binoculars. I wrapped my arm around her and directed her gaze.

"One o'clock. There's a house in the forest. A patch of greener grass near the driveway." I whispered.

She held still. "Got it. It's a wooden structure. A log cabin, not over twenty by twenty, windows covered with cardboard. A simple home turned sideways, both front and back yard visible."

"That's right."

"There's no one outside."

"Then make him come out."

"Who?" Her voice trembled. She pulled the binoculars away from her eyes and looked up. I held the rifle out to her. She looked at the gun, then at me again.

"Exactly who you want, Allie."

"Impossible." She shook her head while I nodded mine.

"Nothing's impossible. It's what you want, isn't it?"

She hesitated. "This is the business you had in Charleston?"

"No. That's unrelated. This came up last night."

The drunk and fun Allie was also the honest and vulnerable one. I doubted she had a clue how she'd cried on my lap before falling asleep.

She swallowed hard and reached for the rifle. She set up the machine like a pro, lowered herself back to the ground at the rifle's end, and positioned herself. I lay down beside her.

"Breathe, Allie. Please remember to breathe," I whispered.

Her body shook as she focused on the scope, but the trembling settled when she refocused on the target.

"He lives closer than you thought, doesn't he?" I asked.

Her jaw tightened, and I couldn't imagine what was going through her mind. Peg hadn't provided many details. Records showed a stillborn baby which had suffered severe trauma and was buried by her father. Allie's mother had revealed a grave burden when she'd told me Allie was in the house when Wright broke in.

She stilled. "He's out."

"Good. Take a deep breath and let it out. Do that three times."

She repositioned her body and did as I asked, all the while keeping her eye on the scope. "He's older—gray hair and a new hump on his upper back."

I watched as the racing pulse in her jugular slowed. She guided her rifle to follow Wright's every move. Her brows narrowed, then relaxed again.

"I can't believe you actually found him," she whispered.

"You've got what you wanted, Allie. Pull the trigger and go back to the force. Life can resume to normal, and your mother doesn't have to fear him any longer."

"What about your girl?"

"Let's deal with one problem at a time."

She remained in position, focused. A light twitch ran along the back of her leg.

"He's sharpening a blade on a whetstone. His clothing is old, but that look on his face…"

She pulled away from the scope. An oval outline from the optic circled her eye. She rolled up her sleeves and pulled on her sweater, loosening the fit. Her lip trembled, but she bit down to stop the twitch. Determination rippled through the air between us.

"You don't have to do this." I barely heard my own voice, but judging by the twitch near her shoulder, she heard me. "I know what revenge feels like. It starts tight in your chest and squeezes until nothing else matters except changing that trajectory. You don't experience vengeance's wrath until it's too late because it's choking you. And all this time, all you needed was change, Allie. Let me be that change for you. Revenge will come on its own."

She shut her eyes and pressed her fingers to her eyes, suppressing tears.

"You don't know what it's like to watch your mother disappear into nothing because of a man. He not only ruined her, but he's also a murderer."

"Who likely covered his tracks, right?"

She pulled her fingers away from her eyes and looked up, searching my eyes.

"If he covered them, we can find how. I know a thing or two about crooked cops and deceitful politicians. They excel at covering their tracks. They break the law without consequence and masterfully plan deadly accidents." Raging fire flashed in my mind. I shook it off. "The elite have funds no one does, but we're not alone in the fight. We have allies. And you're not alone in this either, Allie. You don't have to take that shot if you don't want to."

"I feel this anger inside me. And fear. If I don't take the shot, he'll find her, and when he does, he'll kill her. He's obsessed. This is more than revenge, Tristan. It's saving her life."

"You have two choices. Take the shot or don't take it. If you take the shot, I'll get rid of the body. No questions asked. You can go on with your life as if nothing happened. And on Friday, you'll come to my office and we'll make it official."

"That's it?"

"Yes."

"That's murder."

"It is. But you want him dead, don't you?"

Confusion swam in the tears welling in her eyes. She blinked, releasing them.

"I think you'll like the second option better."

Her eyes darted back to mine. A glimmer of hope sparked in her irises.

"We can leave him be, and I will take care of him. Legally."

"There's no evidence of what he's done."

"Maybe not what he's done to your family, but that's not all he's done. I promise you, I will get him and make sure he lands in prison, where he truly gets what he deserves."

"Before he gets to my mother?"

"Your mother's safe with Julian. I drove them to the airport this morning. She'll be a guest at my parents' house with the best security in the country until Wright is out of the way."

"She trusted you?"

"It took little persuasion once I told her Wright was in the area."

"You what?"

"I need you focused. Will you focus now that your mother is safe at the Silver residence?"

She lowered herself back to the scope. "I've been waiting for this my entire life."

"This isn't you, Allie," I whispered. "As much as you want this son of a bitch dead, you can't fire unless it's in self-defense. You took an oath. This would be murder, and I'd much rather see this bastard climbing the social ladder from behind bars. Once he's inside, he'll get exactly what he deserves. Besides, your father wouldn't want you to do this."

"Wright needs to suffer." She sniffled and blinked repetitively past the tears.

"A bullet to the head is not suffering. Your mother will get the best lawyer in Manhattan."

She turned her head toward me. "The Wagners?"

I tilted my head to the side.

"Yeah. How—"

"I have sources too. They call you guys the Billionaire Trifecta. Investigations, security and law."

"Who's they?'

"I don't know. People. Everyone. You get into trouble, but you never face consequences."

"Our troubles are the consequence. Kendra's the biggest of them troubles out there."

I noted her relaxed shoulders and took advantage of the moment.

"My family will take good care of your mother. I really need you, Allie. If I don't get Kendra, my company and my family will be ruined. More importantly, she will die, along with many others. It's been two weeks since she disappeared, and I fear we may already be too late."

She shivered. I slowly removed her finger from the trigger and her arm from around the rifle. She fell into my arms and sobbed for an hour, staining my sweater with her tears and snot, and I couldn't imagine being elsewhere.

"I'm sorry," she said at one point.

"For what?" I rubbed the sides of her arms and kissed her forehead.

"I wanted this job because I needed to find him, and here you've found him already."

"Does that mean you don't want the job anymore?"

"No. Not at all. I want to help you find Kendra. I want her safe. You work on Wright, and I'll work on her."

"Deal." I held her tighter.

A new impulse ticked inside me like a bomb. The more time I spent with Allie, the more the urge to protect her grew. I protected people for a living, but this was different. It hit closer and deeper, beyond my job. She was young and talented, smart and resilient. We clicked. Add to that her courage and the freckled face, how could I not find her attractive?

We sat on that grass for hours. She snuggled into my chest until cooler air from the north forced us to move. I drove straight to the airport, and we flew back to New York that night. Allie called her mother from the plane before settling in her seat. She would start training within days. James had infiltrated their circle, and Wright... well, that bastard was a battle I temporarily postponed.

The alley smelled of semen and piss. The mini I'd bought from an eighties boutique rose up my thighs with each step. A gust of wind blew, but my hair-sprayed style remained intact. My provocative tube top ensemble showed off my boobs. They hadn't bounced with this much freedom since my days on the stage. As naked as I felt without my bullet-proof vest, by the end of the night, Tristan Silver would know I deserved the job at Silver Securities. He'd already done the unthinkable for my mother, so I owed him.

A poignant aroma of cheap perfume hit me: a blend of exotic blooms with a spice. I strolled to the curb, regarding the redhead at the corner. Her name was Portia. I'd paid her off with three times what she'd earn in a night to let me join her turf. It didn't stop her from glaring at me like she wanted to rip out my throat. She worked the sidewalk toward me with her head held high and her ass swinging behind her like a pendulum. I observed her every move, soaking the appearance into my own.

"Your lips are too pale." She handed me a bright red lipstick. Her forced Bronx accent sold her out. She couldn't have moved here too long ago.

"Thanks." I pulled out my own from the small pouch I used as a purse. "So, you think he'll show today?"

"He drives by here every other day, but he never stops. I figure he goes to the west side, but a girl I know said he doesn't. Why do you think he'll stop for you?"

I pulled out a pack of fresh bubble gum and handed her a piece. "Just a hunch. Any idea why he drives by?"

"What am I, psychic?" She turned on her pumps and strolled back to her corner.

I popped the strawberry strip into my mouth and chewed it with the full motion of my jaw, the same way the redhead did. Each time a car passed, she'd bend over. Portia wore no panties and apparently had no shame. A car stopped at the curb beside her. The male customer rolled down his window, and Portia leaned inside. Her skirt rose at the back, and the under-curve of her ass hung out. After a minute of chit-chat, she jumped into the car, and they drove away. She waved out the window before flipping me the bird.

The sound of screeching brakes echoed from the other side of the road, and I whipped my body around, facing bright headlights. The quiet purr of an engine rumbled, and my stomach tightened. It had to be Silver. I took a deep breath in and added an extra sway to my hips.

It's now or never.

I paced my fuck-me walk the way I'd practiced at home in my new and only pair of five-inch heels. I stopped at the passenger door, and Tristan rolled down the window.

"What the fuck are you doing?" he asked through gritted teeth.

It wasn't exactly the greeting I'd expected. "You interested, hun, or not?" I chewed my gum like a cow, completely committed to the role.

One of his brows rose with amusement. He shook his head

but failed to hide the small lift at the corner of his mouth. "Get in."

"Deposit first." I stretched out my hand.

His mouth softened. Silver reached into his wallet and pulled out a handful of crisp hundreds. His dimple sank in his chin, and my heart skipped a beat. I didn't count how much he gave me, but it was a lot of money.

"You're mine until morning. Now get in."

I hopped into the Bentley. My mini rose to within an inch of my thong, almost showing my crotch. Silver pressed the gas pedal, pushing me back into the leather seat, but eased off within moments. For someone who liked fast cars, he certainly didn't drive them the way most did. The car responded to his gentle touch, purring along the road. Inside, the aroma of a coconut air freshener and scotch overpowered me.

"Do you drink and drive?" I asked.

"No, why?"

"I smell scotch."

"You have a good nose. Now, can you tell me what the fuck you think you're doing?"

His tone threw me off guard, and even without the tequila, it took longer than usual to compose myself. I took a deep breath in. "I'm applying for a position. If it's a hooker you want, a hooker you'll get. But I prefer you call me Katie." I fluttered my lashes.

The scar on his lip lifted by a fraction. He liked Katie.

"Did you know women get kidnapped from that corner? They disappear and never come back."

If Tristan was trying to scare me, it wouldn't work. I'd trained for this; I'd always known I would do something big with my life, and helping women who found themselves in deadly situations was it. Becoming a police officer was a stepping stone, and I wouldn't waste the opportunity Tristan gave me. Whatever our goal to save Kendra entailed, I wouldn't let them down.

"Is that where they kidnapped Kendra? Because that's what my informant told me."

"Informant?"

I nodded with a somewhat cocky smile.

"No, not here. Kendra... she helped the girls get off the street. I don't know how, but she had her ways. She trained and hired many of them. Took them off the streets. Gave them jobs at her club."

"Sounds like she's been saving lives for a long time, and now she's the one in trouble."

He scoffed. "Trouble. That's what you get when you deal with Kendra."

"It sounds to me like she has a big heart."

Tristan's grip tightened around the steering wheel. "She has a big addiction, which overshadows that heart. And now she's missing."

He pressed the brakes harder than intended, stopping on a red light. He turned his head my way and lifted his brow. "You're going to deal with palmy men."

"Nothing I haven't handled before. I used to strip, remember?"

"Right." He growled.

"Relax, Tristan. Think of it as an enjoyable experience. I've dealt with worse than men with sticky fingers and twitchy palms."

"Your rights will be stripped, and they'll treat you like cattle."

"Are you trying to scare me? Because it's not working."

The light turned green, but Tristan waited, doubt rippling through his clenched muscles.

"I can do this," I whispered.

"With your experience, you'll blend in easily. Every single

fucking pimp will wag his tail like a dog when they see you. And then we'll step in and rip off their balls."

"Sounds… bloody and painful."

"It's all they deserve. I'm very grateful you're willing to do this. I have a surprise for you tomorrow; but tonight, you're mine."

That beautiful tightening in my stomach returned as heat flowed along my skin.

"You're looking for someone who can pose as an escort girl, not a hooker, aren't you?" Suddenly my eighties dress-up felt awkward.

The car slowed to a stop, and Tristan turned my way. "You're gorgeous and smart. That's a lethal combination. But I'm not looking for an escort girl either."

"That's good to know."

He focused back on the street, but kept his foot on the brake. I was certain he would go on the empty four-way stop, but he held.

"Tristan?"

Tires screeched in the distance. Tristan gripped the wheel and pressed his foot harder on the brake, shaking like he was losing it. I turned as headlights flashed; an out-of-control Camaro barely made the corner, going well over the speed limit, and came to a stop in the middle of the intersection.

The guy revved his engine and took off, leaving smoke and fumes behind.

I twisted in my seat. "How did you know?"

Tristan sat silently until I touched his arm. He jumped out of his thoughts and shifted my way. "I heard him four streets down."

"That's impressive. Are you okay? Tristan, you're shaking." The tremors flew through his arms and shoulders until he took notice and physically shook them out.

"Yeah, I'm okay. I'm fine. I'm sorry."

"I can drive if you're not feeling well. I'm pretty good."

The side of his mouth lifted and my heart thumped a little harder. The scar twisted his lip into a sexy smirk as the dimple sank, turning on his boyish charm. Gosh, he looked hot.

"You can drive a stick?" His eyes widened.

"I drive all kinds of stick." I winked. "And I'm an excellent driver." I pulled on the door handle, hopped out, and hurried around the car. The mini and high heels constricted my movement to miniature steps. I removed the fuck-me pumps and opened the driver's door. "Come on. You can trust me."

His gaze fell to my feet. "Barefoot?"

"Not the first time." I stretched my smile into the widest of grins possible, and he complied.

Tristan set the GPS he must have never used, and I followed the directions in silence, concentrating on the road. The smooth ride and empty roads led to Manhattan, where the lights switched on a new life. He guided me to a parking spot in a building across from Central Park.

I pulled into the underground garage and parked in a private spot near the elevator. Four other Bentleys, silver and black, were lined up against the wall. Each one shone with a fresh coat of waxed pride. I turned off the ignition and twisted in my seat. He eyeballed my boobs and exposed thighs.

I squeezed my knees.

"That was hot."

"You're welcome. You should see what I can do with a boat."

"Don't tell me you fly as well."

I laughed. "No."

"You surprised me tonight."

"The evening is not over yet, Mr. Silver."

He shook his head, looking at me like I had too many special brownies. Maybe I was crazy, but I needed him more than I could ever have imagined needing someone. I straightened my back. "I wasn't going to bring it up tonight, but what's gonna happen to Wright?"

"He's flying out of the city tomorrow."

"What? How?"

"He'll remain on the west coast until we free Kendra, and then he'll be cuffed. He'll be put away for a long time, Allie."

Years of anxiety bubbled out on a nervous breath of relief and laughter. Was what he'd said really possible? Yet why wouldn't it be? Tristan Silver was part of the Trifecta, and the billionaires always got what they wanted.

"You're a careful driver," I said.

His brows narrowed.

"I mean, for someone who drives a Bentley, you know. You're careful."

One brow lifted, and that dimple sank into his cheek again. He pulled his fingers through his hair, and I melted.

"My roommate says the car a man drives reflects his performance in bed." I bit my lip and gripped the steering wheel.

"I promise no correlation between my driving and my fucking."

"I wasn't implying—"

"No?"

Of course I wasn't.

"Were you thinking about me fucking you in my bed?"

Yes. "No."

Tristan's smug grin layered with sexiness remained pasted on his face as he clicked his seat belt free and reached over my legs to a side pocket in the door. I gripped the seat sides. His warm breath trailed along my thighs and I could have sworn he took a longer inhalation while near my apex. Everything inside me turned into mush. My stomach swirled, and I bit my lip at the sweet pulse between my legs deepened. Tristan sat up, his jaw set firm and dick hard, and I could barely breathe.

Concentrate, Allie.

"This job requires you to be on duty twenty-four seven. Sign it." He handed me the sheet.

"What is it?"

"An NDA. You will not speak to anyone about the work you do for Silver Securities, understood?"

"Of course." I signed on the last line.

"You didn't read it."

"I trust you."

"Mistake number one. Don't trust anyone. Do you really want this job or not?" His brow lifted.

The bossy Silver was not as much fun as the flirty one, but Tristan was wrong about this.

"You're not just anyone, Tristan. And if I can't trust my employer, who will keep me safe, then who can I trust?"

The silence between us sizzled with desire and hormones. If it weren't for the light directly above us, I'd have straddled his lap and tasted the scar on his upper lip, just to convince him I was right. We breathed in sequence. This was it. To succeed, Tristan had to trust me as well.

"It will be dangerous." The obvious reluctance in his voice gave me the shivers.

"I never thought otherwise."

"If something goes wrong, they could sell you to a pimp who'll use you to service fifty men a day."

My breath stilled. Human sex trafficking. And he was still trying to scare me because Tristan would never allow me to be sold.

"Then it's a good thing we trust each other," I whispered.

"We do, don't we?"

His eyes softened, and the tension in his neck eased. And as much as my mind urged me to think twice, every nerve in my body guided me to trust him with my life. After all, it would be my life we'd be selling, wouldn't it? But we'd also be saving Kendra.

"How did you know where I'd be?" he asked.

"You're not the only one with sources," I said, remembering the past couple of evenings I'd spent driving around the city asking about a man in a Bentley. "Why would you say a hooker?"

"I wanted to see if you were up for an odd job. You took it to a whole new level, looking for strangers on the street."

"You're not really a stranger, though."

"True. But I am a man with needs, and you're testing them all." The tone in his voice zapped me below my belt and my panties dampened. The pressure to give into the carnal need grew.

"How can you handle so much tequila?" he asked out of nowhere.

I welcomed the change of subject and wondered how he'd known what I was thinking. "Practice."

"Drinking won't be a problem, will it? You should know that I have an issue with substance abuse."

"Yet you smell of scotch all the time." I rolled my eyes.

"A sip is not the same as addiction."

"I'm not an addict. And no, it won't be a problem. I may like a drink or two..."

"... or three." He cleared his throat.

"Or three, when I'm off duty, but I take my work seriously. Lives depend on it, and I wouldn't do anything to jeopardize people's lives."

"That's what I thought." He opened his door, walked around to the driver's side, and opened mine. I took his offered hand and stepped out of the vehicle with as much grace as the mini allowed me. "We'll go over the details this weekend, but tonight, I'd like to forget about reality."

Delectable shivers scattered over my skin, reminding me how much I'd yearned for his touch. He hadn't touched me in

Charleston, but I wanted him to. I craved his touch more than I craved tequila to calm myself.

Tristan locked the car and tightened his grip on my hand. My pulse raced with every step. The exclusive elevator opened as soon as we approached. He guided me with a light touch on my lower back, and we stepped inside. Tristan scanned a card and clicked the penthouse floor.

"Welcome home, Mr. Silver," the automated speaker intoned above head.

The elevator lifted against gravity, and my feet pressed to the floor. Tristan turned and pinned me against the mirrored wall. His sultry stare bore through me. Body to body, his strength dominated mine, and I found it difficult to breathe. Goose-bumps peppered my skin as the desire grew deep in my belly.

"If I had a choice, I wouldn't hire you, Allie. I'd keep you far away from the scum. I'd keep you to myself. But you're too perfect for the job. You're beautiful, smart, and strong. And most important, you've already seen the man we're looking for."

I recalled the Saturday afternoon as if it were yesterday because I'd agreed to swap a shift with Laura. We usually tried to stick to our schedules, as switching meant sleep deprivation for a day or so, but her baby boy caught a bug, forcing her to stay home.

"You're sure Martinez is our key to finding Kendra?"

"Right now, he's our key. They'll sell Kendra to the highest bidder at one of two auctions. If he's successful, we'll lose our chance to get her."

I forced my cop instinct to return to my brain. "So, we go to the auction and get her back. What's the problem?"

"It's not just any auction, Allie. If we don't get her that first night, if she's not there, you won't be able to attend another auction. We've infiltrated the group, and if everything goes our way, James will buy you both and you will be home before midnight."

Like Cinderella.

I slightly recalled James from the station when I'd booked his younger brother.

"I trust you, Tristan. You will not fail me."

"You remind me of someone who was as strong as you. Someone I failed. And—trust no one," he said.

"Who do you trust?"

"My family. Same way you do. And I trust you."

Did he realize he was a hypocrite? A cute one, so I had to forgive him. His words relaxed me, and warmth filled my chest before a devilish grin returned to the side of his face.

"Help me forget about work tonight. I'd much prefer to concentrate on you."

He slid his hands up my bare arms and cupped my face, tilting my head to that perfect angle. I closed my eyes and parted my mouth. His lips naturally found mine. The delicate kiss bent me to the knees, forcing my body to lean on him for support.

It wasn't supposed to be like this. He wasn't supposed to hold such power over me. You know, the kind which messed with your head and heart. I was a cop. A strong cop tortured by crying babies, cute puppies, and gorgeous billionaires in their Bentleys who offered everything they owned and more. Was that what he was offering? He'd lived through more than I had and skipped right through the bull-shit years of life long ago. He didn't live in his mom's basement and knew what he wanted from life. Just like I did.

He pulled away, robbing me of his heat, and searched my eyes with his.

"Where are you at, Allie? I wish I could read your mind." His jawbone tensed, and his eyes filled with pain.

"Tristan, you're personally invested in this job. That's not a good thing for you or anyone else."

"No talking about work today. Now, what will two thousand dollars buy me, sweetheart?" He lowered his mouth to mine for a promising smooch and all the trepidations in my head sailed away on his lips.

Fine. I could play his game for now.

"Whatever you want."

My body had secretly ached for his touch since he'd walked into the auditorium. And that kiss we'd shared in his car and tonight, everything was like a teasing spoonful of chocolate cake. I craved the whole cake, and not just a bite.

Tristan crushed his mouth to mine, like he'd heard my craving. He captured my mouth like he owned me, parting my lips with his needy tongue. And at this moment, he owned every single piece of me.

A hint of scotch lingered along his gums. The taste had grown on me. He gripped my wrists and lifted my arms above my head. His demanding fingers wrapped around my hands like cuffs. The forceful grip brought out a long-forgotten yearning in my belly. Tristan matched my every move and swallowed my every moan. Robbed of my breath, my limbs turned to jelly.

He let go of my mouth and trailed his lips along my jawline, over my cheek, and up to my ear before lowering down my neck. He pinned me harder against the wall. I breathed in the oak scent on his skin and in his hair. It messed with my head even more.

The elevator halted and Tristan jolted up as if he'd just realized what he'd done. And for the first time tonight, doubt crept in. He leaned his forehead against mine and shook his head like he'd made the biggest mistake of his life.

Chapter 9

Tristan

"We can't do this. I'm your employee," she whispered into my mouth before I told her I could no longer keep my hands to myself. The open elevator chimed for the third time. The urge to have her home and in my bed grew.

"Your body says we can." I kissed her again, gently tugging on her lip. My hands lowered to her engorged breasts. I skimmed my thumbs over her pebbled nipples. She responded with another soft moan that drove me crazy. This was so wrong and so right, but I'd known the outcome of tonight the moment I saw her in that mini. Her risqué outfit might have been the perfect one for a hooker, but many girls wore minis back in my time, stirring all kinds of dirty thoughts. The urge to get it off her ass grew as fast as my dick.

"You have doubts." She writhed in my grip, and so I lifted her into my arms.

"Quite the opposite, Allie. And technically, you're not hired until you sign the papers. Anything else doesn't matter right now."

I kissed her again and stepped off the elevator. When the

door closed, she slid down my body and removed her fuck-me pumps.

"We're gonna go on technicalities?" she asked.

"No, we're gonna go by your needs. All your needs."

I kissed her again. Jesus, she tasted like freshly picked summer strawberries warmed in the sun. She was the beginning that could end my struggle.

"Come." I took her hand, dropped the keys in the bowl, and led her to the kitchen. "Make yourself comfortable."

I opened the fridge and removed the champagne while Allie looked around the penthouse.

"I don't think I've ever stepped inside anything this fancy." She admired the sleek furniture in white and charcoal tones and Scar Wagner's red-toned artwork hanging on my walls before she turned around to face me. Her flustered face and prominent freckles glowed. She breathed hard, in and out. "Why do I feel you're way out of my league?"

Did she even know how wrong she was? I cocked my head to the side and took her in. Her strong yet delicate physique sang to all my senses. Her humility sang to all the years I'd spent realizing money couldn't buy a decent woman, though it could still impress her enough to give me a chance. Between the two of us, she was the one out of my league.

"Come here."

I set the champagne to the kitchen counter and lowered my hands to her hips and caressed her lips with mine, teasing and prepping them, showing her how much we synched. She swelled with every kiss and touch, wrapped her arms around my neck, and raked her fingers through my hair with approval. Her finger pads raked through the tension on my scalp. I slid my hand down to her thigh and scrunched her mini upward until I reached a strapped holster. I smiled against her mouth.

"You're prepared."

"You never know what weirdo you'll run into on the street."

I pulled the buckle open and set her piece aside on the table.

"It's a good thing you didn't run into one tonight." I drew my thumb along her lower lip while my other hand returned to her thigh. Her silky thighs drove me crazy.

"Right, that's an excellent thing." I reached to the small of her back and lowered the zipper. The mini slipped off, revealing a black lace thong. My dick pulsed harder, tenting my pants. I grabbed her ass and lifted her to the kitchen counter.

She squealed.

"The marble is cold."

"Not for long."

She laughed.

I reached her tube top hem and pulled it over her head. Her beautifully young breasts bounced in front of my face. I cupped them and lowered my mouth to hers, stealing her next breath, then dragged my lips along her jawline and down her neck. Her lower back arched as she pushed out her chest. Her head lolled back, and she closed her eyes, waiting. I trailed a line of kisses to the valley between her breasts and pinched the pink nipple. She writhed underneath my touch. I lowered to her navel and the edge of her panties, where I left a row of kisses along the lacy rim. Her sun-shy skin blossomed with flushed patches of heat, yielding to my mouth and touch. I ripped through the delicate fabric with my teeth and removed the panties from her hips. I lifted her feet to the top of the counter and spread her feet apart, exposing her. Her pussy glistened with need, and her skin sprinkled with excitement. By then, my dick was hard and ready.

"Tristan," she breathed. "Please."

I kissed a downward path from her inner knee down to her beautifully waxed pussy.

Fuck!

She pulsed with impatience underneath my lips, urging me to soothe her swollen clit. I locked my lips around her and flicked my tongue. Her hands flew to my head, holding me steadily over the spot. I slid a finger inside her, stretching her while devouring her. The tender strawberry taste was driving me nuts.

I hummed against her pussy, "You're fucking delicious."

"Tris-tan!" Her words hiccupping as she pushed herself harder into my mouth. I sucked on her clit and added another finger inside her before closing my mouth over the bud. I flicked my tongue around the delicate flesh, back and forth. It swelled under my tongue's strumming. I pumped harder in an unforgiving rhythm until a tremble flew through her body. Goosebumps scattered over her skin. She held her breath through the next zap before she released a scream.

"Tristan!"

It was the most beautiful scream I'd heard in my life.

I closed my mouth over her clit, triggering her full orgasm. She shook underneath my lips, and I didn't let go until she pushed my slobbered face off her pussy. I grabbed her wrists, pinned them to the counter, and dove in once more, reviving her orgasm and forcing a stronger one out of her limbs until she lost all strength and lay flat on the counter.

I grabbed a kitchen towel and wiped my mouth down, listening to her spent breaths.

"That was incredible."

"The night is still young." I pulled her up and lifted her petite frame into my arms. She squealed. That was the second best sound I'd heard in the world. I wasn't sure what was happening to me, but suddenly I wanted a collection of all the sounds she made when I took her in every way.

"I want to fuck you, Allie. Hard."

"It's a good thing two thousand dollars buys you a fuck," she breathed. "Katie's at your full disposal tonight, Mr. Silver."

God, she was good. Too good. She attracted all the wrong attention.

I carried her across the apartment to my bedroom. She held onto my neck, weaving her fingers through my hair, curling the single genetic silver strand I shared with my family around her digit, inhaling me. I lost my balance twice.

"Whoa, you okay?"

"Ever try walking with a hard dick in your pants? I don't recommend it."

She chuckled lightly as she slid down my body and grasped at the buckle. I sprang free five seconds later. Allie stared at my dick and licked her lips, and I couldn't wait to feel her tighten around me. Her focus shifted to my shirt, and she unfastened the buttons as fast as her little fingers could manage. I took a step forward, backing her onto my bed. She climbed backward with a sultry look that slowed time and made seconds last for hours. She looked up from underneath her mascara-heavy lashes, blinking innocently. I made a note to wash the makeup off later.

I walked around the bed to the nightstand and opened the drawer. I pulled out a condom, ripped the packet open with my teeth, and rolled the rubber onto my dick. She watched with intent as I joined her on the bed. I crawled until I hovered above her and lined myself at her entrance. I rested my arms at her sides, connecting my hard muscles to her warm skin, perky breasts, and nerved nipples hardening right against my chest. She yielded to me, opening her legs. Her lips parted as I slid inside her.

She closed her eyes, wrapped her legs around my hips, and tightened her hold on my dick. I grabbed her underneath her back and lifted her into my arms while I sat back on my legs. She held onto my neck and straddled me: body to body, skin to skin. Supporting her on my thighs and in my grasp, I plunged deeper, worried about the pressure her petite frame could withstand. That was, until she took over. Allie rode me like she fucking came out of a Western. Her hips controlled the motion, ensuring my length slid in and out of her pussy with ease. She picked up the momentum. The smell of our sweat, my cologne, and her floral perfume wafted around us, blending into a sexy mix. She threw her head back, her beautiful brown curls sliding from her chest to the back.

My balls tightened. A growl, thick with lust, vibrated in my chest before it escaped from the back of my throat. I withdrew, adjusted my condom, and lowered her to the bed on her side. With her back against my chest, I smoothed my hand along her soft ass and slid back inside her. She moaned, tilting her pear-shaped ass towards me. It was a young pear, but a cute and giving one.

The smooth rocking motion of our bodies, fused and working together, reached a fevered pitch. I slid my hand forward to her breast and played with her nipple. She angled her head backward for a sensual kiss. I kept her there, letting my hips work with hers. My hand inadvertently slipped down her belly and then to her pussy.

She gasped, and I crushed my mouth back to hers, sealing her breath. I slid my fingers down to where we connected and dragged the moisture upward to her clit. Her mouth opened as soon as I touched the spot. I circled my fingers in slow motion. Her body yielded to mine, begging for more.

"Fuck me, Tristan. I want you to fuck me. Please."

Her words sang with an invitation I couldn't resist. I withdrew again.

"Get on your knees." I said.

I adjusted the slippery condom. The right thing to do would be to get a new one, but when Allie lifted to her knees and stuck out her flushed ass, my attention swayed. She lowered to her elbows. Her slick pussy had swollen. I grabbed her ass and kissed each cheek before I got up to my knees behind her. I took hold of her hips and slid in with ease. The deeper entrance was everything my dick needed. I reached forward to her neck and covered the area with my palm. Her pulse thumped underneath my thumb as I traced the hollow in her neck. She yielded to my touch and, with her permission, I pushed my hips to the sweet rhythm of her pounding pulse underneath my fingertips. She braced one hand against the headboard.

I thrust forward. The skin to skin slaps echoed through the bedroom. That, along with her bursting yelps, created an orchestra. Feeling that point of no return, I held her hips steady. Each push jolted her forward harder than the previous one. I circled my hips, hitting her depth. The sound of her needs delivered with each moan drove me crazy. We moved in tandem. My fingers dug into the skin at her hips. Allie glanced back over her shoulder and whispered, "Cum on my back."

My balls zapped at her command. I removed my dick from her pussy, slipped off the condom, and watched as I spilled over her ass and back. She watched me with a devious smile until the last drop hit her skin.

"That was incredible." I lowered to kiss her. I hadn't smiled like this in a long time.

"There's more where that came from." She bit her lip.

"If that's so, I promise you'll be sore tomorrow." I grabbed her ass cheek in my palm and squeezed it enough to leave a bright print. She jumped with surprise and turned her head my way with a calculated glare.

"I'm looking forward to it, Mr. Silver."

I shook my head. "Stay there. I'll get a towel."

I cleaned her up and flipped her over on the bed. She squealed with happiness.

"You're fucking amazing." I lowered myself to a hover above her delicate body, supporting my weight on my hands, and kissed her. She inhaled my essence, which drove my dick back to its ready state. I centered my hips between her legs and slid inside her while stroking her eyebrow with my thumb.

Her eyes sparked with confusion, so I lowered my mouth to hers and kissed her again, hoping to comfort her. She moaned. Pleasure painted her face with a pink shade. Slow and steady, I rolled my hips with hers, her delicate belly against my pelvis and breasts mid-torso. I encased her in my arms. Her delicate moans confirmed everything I feared happening inside my chest. Doubt, insecurity, fear for her safety. Everything.

When I pulled away and looked at her, an unspoken understanding passed between us. Like this was fucking meant to be. I fell lost in her captive face and the slow rhythm of our bodies.

Her hips reached higher and rolled quicker. She rubbed herself against my pubic bone, giving me no choice but to quicken my thrusts. I lowered my mouth to her breast and caressed her nipple. I rolled it with my tongue and squeezed it with my lips, pulling up and releasing. The bud bounced over her breast and I gripped it between my teeth, teasing. She moaned, and I pushed harder. The nipple slipped out of my mouth, but I had no strength to catch it again. Instead, I watched her beautiful body coil into my need. On my bed. In my home.

And it was everything I never expected.

The next jitter flew through my balls, zapping me right up my shaft, and before I realized what was happening, I lost control. My hips buckled, and I stilled inside her, spilling everything I had.

Fuck!

My face must have had contorted like fucking Frankenstein's as the orgasm forced the last drop of my cum straight into her uterus.

Fuck!

"Hey, hey, hey!"

She brought me back to the moment. I realized I was still inside her warm pussy and pulled out as quickly as she allowed me to.

"Hey, Tristan. Relax. It's okay. I have an IUD."

"Fuck!" Relief dripped off my body, along with the sweat.

I fell to the bed beside her and turned my her way.

"It's not that I don't want kids. But they complicate life, and my life is complicated enough. Dangerous, in fact. It would be selfish to want to build a family."

"I agree. My roommate has a toddler. He's amazing, but I have no idea how she does it all."

"A single mother and a cop?"

She let out a long yawn, "She was the best partner ever. I'm going to miss her."

She stretched out her arms, taking note of the mess we'd made. "I'll wash the sheets in the morning."

I chuckled. "You'll what?"

"I'll wash the sheets in the morning." She yawned again.

"You'll do nothing of the sort." I lifted to my knees and scooped her into my arms.

"Tristan!" she laughed. "What are you doing?"

"Shower." I growled like the caveman I felt like at the moment, and she laughed again. I was enjoying the joyful sound more and more. It had been a long time since I'd lost myself in a moment.

I lowered her to the warmed tiles and turned on the overhead rain shower. She tilted her head back underneath the water. Hair spray and makeup streamed over her skin as steam filled the glass enclosure. She stepped forward, opened her eyes, and took my face into her hands, pulling me closer and tasting my mouth. I lifted her by her naked ass. Her legs wrapped around my waist and I braced her against the marble wall tile. She slowly uncoiled her legs and slid down my body, her soft curves slipping over my hard muscles, pale skin against my Kiwi tan, never letting go of my mouth. Her fingers weaved through my tussled hair, pulling slightly. I let her go with reluctance and squirted shampoo into my hands. I dabbed the soap over her wet hair, gently massaging the scalp. The hairspray gave into the suds and let go of its last hold.

"I must look awful," she said through the soap cascading down her face.

"You look beautiful, Allie." I touched my lips to hers and continued the wash. She held onto my arms. My muscles ripened underneath her delicate fingers. The hum of her breath vibrating off the water flowing down her face was beautiful. I slid my hands down her neck and to her shoulders, then to her chest, caressing each breast with my slick hands. The lower my hand skimmed, the longer she held her breath.

"Breathe, Allie."

She sucked in air like it would vanish. I lowered my hand to between her legs.

"Are you wet for me, Allie, or is this just the water?"

"For you."

"For me what, Allie?" I pulled my fingers between her pussy lips.

"I'm wet for you, Tristan."

"What do you want me to do about it?" I asked.

I knew exactly what she wanted, because it was exactly what I wanted to give her: attention and care and a fuckload of orgasms.

She looked up through her soaked lashes. "How are we going to make this work? You're supposed to be my boss."

"Fun now; work later." I slid my finger higher, washing gently and with intention. "I don't do showers like this every day, Allie."

My stare hardened. She watched my chest lift and lower, waiting for more. And I had so much more to give.

"You're unlike anyone I'd ever met. I—I've been locked up in here for years." I placed my hand over my heart, where the white scar marked my chest. "And you make me forget... about everything."

I brushed my thumb over her parted lips where a shadow of her red lipstick remained. She lifted her palm to my heart, drawing her finger over the faint scar. I sucked in a sharp breath and stepped back as if she'd burned me. Pain swam through my body at the memory.

"What happened there?" she asked.

"Car accident." I lowered my head. "It was a long time ago."

"Is that why you don't go over the speed limits?"

"Likely."

"But there's more to it. I can tell."

How could she tell? I never talked about that day. Hartley was difficult enough to remove from my life as it was. My fiancée's dead shadow followed me from morning to night. I didn't know whether it was the cop in Allie or her youth and the everlasting hope, but it took my mind off all the shit sitting on my psychologically disturbed shelf. Allie worked for me in more ways than an employee.

"You can really tell?"

She nodded and waited. I wasn't sure where to start. The damage from that day gripped my heart strings and never let go.

"Fifteen years ago, I was involved in a car accident. We were driving up a mountain in Austria, and I was behind the wheel. The brakes failed as soon as we passed the peak, and when I say it was a mountain, it was a mountain."

"You drove off a cliff?"

"Technically, I tried not to. But the mountains we planned to cross that day were steep and unforgiving. The brakes failed. The convertible flipped upside down before it landed in a tree crown. My seatbelt held me in, but Simone's didn't. My fiancée fell to her death. They found her mangled body the next day. All I got were two scars." He pointed to his upper lip and chest. "And a shattered heart."

"I'm so sorry." Allie touched her hand to her lips.

"After Simone died, I lost myself to work and… well… time flew by, and it's never felt like the right time to immerse someone in this crazy life."

I knew I met the wrong girl. At least that's what everyone around me said, but I never saw Simone that way. We were nineteen and silly. Fucked like bunnies, blind with lust. Our parents mingled in similar circles, until the strain between our families tore us apart. We were at a party when the news about Jeff's private island and perverse obsessions came out. I escaped with Simone on a boat and hid while her father hired a mutual friend lawyer, Frank Wagner, to defend the 'misunderstanding'. He won the case because the Wagners didn't lose, but the victory came with consequences. Hartley's obsession continued. Then came the funerals and Hartley's ugly divorce. I wanted to protect Simone from it all, but I failed.

My heart was beating hard in my chest. I hadn't noticed I was lost in the past until Allie's touch brought me back. Her eyes softened as she waited for me to continue.

"Many of my friends are also my enemies, and the rush never stops. Someone always needs saving. I love my work, but the consequences that come along are not the happily-ever-afters you read about in books. Although financially rewarding, it's difficult, draining, and dangerous."

I waited for her reaction, and it felt like hours passed before she spoke again.

"Everyone has baggage," she said. "And it appears yours is just as heavy as mine, so who am I to judge?"

She couldn't be twenty-five. She was too mature for her age. Too perfect.

"Kendra's relying on us, and I'll do my best to keep my mind clear. I promise you that."

"I don't know where you get that strength, but I'm thrilled to have you in my life."

It had been a long time since anyone had brought this level

of comfort. I lowered my mouth to hers before she said anything else. Allie was the priority now. When she pulled away, I squirted body wash onto my palm and continued with the lather over her skin. Thankfully, she didn't mention Kendra again. I started at the neck and made my way over her breasts and stomach, and down to between her legs. She winced when I touched her there.

"It hurts?"

"Yeah, but it's a good pain. And don't freak out if you see my skin change color. I bruise easily."

Good.

I continued with her legs and feet before scrubbing her back, rinsed the soap off, and washed myself. She stood underneath the shower, watching me. Unfortunately, she had the kinds of questions I had no answers for. Moments later, we were back in bed, underneath a layer of fresh sheets.

"How did you do that?" she asked.

"Not me. Melissa."

"Who's Melissa?"

"My housekeeper. If you need anything, just holler."

"Housekeeper. Holler. Right."

Tired, she laid her head on the pillow. Her limbs relaxed into the mattress. She turned toward me and slowly closed her eyes, smiling. I pulled her in, wrapping my body around hers. She lay at my side, resting her head over my chest. My breathing slowed and my heart settled. It would be the first night in a long time I had no bourbon before sleep, yet doubt crept into my mind. I didn't want Allie hurt, and I worried that pawning her at the auction was a mistake.

ristan's chest moved with even breaths. The white sheet was wrapped around his hips, covering everything that had made last night absolutely magical. I lay still beside him, watching his eyes twitch as he dreamed. My heart beat steadily in my chest. He wasn't quite part of the plan, but who was I to argue against the mutual attraction? For the first time in my life, it was nice not to have a plan. But he was my boss, and I'd agreed to a serious job. We could figure out the rest later.

His cheeks sank in and his eyes rolled underneath their lids. I inhaled, breathing him in. The room still smelled of us and delicious sex. The digital clock on the bedroom ceiling shone six in the morning. Beyond the window, the sun glowed upward, lightening the sky from below.

Last night was so worth it.

I slid my legs over the bedside in slow motion and stepped onto my tiptoes. I grabbed Tristan's longer sweatshirt out of his walk-in closet and pulled that over my body. Although large, it was much better than the tube top, almost like a mini-dress.

Since his pants were at least twice my size, I slid the mini over my hips and tiptoed to the full-length mirror by the door. As expected, you couldn't see the skirt from underneath the sweatshirt. My freckles popped and my lips swelled, but the inch of makeup and pound of hairspray had been washed off last night. Besides, if Pretty Woman could do it, so could I.

I scrunched the fluorescent tube top and panties in my hand and crept to the bedroom door.

"Where do you think you're going?"

I froze mid-step and turned around in what felt like slow motion. Tristan hopped off the bed naked and rushed across the room, scooping me into his arms. I lost my grip on the tube top and shoes as he carried me to the washroom.

"What are you doing?"

"Making sure you don't leave."

"But—"

"Exactly,"

The icy stream of water hit me before I realized what he'd done.

"Tristan!"

"Beautiful." He kissed over my shoulder, removing his soaked, oversized sweatshirt down my body through the wide neckline. My head rolled back and water streamed down my face.

"Tristan," I breathed.

The mini lowered next and, just like that, I was standing naked in front of him. He spun me around in a swift move. I braced my hands against the wall, tilting my ass up for him, like I knew exactly what he was after. He slid his right hand around to my front and held onto my hip with his left. His full palm cupped my sex. He spread his fingers through my folds and rimmed my clit. I closed my eyes and pressed into his touch, circling my hips to the gentle rub.

God, that felt so good!

The delicate patting and nudging awoke my need. He

frisked me with gentle strokes, slowly speeding the motion. My tip ripened with the friction. I pressed my forehead to the shower tile.

He shifted, and his cock brushed over my ass. I looked back just as he drew his length down my crack and between my thighs. I shifted, parting my legs.

"Tell me what you want, Allie."

"I—I want you inside me."

He rammed into me without warning, hitting my depth.

"Ahh!"

He stayed pressed against me. "Are you okay?"

"Yes," I heaved. "Harder."

He pushed again, and I jolted up. Tristan held still, his chest against my back, my front flat on the wall, and his cock deep inside me.

My pulse hastened. He gripped my hips and held steady, finding a building rhythm. I braced my hands against the tile and lowered my front, legs wide apart. My ass stuck out, and his deliciously slow momentum grew. My breasts bounced in the air. Arousal tightened below my waist as I watched Tristan's bare feet standing behind mine.

"You're so fucking tight." His merciless rhythm was driving me crazy.

"Shut up and make me come." Oh, God! What was happening to me?

Tristan was so much. He was everything all at once.

"Be careful what you ask for." He withdrew from inside me and turned me around, dropping to his knees.

He looked up with a smirk. "We call this MTP care."

"We? What?"

He lifted my leg and bent it over his shoulder. His breath trailed up my thigh as he slid two fingers inside me. He watched me from below as he closed his mouth over my pussy and his tongue did its magic. Oh my God, that tongue! He basked in my folds, sucking on the tender tip. Pleasure zapped through my limbs with every flick. I pushed my arms out to the sides, in desperate need of support, but the shower was too wide. My toes curled, and I grabbed Tristan's shoulders, digging my fingers into his skin. My back arched as I pressed into his face and unforgiving mouth.

Tristan spared no moment of rest as he sucked on my swollen clit. The tender spot ripened under his strumming tongue. He pumped his fingers so fast I barely knew what was happening. I tightened around his digits. He hooked his fingertip, pressing against a spot on my inner wall. My skin ignited, and my mouth opened with laughter from deep inside my belly. I grabbed his head, pressing him into me, exploding into his mouth. My body spasmed until I could no longer stand.

He stood up and held my spent body against his.

"I planned breakfast in the kitchen, but this was much, much better."

My brow rose. I wiped the dripping water off my face and wiggled my thigh where he was hard against my leg. "Is that part of the breakfast?"

"If you want, it could be." The coy look on his face made my heart skip a beat as I imagined him as my breakfast.

The smell of a chocolate-vanilla brew wafted inside the shower.

"Is that coffee?"

"I told you—I planned breakfast."

He kissed the tip of my nose and gently touched me between my legs. "Are you sore?"

I was, but not sore enough to deny him, so I shook my head.

"Liar," he laughed. "Come on, we've got a long day today."

"I know. I'm going home and handing in my resignation."

He lowered his lips to mine and suddenly that resignation wasn't as important as it had been a moment ago. A needy growl vibrated from the back of his throat. Tristan pulled away from my mouth with reluctance.

"What's the matter?"

"You are home, and we need breakfast."

My heart stilled. Did I hear him right? And if so, what did he mean by that?

He wrapped one towel around my hair and semi-dried himself with another, and then draped an oversized fluffy robe over my shoulders.

"You can wear this for now." He hopped into a pair of jogging pants. I stared at him like I was living someone else's life.

Never in my life had I been so willing… with anyone. Not like that, and definitely not that quick. Commitment wasn't my thing, but then again, no one got me until Tristan. I had set my path, focused on Wright and Mom's well-being. The life of a police officer and vengeful daughter didn't allow for the luxury of new things and relationships. Yet here was Tristan, offering me everything, it seemed. I took in his hard body. The maturity, experience, and stability were definitely a bonus I'd never expected. There was no bullshit. Tristan knew what he wanted and worked hard for what he had. Judging by that scar near his heart, and the trauma brought on by his accident, he'd lived through moments as hard as mine. Some maybe harder.

I dragged my gaze down his sculpted body to where his morning wood had settled. The need returned to my apex at the thought of making him hard again.

No, no, no.

This wasn't some fucking escapade. This was Silver, and he was my boss.

I cleared my throat. "Is Melissa making breakfast?"

"No. I am. Breakfast is the most important meal of the day."

I laughed. "That's old school."

"Let's talk again after you try my omelet."

I definitely wanted to try something of his, but it wasn't his omelet.

I followed him to the bedroom, where he paced barefoot around the bed, straightening the sheets. Now, I didn't know many twenty-five-year-old men who made their bed, let alone ones who supported themselves. In contrast, here was Tristan... making the bed. Most men I knew lived in their mamma's basements. So yeah, Mr. Silver came with all kinds of bonuses.

"Is that something your parents encouraged?"

He looked at me in confusion. "What? Bed making?"

I nodded.

"No, that's from Admiral McRaven. YouTube. He says if you get nothing else done in the day, you'd at least have accomplished something."

"I'll look it up."

"It's from a commencement speech. He's a smart man. You had no allergies listed in your file."

He beckoned me with his index finger. I hopped over the bed and strolled to stand in front of him. The sneaky grin on his face held promises I couldn't read. He lowered his mouth to mine, where he left a heartening kiss.

"How do you like your coffee?"

That dimple, the scar on his lip, and the constantly genuine smile were messing with my head. What was happening to me?

"Wasn't that in my file?"

He kissed me hard, pulling the answer straight out of my lungs.

"Black. Please."

He took my hand and led me through the hall into the main living area, which was connected to the kitchen. I hadn't noticed all the luxurious details last night when we kissed our way to the bedroom. Now that I had my senses turned somewhat back on, I could appreciate the luxury of his home. White and charcoal tones contrasted the light furniture against the dark walls. The home's open concept gave the illusion of more space than there was—not that it was small. In fact, the living room alone was larger than my apartment. Decorative sheers hung at the window sides, draping to the hardwood floor where they fluttered in the air-conditioned breeze. The sun blazed through the full wall windows. Beyond, the breathtaking view of Central Park predominated with fall colors, the perfect backdrop to Tristan's monotone penthouse.

"If there's a way to impress a girl, I think this is it." I stared out the enormous window.

"I'm glad you like it, because this is where you'll live now."

"What?" I whipped my body around and followed him to the kitchen.

"It's part of the job."

"Conveniently enough."

"The auction will be in Manhattan, and it's more private than a hotel. "

As much as I doubted that was his true reason for keeping me in his penthouse, the reasoning made sense. Laura would appreciate the time she'd have with the baby, and I'd appreciate the restful night of sleep here... with Tristan.

The coffee machine beeped as the last drops trickled into the pot. Tristan poured two cups of coffee and set them on the kitchen counter. There was nothing better than the first sip of morning coffee. Okay, perhaps there was, and Tristan had proved it last night and this morning, but that first sip came pretty damn close.

"All right, so I may also have a selfish motive, but I promise you'll reap the benefits of those motives when I eat you out at night."

Instant heat covered my body.

Tristan pulled out a stool from under the counter and motioned for me to sit. The leather seat made me suddenly aware I wasn't wearing any panties. He must have noticed my discomfort and glanced at the clock. "Don't worry. The clothes are on their way."

What clothes?

Tristan was one of those people prepared for anything and everything. The notion brought comfort to my soul, because suddenly for the first time in my life, I didn't feel prepared for anything at all. He lowered himself to the counter, where he leaned on his elbows and gripped the cup of coffee into his hands.

"You know, I've never had a woman leave my bed willingly."

I didn't doubt that. I also didn't doubt there'd been quite a few women here before me, and that I wouldn't be the last one. Which led me to another important question. I crossed my arms over my chest. "Was last night a mistake?"

"The noises that came out of your mouth sounded very right to me."

"I'm serious, Tristan. I don't want to jeopardize my job."

"Aha, sleeping with the boss. I think we're beyond that, Allie, don't you?"

What did that mean?

"So… what are we? Because I don't—"

"You're overthinking, so let me clear up the confusion. I'm not your boss. Silver Securities is, though, which makes me your"—his eyes darted to the left and up, like he was searching for the right word—"it makes me your partner. I'm your partner, and you're mine. Simple as that. Your life depends on me, and mine depends on you."

No pressure.

"Are you going on some technicality again?" I asked. "Because technically, you own Silver Securities."

"Technicalities save lives."

I rolled my eyes and dropped the subject.

"So, any way you can give me more details on this job?"

He set his coffee aside and moved to the fridge, from which he removed eggs, vegetables, herbs, and cheese, and placed the ingredients on the counter.

"We're starting auction day rehearsals this weekend and training tomorrow. You'll change the way you breathe, walk, and talk. Hold on."

Tristan hurried to the foyer and brought back his cell phone. He texted someone while mumbling under his breath. "36C..." He looked me over as if I were an item in a grocery store, and continued. "28, 36, 8.5."

"What are you doing?" I asked, intrigued.

"Unless you want to wear that fucking hot outfit you wore last night to dinner at my parents' tonight, I'm getting your wardrobe."

I hopped off my seat. "Wardrobe?"

"Don't panic. It's for work. And you wouldn't want your mother seeing you in my shirts, would you?"

Right—we were attending a dinner with his family.

"My mother will be there? Tonight?"

He nodded.

"Thank you, Tristan," I whispered, and took his face between my palms, kissing him, forgetting all about the wardrobe.

"You're welcome." He breathed against my lips. "The people we'll be dealing with cater to the wealthy and disturbed. Your outfits will be custom made. Also, I want you here. With me."

Tristan removed a knife from its holder on the counter and proceeded with the vegetables.

"I hardly get the time to cook." He smiled.

"Looks like it's something you enjoy."

I watched as he sautéed sweet pepper and onion. He cracked two eggs onto the pan but didn't break the yolk. He slowly stirred, cooking the whites, then broke the yolk at the last minute, swirling the creaminess between the whites. The vegetables added beautiful colors throughout. My mouth watered.

"My grandmother used to make them this way."

"She's gone?"

"It's been some time. Liver failure. Seems to run in the genes. Not mine, though. It's predominant on our cousin's side."

"I'm sorry."

"Thank you." He pulled on a drawer handle, reached in, and removed a folder, setting it in front of me.

"We may as well do the paperwork here. Read it over and sign."

"You had an extra copy in your kitchen drawer?"

"I like to be prepared."

I read over the agreement while Tristan refilled my coffee and cut up the vegetables.

"No sexual harassment clause?" I asked.

"No. I can harass you anytime I want. Will that be a problem?"

The only problem I could see was my heart shattered to pieces.

"No problem." I flipped the page.

Tristan pulled out a stool, sat beside me, and turned my body to face him. His knees hugged the sides of my legs. He took my hands into his, and his face turned serious. His hazel eyes darkened.

"Allie, the job will be dangerous."

"I understand." I squeezed his hand. "And I'm not afraid, Tristan."

He took a long breath in and slowly released it.

"You should be. A little fear is good for everyone. It keeps us on guard. The dogs we're dealing with can smell a trap from a mile away, and the girl you'll be posing as needs to be afraid. Imagine—no future; and if there is one, it's a nightmare."

I shivered.

Tristan reached for his phone and opened a gallery of photographs. The first one was of a beautiful girl. Late afternoon sun lightened the side of her bronzed face as she held her arm up to remove a few blowing auburn strands from view. The carefree photo captured a stolen snapshot of her life.

"This is Kendra. They took her three weeks ago, and she likely looks different now. Thinner and bruised. I don't think they'll care to cover her wounds. But my sources tell me she's still alive."

He reached to the kitchen drawer, which seemed to serve as his office, and handed me a folder. I flipped through the papers, scanning every page. Adrenaline pushed through my veins, waking up the cop inside me. I'd need to look over the details later, but for now, some words stood out more than others. I cringed. Kendra was about to become a single man's commodity on his private island, where she'd serve him as a sex slave.

"We're meeting your handler in a couple of days. Friday night. If your roommate has time, invite her too."

I flipped the page to a photograph of a luxurious room and a row of naked women. My skin crawled with everything you don't want crawling over your body.

"Kendra will be at one of two auctions, and I'm hoping it's the first one. Once you or James recognize her, we'll get you both out."

"And if she's not there?"

"You're coming home either way." His tense jaw outlined the chiseled cheeks. "Are you sure you want to do this?" he asked.

Kendra must have been a special client to be worth the effort, but wasn't every woman worth it? My stomach turned at the sudden urge to save every soul from palmy men. When I scouted for Tristan and met Portia, I'd seen streets lined with minors. Women of all ages, shapes, and sizes filled dark alleys while their pimps lurked nearby. Sex trafficking was a combination of slavery and prostitution. Once in, there was no way out—not unless you knew someone like Tristan Silver or their missing client Kendra.

"We'll get her out, Tristan. I know we will. But what about the others?"

His shoulders eased. His phone sent through a notification chime.

"One sec." He slid his finger across the screen a few times before setting his phone aside. "I'm sorry about that."

I pressed my fist to my sternum. "Doesn't it break you here knowing you can't help the others off the street?"

"With every beat of my heart. I'm hoping once Kendra's safe, we can shift Silver resources to the cause."

A firm knock on the front door startled me.

"Aha!" Tristan jumped off the stool and hurried through the hall and to the door.

"You don't ask who it is?"

"I already know who it is."

He opened the door wide. A pleased smile stretched across his face. "Set it all in the living room."

An entourage marched into the penthouse. They were carrying boxes and pushing racks of clothes, lining them all around the living room until there was no more space to fill. It all happened so fast I barely reacted. Moments later, it was Tristan and I, alone in what looked like the women's section of a famous house I couldn't pronounce.

"Is all this necessary?"

But Tristan didn't reply.

"I mean, it's too much."

I paced between the boxes marked, boots, toiletries and delicates.

"You really want me to move in, don't you?" I couldn't help

but feel giddy all over again. This had never happened to me before. I thought I'd missed those heart-skipping teenage moments, yet here I was, with my heart skipping for a man I could see in my life forever.

This is just a job, I reminded myself.

But was it?

"It makes sense, you know... work-wise. Speaking of which, I have a meeting."

"May I ask with whom?"

"Jeffrey Hartley. We have some business to settle."

"*The* Jeff Hartley? The real estate billionaire?"

"Yes. One and the same."

"Wasn't he charged with pornography or something like that?"

"He was actually charged with more, but Wagner got him acquitted on technicalities. He didn't have a choice."

"I thought you said technicalities save lives."

"True in this case as well. Technicalities saved Jeff's life though he doesn't deserve to live. He's protected, and we can't get to him until his safety net is gone."

"Sounds personal."

But he didn't reply, which meant it *was* personal. And... were those nerves I'd heard in his voice? Tristan didn't get nervous, which for the first time made me feel a little uneasy.

"Right. It makes sense."

"Breakfast is ready."

He set an omelet with a side of toast in front of me. I refilled our coffee mugs, grateful Tristan's coffee addiction matched mine. With his luxurious coffee machine at home, I'd never have to visit a coffee shop again. But this wasn't forever. This was work. And sex. With the most mind blowing orgasms I craved every time I thought of him between my legs.

After breakfast, Tristan left for his meeting, while I stayed in his Manhattan penthouse like I was... his. I shook off the stupidity, organized the clothing, changed, and went down-stairs to get flowers and wine for the Silver dinner tomorrow afternoon.

As I walked through the private store in Tristan's building, the eerie sensation of someone following and watching me wouldn't let go. I stopped by the flower section, searching for the perfect bouquet. A girl with her mom went inside the flower shop, an older gentleman tipped his hat with a good afternoon, and an elegant woman with platinum hair and sunglasses picked out a bouquet of tea roses. But I couldn't see anyone suspicious.

Chapter 11

Tristan

An Uber pulled up to my rental, blocking the driveway. Simone hopped out of the vehicle with a backpack over her shoulder and closed the door. She ran to me in a hurry, her lightened blonde hair blowing with as much life as she had in her skip. She dropped the bag and jumped into my arms, clinging to me like an octopus and kissing me hard. I welcomed her mouth and body, wishing I'd taken less time to propose. I wanted Simone in my home and in my bed now and forever, but her father had some fucking pre-conceived notion that a couple should marry before they lived together. So that's what I'd do.

I'd met Simone as a teenager. Our families spent every vacation together. But as we fell in love, Hartley's criminal secrets mounted. Candice Hartley, now Watson, divorced her husband, and Simone distanced herself from her father. And for that, Hartley blamed me.

At the rate our family relations were deteriorating, an amicable wedding was impossible, so we agreed to elope in the Alps.

"Hey, I thought I was picking you up at the resort?"

"I told my brothers I was going with my father and vice versa."

"That will work." I laughed.

I'd rented a secluded cottage by a stream down in the valley, and it came with everything except the Hartley family. It was perfect.

"You know they'll want to kill me and lock you up in a castle once they hear what we've done."

She laughed. "They don't have a castle."

Maybe not a castle, but the Hartleys had dungeons and chains where they kept little girls. The thought made me sick to my stomach every single time.

The news Ace Wagner had announced last week sickened the entire family. It wouldn't be long before the media discovered Jeff Hartley's disgusting activities. While Simone's father had shielded her from the spotlight, I vowed to shield her from him.

"Once I'm Mrs. Silver, they'll have nothing to say."

"When we come back, you're moving out. It's time."

"I know. I can't wait to have privacy and a home and no brothers in the kitchen when I come downstairs in the morning."

I wanted the image of Simone's siblings gone for the weekend. The family was staying at a hot springs resort further up the range. All the more reason the next few days in Austria, alone with my fiancée were so precious. "I'm glad you're here. But we're triple-checking their itinerary before the next getaway."

"I was sure my father planned to go to the Maldives."

"Maybe at one point he did."

Simone sucked at keeping secrets. Jeff Hartley had come to Austria to hunt my ass about any evidence against his organization. Little did he know, the address he thought we'd booked was a decoy. Dating a criminal's daughter had pitfalls, and this trip away from the Hartleys couldn't come at a better time.

"I'm ready to go if you are. Jump in."

She hopped over the door and slid into the passenger's seat, securing the backpack between her legs.

"We can put that in the trunk."

"No, it's good here. I'm ready when you are. Let's go." She gripped her trembling knees.

I hopped into the Miata and pulled out of the driveway. The road up the mountain wound in tight turns up the scaling cliff. The low traffic eased my worry about the drive. Adrenaline spiked with each view of a bottomless gorge. This road ended past the second peak at the thermal spa resort, but nothing could beat our secret destination. The cottage by a stream was hidden in a deep valley.

I turned up the radio. Simone's hair fluttered to the wind's tune, but she was sad. On a normal day she would be belting along to ABBA, swinging her arms in the air, yet she just sat there, paying attention to the road. I passed a parked empty SUV at the top of the mountain. Simone rested her elbow on the door's edge and squealed when I pointed to our destination below.

The car rolled down the hill, and I sensed trouble before the next turn. I pressed the brakes, but they didn't work. I pumped my foot harder and harder, but it was clear they had failed. The wheels squeaked, and I turned left.

"Tristan!" Simone gripped the seat.

"The brakes!"

I slowed the car with the gears, but it wasn't enough. The hand brake failed on the next turn as well. The car tipped and bounced back on its wheels as we turned. Black smoke and a distinct smell of burning oil lifted from the hood. The tires screeched, pinning the sound of permanent trauma in my brain. We wouldn't make the sharper curve ahead.

"Tristan!"

"I'm sorry, Simone. I'm so sorry."

* * *

Drenched sheets wound around my body. I twisted and groaned, peeling them off. The nightmare pulsed through my mind and I gripped my hair, pulling on the long strands, like the pain would bring me back to the present and erase the memories. The terror eased, but it didn't pass. 5:00 am flashed on the clock. I showered and was zipping up my slacks when my phone rang. It had been a while since I'd seen the familiar number.

"Joe? What's going on?"

"They're at Magnet. Came in about ten minutes ago." Joe, one of my surveillance guys, had watched the elite spot for months.

"How many?"

"All three brothers. Plus their sons, Donaldson, and his guests as well. I called you at once but couldn't get through, so I called Julian as well. He's on his way."

"Good. Thanks. Let me know if they leave."

I changed into jeans and a sweater and hurried downstairs. The ten-minute brisk walk down 5th Avenue to Magnet, the exclusive billionaire club, burned in my lungs and cleared my head.

"Good morning, Mr. Silver. The usual?" Walter unfastened the red barrier rope, and I passed through.

"Good morning, Walter. Just a coffee and a private booth."

"Your brother is already here. Follow me, please."

Walter had worked at the club for three decades. Few knew this, but my uncle Jacob got him the job, and Walter's allegiance to the Silvers never faltered. He knew everyone and anyone who passed through Magnet's front door. He led me to

Julian's table, where I lowered my hand to his shoulder and leaned in closer. "Turn off the hallway cameras by the bathrooms."

He gave me a brief nod. "Sir, there was a new woman here."

"Who?"

He kinked his head. "It wasn't my shift, and no one logged her. Someone erased the cameras."

The fucking log books were useless. No one had signed in since the nineties, myself included.

"Anything else?"

"She never spoke. Just listened and observed."

"Would you recognize her?"

"I never saw her face, sir. She wore an oversized hat and long gloves; showed barely any skin. Very elegant."

"Thank you."

I slipped in past the curtain to the booth, where Julian had started a pot of coffee.

"Morning. Looks like a fucking godfather meeting in there." He poured me a cup and slid it my way.

"That's the least of our worries. There's a new bitch in town, and he's smoother than Hartley and Martinez combined."

"No names?"

"Not yet. Hartley's fucking planning a new exchange, but I have no details. I called in a new team, but I have a feeling he's trying to distract us. Also, Wright is missing from his apartment."

"Shit."

"But guess where he's at?" He slid his phone my way with a screenshot.

"Working with Hartley?"

"Donaldson got him in on a trade. It's a perfect set up. If he shows. James is in as well. The prosthetic looks great. We got him in set up as a seller and a buyer."

"Good."

"You're hesitant."

"I need to tell Allie Wright could be there, but if I do—"

"She'll run?"

"I don't know." I cracked my neck from one side to the other. "But there's no point in worrying her if he doesn't show. You better keep it cool tonight, my brother."

"I'm here for Kendra, and I know my limits."

"What are we going to do about Hartley? I have this gut feeling he's getting ready for something. It would be wise to get a warrant." I tucked the curtain aside and checked our privacy.

"You and me both, but we can't get the police involved until Kendra's safe."

"He just fucking gets away with everything. Simone, Joanne, and now Kendra."

My brother shifted in his seat. I hit him where it hurt us both.

"Did Walter tell you about the woman? Could be someone new on the scene."

"Or someone who hides well." I sipped on my coffee. The first sip of caffeine jolted me awake.

"Possibly a new mule."

My brother re-filled his cup and took his phone out of his pocket. He placed an earpiece in his ear and gave me the other one.

"We're filtering through fresh girls, so let me know what you'd like on the menu." He clinked his champagne flute with Donaldson's. *"Young, white, brown, black, experienced, virgin, you name it."*

"And when are we picking?"

"A couple of weeks. The plane will be fueled and ready for the island after the auction."

"Perfect."

I removed the earpiece, "Sounds like it's happening soon."

"It can't be soon enough. The plan better work. Once

Hartley takes Kendra to that fucking island, we'll never get her back."

I peeked through a slit in the curtain again and set my coffee down. "One step at a time, my brother. Keep listening and wait here. Hartley's on the move."

Julian remained in the booth while I took the back hallway to the washroom. Hartley turned the corner moment later.

"Family reunion?" I leaned back against the wall. It had been years since I'd seen him.

Hartley paused. He adjusted his suit and stepped closer. I straightened and secured my stance.

"Silver. I've been wondering when you'll show up. You should join us for a drink."

"No, thanks. I prefer to breathe."

"You know, if it weren't for that accident, I think we would have been excellent partners."

"You're a fucking lunatic. Your daughter died in that accident." Hartley had a nerve.

"It was a tragedy. Simone shouldn't have been in that car."

"Right. Because they meant the cut brakes and leaking transmission just for me."

"Let bygones be bygones, Silver. And you're not the only one who grieved my daughter."

"You killed your daughter."

"Are you back to that again? There was no foul play."

"Because you fucking disposed of my car. Simone wanted nothing to do with you."

"I wish she were here so we could ask her. And for once, you'd see the Hartley family for who we are."

Hartley was exactly whom I feared: capable of anything.

"You're forgetting I've known you for decades," I scoffed. "And you don't know the first meaning of family. Families don't sell underage girls to predators or burn clubs downtown."

"You know what your problem is, Silver? You enjoy baseless accusations. I had nothing to do with Wagner's club."

I called bullshit on that. *Stick to the plan.* Once we had Kendra, Hartley would get what he deserved: life in prison.

"What's Donaldson buying from you now?" I asked.

"It's just a friendly gathering, and it's none of your business."

"Your congressman is under watch, and the FBI is listening to our conversation right now."

"You think that's news to me?"

It wasn't. I was fishing, and Hartley was about to fall into my trap.

"Donaldson's going away for a long time, and once he faces prison time, he'll quack like a duck."

Hartley laughed before his face darkened, and he stepped a few inches away from my face. I fisted my hands and breathed through my nose.

"Quack, quack."

His face reddened. "You're talking fairy tales, just like you did when Simone was alive. You simply weren't good enough for my daughter, and you will never be fucking good enough for her. Blood is thicker than water, Silver, and Simone knew that. You of all people should know it too."

I stepped forward, backing him into a wall. "She wanted nothing to do with you and your family."

Hartley pushed at my chest. "Keep your distance, boy, or you'll end up where you should have been long ago. Simone should have never gotten in that car with you. Murderer. They should have suspended your license. And stop surveilling Donaldson. I won't repeat myself."

Simone's death had been a heavy punishment to bear for us both, but Hartley's little performance about how much he loved her was just that: a performance. Hartley had tampered with my vehicle. I just had to find the proof, which I hadn't, so I focused on getting him for the sex trafficking.

"Donaldson's going to prison. Once he does, he'll sing."

He sneered. "It's been over ten years, Silver—"

"Fifteen."

"It's time to drop it."

"Something tells me it's time to pick it up again. The complete family's here. The DA will issue that warrant the minute we tell him."

"You have nothing. Shouldn't you worry about your missing friend?"

I tightened my jaw until the molar in the back ached. I massaged the area on my neck where the jugular vein thickened.

"Let Kendra go before it's too late. That's all."

"Who's Kendra? I don't name the bitches I fuck."

My calculated swing connected with his jaw before he could blink. The crunch echoed from my fist. Hartley swung back, but not before a second punch sank into his gut. He bent in half, groaning.

"You're going to pay for this, Silver."

"Fuck you."

I turned around and left. I already had paid. I'd lost the woman I loved.

The driveway weaved three curves past the main gate. Oak trees lined each side of the paved entrance, the width of each one spanning at least six arm lengths. Surveillance cameras marked every lamp post. I rolled down the window. Warm wind tousled my hair. The landscaped terrain reminded me of a golf course, but more luxurious. Groomed grass, sculpted trees, statues, scattered resting benches and birdbaths gave the landscape the aura of the Palace in Versailles; that was, until we parked by the garage next to a ride-on mower. The smell of fresh grass mixed with a fragrant bouquet of over-bloomed roses overpowered the air.

Tristan turned off the ignition, and my gaze was drawn to the two Rottweilers running toward the vehicle. The dogs sat in front of the hood and waited patiently. Tristan opened the door and stepped out with confidence while I remained seated in my comfortable fall dress, one of the outfits Tristan's entourage had brought this morning. I liked the ensemble enough I preferred not having it ripped to shreds.

He walked around to the front. The dogs wagged their tails, sending dust up in the air. They reminded me of my chocolate Lab, Millie.

"They're friendly." Tristan lowered and scratched their heads.

I opened the car door, and Tristan lost their attention. They ran around the car, sniffing and circling me.

"Pebbles, Bamm-Bamm, sit," he ordered.

Wh-what? I whipped my head his way.

"Flintstones? Seriously?" I walked with the dogs to Tristan, one on each side, scratching them behind the ear.

"My little sister named them. They were a gift, so technically they're hers."

I crouched to the ground. That was a mistake. Pebbles pushed his nose right in between my legs, and the other one walked behind me, sniffing my butt. I took Tristan's offered hand.

"Pebbles, Bamm-Bamm. Off!"

My head flew up to a young girl standing on the porch. She was wearing a cowboy hat, matching brown boots, and Daisy Duke cut-offs. She set her hands on her hips and tilted her head to the side. I let go of Tristan's hand as if it burned.

"Relax. That's Emma. And she's not as innocent as she looks."

The teen hopped towards us, like a movie star. The genes in the Silver family were definitely movie-star quality.

"Allie, this is my little sister, Emma. Emma, Allie."

Emma reached out her hand while I just stood there, staring at her adorable smile. She carried the charm and looks of a big city and the heart of the entire country. The ocean breeze fluttered her hair. A brown streak, a single lowlight among the blonde strands, tickled her face, and she tucked it behind her ear.

"Is she okay?" Emma asked, and Tristan squeezed my hand.

"Ahem… yes. I'm fine. I'm sorry. Hi, Emma. I'm Allie. I've heard a lot about you."

"Likewise."

My forehead creased.

"Oh, your mom told me," she explained. "She's awesome, which means you must be awesome too. Welcome to *Casa Silver*."

"She's into Spanish." Tristan leaned in from beside me.

"Oh, that's great! It's nice to meet you, Emma."

"And Italian, German, French, Mandarin... I think I'm missing one, but I'm sure she'll tell you all about it if you ask."

"Wow! I'm sorry to disappoint, but I only speak English."

"Same here." Tristan laughed. "Emma's smart and special."

"He means to say I'm the baby of the family, or at least that's how I get treated. They never let me do anything fun. Okay, that's a lie. They do, but you know, not their kind of fun. Boat rides, scuba, motorcycles, parachuting, diving for treasures. That's the real fun stuff."

"You're fourteen, Emma."

"Almost fifteen. I can drive a car and ride a boat and I successfully completed a..." She paused and quickly glanced at her brother. "Well, I can't really talk about that."

Her brows drew together, but after a doubtful pause, she perked up. "At least not until you're family, if you know what I mean?"

Did I know what she meant?

If she meant I'd be marrying a man I'd barely met, then Emma was living in a grander fairytale than me. I might enjoy Tristan's company — likely a little too much — but he was my boss. And I was his employee. Almost. Marriage was off the table for so many reasons.

Tristan's fingers skimmed the back of my arm, bringing me back to the present. "It's true. She can drive a car and ride a boat, but she also has a wild imagination. We don't dive for treasure. We do it because we can. Let's go in."

But Emma stretched out her hand and blocked our way.

"Wait! I have to clear something up because they're all

arguing in there. Are you two dating?" She then pointed between me and Tristan, wiggling her brows like I was supposed to read their wavelengths.

"Who's arguing about what, Emma?"

"Julian made a bet with James that you'd shagged."

"Shagged?"

Tristan's phone buzzed.

"Austin Powers."

Right.

She took my hand, guided us to the front porch, and continued. "My brothers never bring anyone home. They say it's for my own good and that I should hang out with kids my age, but kids my age are boring. So I put a spy camera on Tristan's tie once, but the connection on my phone broke, and when it finally worked, Tristan spilled something so I couldn't see, but I heard a girl say she'd love to see his..."

"I think that's enough, Emma!" Tristan interrupted before returning his attention to his phone. "Excuse me for a moment."

He let go of my hand and stepped aside. Emma's solid grip remained on my other hand as she pushed open the mansion's front door. The cozy exterior matched the interior. An oval entryway with a skylights overhead brought the outside in. I followed the floating staircase to the balcony above, but Emma quickly brought my attention back to her face.

"I was gonna say, the girl wanted to see his Bentley collection. Are you two going on a date? My mom says she'll do your hair, and I really want to help if you'll let me. Pleeaassseee."

I glanced over my shoulder to where Tristan was lost in a phone conversation, and I nodded to Emma, who ended the long plea before she ran out of air.

"Yay! Finally, the curse is broken! When I trimmed Tristan's hair and gave him highlights, I made a tiny mistake." She squinted. "But the purple washed out pretty fast. I don't know why Tristan insisted on working from home for a month. He looked real good."

Emma led me through the foyer, and before I could ask where we were going, she continued. "Tristan finds dark-haired women hotter than the blondes. So does Julian. I think blondes have more fun, don't you? I did when we went to New Zealand. I was posing as a boy, so I wore a ball cap. It was the first time my brothers let me take part in a job, and I did great. You should ask them. Actually, don't ask them. I'm under strict secrecy, so technically, you shouldn't know about that."

I guessed the technicality streak ran in the family.

"So that's why I think blondes have more fun." She let go of my hand and took a strand of my hair between her fingers. "Well, take my word for it. If you stay here, you can sleep over. You can use my room. I don't mind sharing."

"Thanks."

I imagined the Silvers had guest bedrooms because my mother was staying over, but I appreciated the offer. We paused in the hall together, and I smiled. Emma's eagerness to grow up shone in her every move and word. She told me how she wished she could join the family business sooner than later, and I loved listening to her every word. I hadn't noticed when we sat down on the bottom step of the Scarlett O'Hara stair-case because she absolutely mesmerized me.

"But they're the best brothers ever because they let me play with their gadgets all the time because I take secrets to my grave."

How in the world could her chatty mouth ever hold a secret?

She froze mid-sentence, made sure no one was near, and leaned in closer, lowering her voice. "I want to be an aunt, but I can't be an aunt until one of them marries and has a baby. Which is wrong because Uncle James is not married and has a baby. Sometimes they tell me things that aren't true, but if you marry Tristan, you could be my sister-in-law." Her eyes nearly doubled in size, and so did mine. She looked around the room conspicuously once again and leaned in to whisper, this time right into my ear. "Tristan loves black lingerie. Women think he likes red, but he really loves black."

My cheeks heated. And with a closing wink and a straight face, Emma planned out my life and possibly arranged our marriage.

"Tristan's just my—"

"Boyfriend."

I was going to say *boss*, but I liked his version better than mine. He stood in the doorway. The sun shone through the skylight, outlining him like a halo. He pulled out a little box from his pocket and presented the gift on his palm.

"I've got something for you, Emma."

She hurried off the step, grabbed the box, hopped up to kiss him on his cheek, and hugged him tightly. "You're the best brother ever!"

Now that we'd shared the secrets of my arranged marriage and Tristan's lingerie preferences, she turned to wink at me and ran off screaming, "Mom! Tristan's dating! And she's cute, and she's gonna be my aunt!"

I burst out in laughter. Tristan's sister was my Emma. No matter what my future held and what happened between Tristan and me, I'd make sure this little girl remained in my life forever. He wrapped his arms around me and brought me in close to his body. I calmed under the support of his steady chest.

"I'm sorry."

"Don't be. She's awesome. I think I already love her." I smiled. "It's just... you know... realizing my sister would have been around her age brings up all these feelings inside of me, and I... I get anxious."

He pulled lightly away. "She hasn't said anything inappropriate to you, has she? Because she has a way with her mouth, and—"

"No. Not at all. She's perfect. You're a lucky brother. Forget I said anything." I waved my hand in dismissal. "So... boyfriend?"

"I thought it sounded better than screwing your boss." He lowered his hands to my hips and brought me in for a full kiss. I could have gotten lost in those lips forever, but the commotion in the back of the house grew louder, so I pulled away.

"No, it's not too forward. We should probably go. Where can I put the wine?"

"Ahem..." Someone cleared his throat, and Tristan removed the bottle from my hand.

"And you already know Julian."

Tristan's older brother was wearing a V-neck sweater with nothing underneath and could have passed for his twin. Except for the scar on Tristan's lip; that definitely set them apart. While the Indian summer didn't call for sweater weather just yet, the light knit fabric fit him so perfectly, it was difficult not to stare at his taut physique.

"A little better than I should." I remembered kissing him at Planters Inn in Charleston.

Tristan pulled me in to his side like he knew where my thoughts had meandered.

"How do you know Julian?" Emma popped back into the hallway. She hurried my way pulled on my hand, forcing me to let go of Tristan.

"Allie here is refusing to greet me as nicely as she did before," Julian teased.

Emma stopped. "Why?"

I threw him a dirty look before I explained. "We ran into each other at a hotel, and I mistook Julian for Tristan."

"Oh, it happens all the time. The girls usually like one and think it's the other. My brothers used to double date, but if you ask me, it doesn't count as double dating when one goes out with a girl and then the other goes out with the same one next week. They say 'sharing is caring,' and I say, 'men are confusing,' and—"

"How do you like your new toy, Emma?" Tristan asked.

Wow!

I knew I liked her for a reason. Oddly, she reminded me of a younger version of Laura as well. Without the statistics Emma guided me to the back of the house, where the aroma of delicious scents foreshadowed a feast.

"I love it. And I intend to find out how it works on you both." She pointed between the brothers.

Julian sped up a few steps and blocked our way. "Hey, hey. What did you get her? I'm still not over the drone."

Tristan patted him on the shoulder. "Don't worry. It's preset."

"I already disabled the factory settings and made it my own." Emma's irresistible smile pulled at the strings of my heart, and I completely understood how well she had wrapped her brothers around her little finger.

Julian cocked his head to the side and made an *I-told-you-so* face.

We stepped into what I would call a chef's dream kitchen. A *Welcome to Bedrock* wooden sign caught my eye above a window. The smell of a barbeque marinade, pastries, and fresh fruit filled the air, and a familiar smile greeted me from near the sink.

"Mom!" I rushed toward the counter where she was drying the dishes and took her by the shoulders, scanning her over like I hadn't seen her in weeks. "You all right?"

I hugged her.

"Of course I'm all right. The Silvers have been wonderful. I'm staying at their guesthouse, five times the size of my apartment. I just don't want to be a burden."

"Oh, Peg, don't be silly. We love having you here." A lady with a funky haircut for her reddish hair with blonde streaks turned around. She wiped her hands on a towel and hurried over, bringing me in for what I could only describe as a mother's hug. I melted in her embrace as if she were my mother.

"Welcome to the Silver residence, Allie. I'm Maggie Silver, but everyone in the family calls me Wilma." Her arms tightened. "We're delighted to have you here. I've been waiting for this moment for so long!"

"Mom! Stop!" Tristan warned.

"Allie's gonna make me an aunt."

My mouth dropped open, and the room fell silent. Everyone's attention turned to Emma, then to my belly.

"She's kidding. Emma, please tell them you're kidding."

"But I'm not. You two are obviously dating. You know, first comes love, then comes marriage… and you know the rest, and the rest makes me an aunt. I won't have it any other way." She lifted her chin up and dramatically exited to the backyard.

"These are for you." I handed Wilma the bouquet of sunflowers I'd bought in the downstairs store. The Manhattan prices were definitely suitable for billionaires only, but I couldn't resist the bright bunch.

"Thank you. Oh, they're gorgeous! Thank you. But a baby wouldn't be so bad, would it?" Wilma asked.

"Oh, we're not there yet," I chuckled.

"But we can get going on it asap." Tristan wrapped his arms around me from behind, resembling nothing close to the professional bodyguard from the auditorium, though it was the same body that had held me safe and made me feel too comfortable. I should have known the mess I was getting myself into the moment I saw him in the burned club.

Wilma's cheeks tinted with a rose shade. She hurried to the sink where she filled a vase with water.

"Guesthouse?" I looked up and over my shoulder in a whisper. "My mom's at the guesthouse? I mean, I love her and all, but it's too much."

"What's the point of a guesthouse if you can't have any guests?" He let go of me and paced over to the sink.

"Peg has been the perfect guest." Wilma removed a sack of potatoes from underneath the sink and set them on the counter. "Besides, the security at Casa Silver is top notch. It's the safest place she can be until the boys finish what they started."

Finish what they started?

I tilted my head. I found myself doing a lot of that lately.

"Hey, Mom, do you need any help?" Tristan asked.

"Wash the baby potatoes, mix them in the big-ass bowl over there, and add olive oil, sea salt, and black pepper. Wrap them up and Fred will put them on the grill."

While Tristan busied himself with the potatoes, I helped my mother dry the dishes and put them away. She moved around the kitchen like she'd lived there for years. Small glass bowls full of spices lined the marble counter. Something was simmering in a pan, and I took a whiff: mushrooms and onions. Mrs. Silver lifted the lid, stirring before she turned down the gas.

Further back on the counter, a fruit bowl in the shape of a peacock made of pineapple, watermelon, and berries caught my attention.

"Wow! Who made this?" I asked.

"That's all Wilma!" my mother chirped.

"She worked as an undercover chef." Tristan moved the peeler over the skin like he had some culinary experience as well.

"She did that for work?"

"Silver Securities is a family business."

Family.

This was the second time today I experienced a butterfly effect in my stomach.

Except every time I looked at Tristan or wondered when someone would slap and wake me up, he seemed… perfect. Too perfect.

"Wilma!" a voice bellowed from the backyard.

"Okay, what's with the Flintstones?" I asked.

"It's an inside joke no one gets. He calls her Wilma and she calls him Fred when it's just the family around. Otherwise it's Maggie and John."

An older gentleman who definitely didn't look his age stepped through the garden door.

"I thought I'd heard you on the monitor! Is this the lovely Allie?" His bear arms caged me in and he held me there for a longer moment than I'd expected. Something deep welled inside my chest, and I traveled back in time to when I'd lingered in my father's arms.

He pulled away, leaving me warm and fuzzy.

"It's nice to meet you, Mr. Silver." I stood tall.

He lifted his finger and warned. "Don't let this boy boss you around. Listen to your instinct. There's nothing better than a woman's instinct."

"Agreed." Mrs. Silver looked away from the stove where she was stirring.

"I'm done with the potatoes."

"That fast?"

I saw Emma continuing the work he hadn't finished.

"Don't worry, Allie. She's getting paid for this. It's good for her. Mom? Work now, or later?" Tristan kissed his mother on the cheek.

"Go do what you gotta do. Dinner will be ready in forty minutes. We'll meet you outside." She wiped her hands on her apron and removed the spare peeler from his hand. "I'll help Emma."

"Thank you."

Tristan took my hand and led me to a kitchen cupboard, where we stopped.

"What are we doing?"

I stared at the cupboard as he gently pushed on the cabinetry. The shelves sprang open to reveal an entrance. Beyond, a staircase led downstairs. I followed Julian, and Tristan closed the door behind us. An automatic light flashed on. We reached a door, where Julian keyed in a code, pushed another door open, and we entered into another room. Lights flickered on in the secret room.

Photos, maps, and sketches decorated a wall. A sequence of shots of the auburn-haired woman, Kendra, had been pinned in a row. The gruesome progression of her failing health twisted my stomach. The unkempt hair, sunken cheeks, and hollow look in her eyes tugged at my heart strings. Below her was a photograph of the guy I remembered from the park a month ago.

"Martinez?" I asked.

"Yes," Tristan replied.

I'd memorized his bushy eyebrows and deadly stare the first time around. Martinez had the sort of face you saw once and remembered. It was the face of an asshole-you-should-never-run into. The unforgiving stare brought a chill to my bones.

On the next wall over, a desk was lined with monitors.

"Have you tagged her yet?" Julian asked.

I turned around at the sound of Julian snapping a latex glove. "What?"

"Obviously not," Tristan answered, before looking at my puzzled face. "We're implanting a tracking device in your neck, just underneath the hairline."

"Wouldn't a button on a dress work just as well?"

The brothers exchanged a knowing look.

"We find buttons and jewelry have a way of getting lost. And what if they strip you naked?"

"Strip?"

"Has my brother not explained the job?" Julian picked up a metal syringe.

Was that thing made for elephants?

"He has—" I started.

"I didn't mention the tracking device. I'm sorry."

Tristan grabbed my hand. I was almost sure I wasn't shaking until then. "It's for your safety."

"Lie down on your front." Julian pointed to the long seat. "Hair up."

Tristan sat at the end, closer to my head, and held my hair to the side. A dab of alcohol evaporated on the back of my neck, followed by a sharp pinch. The pressure was uncomfortable but not too painful. Julian withdrew the thick needle from my skin and disposed of the tip. He removed his gloves and picked up his phone. After a few keystrokes, a string of beeps marked my spot.

"All good. The bruise will go down in a couple of days," he said. "Allie, thank you for doing this. Thank you for helping Kendra."

"We'll find her," I assured him.

"I know we will."

I sat up and touched the back of my neck where the bump pulsed underneath my skin.

"When was the last time you practiced jiu-jitsu?" Julian removed his gloves and sanitized his hands while crossing the room.

"I work out every day." I noted his predatory steps. "Julian, I promise I can defend myself."

I didn't want to hurt him, but I would if he gave me no choice. He walked around the bench where I was sitting, holding his arms crossed over his chest. If he wanted to intimidate me, he'd have to do much better than that. Tristan swept to the side, giving us room, and watched me with intent. As Julian came behind me, something shifted in the air. My instinct snapped, and I ducked from under Julian's arm as he tried to grab me. I reached back before he stood tall again and wrapped my arm around his neck. Using the bench to brace, I pulled his entire weight over my shoulder and flapped him down on the mat.

He yelped out in pain, but I felt no mercy. If he wasn't ready for the consequences, he shouldn't have attacked.

"The bruising will go down in a couple of days." I stood up and tapped my bare foot on Julian's chest. "If you want another kiss from me, baby, you'll have to do better than that."

A grin stretched across Tristan's face before he burst out in laughter. "I told you she's good."

"Ouch!" Julian moaned.

"Don't be a baby. I didn't do any damage."

And before I realized what was happening, he swung his arm to the side and knocked my other foot from underneath me. I flew onto my behind and then rolled back over my head into a crouch I liked to call *Kung-Fu Panda*, all thanks to the after-hours I'd spent with Sensei Paul. I made a mental note to send him a gift basket because the hours of training were worth every stunned look on the brothers' faces.

Tristan stopped laughing. "Holy shit! That was fucking amazing!"

I extended my hand to help Julian, which he took.

"Yeah, she'll do." Julian slowly sat up, and I let my muscles relax.

"'She'll do'?" I lowered my gaze. "I let you jab me with a needle that looks like a cattle probe. You get an ass-whupping, and I only get a 'She'll do'?"

"I'm sorry. I didn't mean it that way. But the men you'll be dealing with are stronger than me. And they'll have guns."

"Yeah, I'm familiar with those."

"They also have drugs. Most laced with fentanyl. One whiff and your karate or fancy-shmancy whatever that was will not help."

I took his hand with both of mine, and our gazes connected. The pain swimming in his eyes had settled underneath as well.

"I'm well aware of the dangers, Julian, but I can hold my own. We're going to get Kendra back. Focus on that."

"All right." He looked up at his brother. "She's in. Come on, Green. I hope you like barbecued ribs and chicken. It's the Flintstone's favorite meal."

I wouldn't have expected anything less than a table set for a king. My mother had dolled up the patio in twinkling lights, over-blooming cream flowers I recognized from her own garden, white blankets, and pillows. With the setting sun across the lawn and the sound of the ocean's lapping waves, Allie stood at the threshold to my parent's mansion and the gardens beyond, her mouth wide open. The place might have been expansive, but it never lacked warmth and love.

I guided Allie to the table, letting her take in her surroundings. Peggy watched her with the same awe I'd felt. As soon as Allie sat down at the table, Wilma took the seat at her right and Emma on her left. I rolled my eyes. Their little conspiracy to find me a woman who could make one a grandmother and the other an aunt was getting old. Allie was here on a job; that was all. And I'd continue telling the lie until Hartley received all the justice coming his way. I walked around the table and sat across from Allie.

"Bon appétit!" Emma cheered.

"I want nothing left on the table!" Wilma pointed at every

family member with her finger, winking at the end. "No one's getting up until the food's gone. Period."

I loved my mother. I missed my family, and there were times I regretted living in a condo so far away. Long Island was my home, and my heart belonged here. Julian lived on the property beside my parents', who'd bought a house on his other side for Emma. She didn't know it yet, though, because they were determined to keep her home for as long as possible.

Little Miss Talkative had her mouth full of ribs.

I watched Allie pick up a rack and bite around the bone. She noticed my stare and held it. The tiny lift at the corner of her mouth, a smirk she reserved to tease me, played with every reason I'd hired her as a pawn. It also gave me every reason not to pawn her. Those delicate fingers held onto the meat like it was the most precious commodity in the world. And then her lips wrapped around the bone like…

Fuck me!

I knew she would drive me crazy. But she also matched the spirit, adventure, and sense of purpose coursing through my veins. She reminded me of everything I had lost. Like some sort of re-incarnation of Simone had stepped back into my life. Except better.

I physically shook my head.

My brother noticed my discomfort from beside me and leaned closer. "You all right, man?"

"Yeah, just the past fucking with my head."

"You and me both."

Julian's plate remained empty, and judging by the look on his face, he had no appetite.

"Mom will be pissed if you keep that up."

"I can't stop thinking about her. What she's going through… and truthfully, whether she's alive."

"We're closer today than we were yesterday," I reminded him.

"You lost Simone, and Gabe lost Joanne. I can't help but wonder whether Kendra's next."

"That's not gonna happen, brother. We can do this with Allie's help."

I looked across the table at Allie. She wiggled her eyebrows in response and snorted as she peeled the meat off the bone. She followed that with a long swallow of the Ruirita my mother had made her. The orange flavored tequila drink was officially Allie's favorite, but I was certain she underestimated its potency.

It was all worth it to see her settle in with my family.

"I don't get it, Silver. Why are you in a Manhattan penthouse when you have this?"

"That's what I've been saying all these years," Wilma chimed in a high tone. "We need him closer. A little bird told me the Jacobs are thinking about selling their property."

My mother had wanted to purchase the property next to theirs, but the Jacobs had built it over thirty years ago, and I doubted they'd give it up. So I insisted on working from my Manhattan penthouse. The location had its benefits when I brushed elbows with cunning elites. They sort of thought they knew who I was, but they had no fucking clue. We'd infiltrated the organization, and if we got it right, we would save lives. While Long Island was a dream of mine, Manhattan made sense.

"They've been 'thinking about it' for years, Mom."

"My source is pretty solid." She winked at Emma, who winked back.

I drummed my fingers on the table. If my little sister who thrived on knowing everyone's business was the source, it might be worth talking to the Jacobs.

"Because if you lived here, I could help with the kids."

"I don't have any kids."

"Well, maybe you would if you treated a lady the right way.

I mean, Tristan, you're almost forty. The clock is ticking." She tapped her wrist like she actually wore a watch, which she didn't.

Here we go again.

"Sperm lives forever, Mom."

"Look at James. He's so happy with Laila and such a good father."

"And I have a job because of him." Emma piped up.

"You work?" Allie turned her way.

"Babysitting. Unfortunately, that's all they'll let me do."

"My roommate needs a babysitter sometimes. If you'd like—"

"I'd love to! Oh, my God! Seriously? Thank you Allie. I need a job so bad. I knew you'd be the best sister-in-law ever."

Allie looked at my little sister, who didn't seem to know she was living in paradise and lacked nothing, like she'd lost her mind. To be fair, Emma insisted on clothing herself and investing in her own phones and gadgets.

"Ignore her." I waved my hand, but my mother saw an opportunity, and she wouldn't let it slip.

"So, Allie—"

"Come on, Wilma." Fred interrupted. "Let it go. Nature will do what nature should do if you only stop talking." He grabbed a cob and spread butter over the kernels. The ribs on his plate glistened with sauce next to the steaming baked potato with trimmings.

"Well, I just hope you boys get Kendra out in time. You know, for Julian. And finish the shit show once and for all. Hartley deserves to stay behind bars and serve those above his rank, in jail."

She was the right one, except we disagreed on one point: Hartley didn't deserve to live.

"Wilma? Come help me with the dessert." Fred lowered his

corn, wiped his hands on the napkin, and turned to the table. "I baked some special brownies. We'll be right back."

Did Allie notice he'd removed Mom from the table on purpose?

"Wait… Julian and Kendra?" Allie mouthed.

"It's complicated," I mouthed back, and rubbed my chest where the sharp pain from the accident had left its mark on my heart. It was good to remember some mistakes. Mine gave me a proper slap in the face.

"Did your dad just say he baked special brownies?"

"Yeah, he did."

Fred could never wait to share his brownies. He'd started the hobby when he retired a couple of years ago and never looked back. I however, needed Allie sober because I didn't take advantage of stoned women. And tonight, I wanted to take every advantage with her that I could.

"I think it would be wise to start with dinner."

She followed my lead and grasped another rack of ribs. She reached forward with a wide smile on her face, saying, "Cheers."

I touched my meat to hers, and her smile twisted into a smirk. She lowered her lips to the rib and slowly sucked off small chunks. Bite by bite, she devoured the beef off the bone like it was the best thing her lips had ever tasted, reminding me of her mouth on my cock.

I had to hand it to Mom—her maple-chipotle sauce rocked —but there was nothing easy about watching Allie eat meat. She pulled off the last piece and licked the bone clean, then each of her fingers, all the while keeping her gaze locked with mine.

Fuck me.

I reached my foot forward and slid my toe up her calf, past her knee, heading for the torturous spot. Her freckles popped and her eyes flew wide open. That rush of need shading her skin in darker tones of pink played with my head.

My dick strained against my shorts.

She retaliated with her foot, sliding her toe up my leg right to my hard dick. She smiled when she reached my bulge, and I longed for alone time with Allie.

"Why do you have that funny look on your face, Tristan?" Emma licked her fingers clean.

"I'm hungry," I growled.

"Well, have some chicken waffles. Peg made them."

At the mention of her mother's name, Allie pulled her foot away. I lowered mine and searched for an exit as Fred came around with his brownies.

Allie declined. "They smell delicious, Fred. Would it be all right if I took one home?"

"One? I'll pack a few. They're good for…" His keen gaze fell to his youngest. "Well, I'm sure you kids can figure it out."

"He meant to say sex." Emma straightened in her seat.

"Emma!" Wilma puffed out. "This is the whole reason I don't like her hanging around you boys. She should be with kids her age."

"Let me be clear." Emma stood up from her chair. "Kids my age suck. That's why cowboy romance is a thing."

I stood up and leaned forward and over the table. "Want to get out of here for a moment?"

"That would be lovely."

I hurried over to her side and helped Allie slide out of her chair.

"Mom, the food was delicious, as always. I'd like to show Allie around, but I promise to return for dessert."

Before my mother and sister realized what was happening, I stole Allie to myself. It was the best steal of the day. We strolled through the back garden and toward the shore. The sun had already set, but the sunrise was the money-maker on this side of the world.

"It's beautiful here," she whispered.

"My father takes care of the landscaping. With some help, of course. I mean, the property stretches… well, for a bit."

"And the vegetable garden? I saw we passed one on the way."

"That's Wilma's baby. The potatoes, squash, peppers, and everything else we had tonight were all hers. Including the chickens. The coop is further back."

"And the ribs?"

"Store-bought. Fred knows a butcher by the river."

"Butcher by the river." She chuckled. "You brought the country to the city."

"Is that funny?"

"No. It's just real. Unbelievable, actually. I mean, I never thought I'd be listening to the Atlantic a stone's throw away on Long Island yet feel like I'm hundreds of miles inland, on a farm. This is exactly why Emma's drawn to the country."

"Emma's drawn to a lot of things, including our ranch."

"Ranch?"

"What can I do to take your mind away from all of this?" I asked, and didn't wait for her reply. Instead I grabbed her hand and spun her in a circle to the distant music. Unfortunately I forgot how close we'd come to the property's edge, and when I steered Allie's spinning body away from the electric fence, she lost her balance and slipped, and it nipped her ass.

An alarm went off. I quickly removed my phone from my pocket and turned it off, sending a family message that it was accidental.

"Ouch!" She grabbed her ass cheek. "What the heck was that?"

"You'll be fine. Come on. I think we should go elsewhere."

I grabbed her by the waist and dragged her underneath a

giant willow tree by the boathouse. She squealed with happiness as I pinned her against the bark, kissing her nose, cheeks, and lips. She seemed so small and frail in my grip.

"Do you fish?" she asked out of nowhere. "I saw the boat by the dock."

"I do."

"My father loved fishing. He would have loved your family. They're all amazing."

Her breasts rose and fell along with her heavy breath. I lowered my nose to the nook between her shoulder and neck, inhaling. Strawberry need oozed off her skin. She was nearly melting in my hold, and I would let no one harm her.

"You fit in perfectly. Allie, maybe we should re-think the auction?"

"Oh no. I'm not backing out. This is important. To everyone and for so many reasons that I could never leave without at least trying."

She couldn't have known what she was risking, and I would owe her for the rest of my life.

"Thank you."

"It's what families do, isn't it?"

I swallowed hard, and only then noticed the sadness swimming in her eyes.

"Hey, are you okay?" I lifted her chin with my finger.

"Yeah, I'm fine. I love your family. They're awesome—"

"But?"

"But it feels like it's all going to disappear."

The willow branches danced around us to the wind's evening sway. The smell of firewood carried in the air, and I assumed Fred had lit the pit for the evening. And all this time I'd imagined Allie at my side, the business on a straight path, and all those responsible for Kendra and Allie's suffering brought to justice.

"You're being silly, babe. It doesn't have to disappear. I

mean, I don't see a reason this should not continue." I lowered my mouth to hers and took her lips just the way she liked me to. Her signature strawberry taste made me pause, tasting her like I had for the first time, wanting this to last forever. Her body molded into mine. Arms around my neck, lips swollen and burning for more, chest to my abs, and her pussy grinding over my thigh. My zipper itched against my dick.

She freed herself from my hold and just stood there as if trying to regain the control neither one of us had.

"Let's go to the boathouse. It will be more comfortable." I breathed the offer inside her mouth, then lowered my forehead to hers and waited.

"How does someone like you stay single? I don't get it."

"Is that what you're worried about? Another woman? Because I promise there are none."

"No, that's not it, Mr. Silver. But I am curious about where you've been all my life. I try to explain to myself that men like you don't choose girls like me."

I moved my thigh, stimulating her, rubbing her clit. I wanted those fucking panties off, and I wanted them now. Her breath filled with a stronger need. She pulled her tongue over my upper lip and then bit the lower one. We wouldn't make it to the boathouse.

"You mean strong, smart, beautiful, and selfless?" I asked, but didn't wait for her answer. Instead, I grabbed her dress and scrunched it upward, gently scratching over her naked thighs. She gave into my hands like a marionette, willing and unbelievably promiscuous. Her smooth skin softened on the way up. She grabbed my wrist before I reached her pussy. My fingers remained on that soft part of her inner thigh, almost there.

"I need to know the truth. Are you looking for more than a partner, Mr. Silver?"

"I don't know. When you're not looking for one—"

"Are you looking for one?" She swallowed hard. While I loved the slight tremble in her voice, I wanted the doubt gone. I wanted my intentions clear.

"No. I'm not. I already found her."

I crushed my mouth and body to hers, ignoring the tree bark behind her back. Fortunately, the weeping branches of the mature willow tree give us privacy. I fucking couldn't wait to sink into her.

Her delicate fingers fumbled with my zipper. It popped open under the pressure and my cock sprang out. Her cool hand wrapped around my hot skin. She licked her lips, looked up to meet my gaze, and lowered to her knees. I yanked her back up. The wind blew, cooling my heated skin.

"Oh no, baby! We're doing this my way."

"Yes, Mr. Silver."

I growled, turned her around, and lifted her skirt. Moonlight illuminated her beautiful ass. I grasped her ass cheek and squeezed it hard enough to leave a print.

"Are you calling me Mr. Silver on purpose because I told you it's sexy?"

She looked back over her shoulder all smug and confident, with freckles and all. "Of course, Mr. Silver."

I smoothed my hand over her shaded ass near where her black thong cut into the center. I snarled and hooked my finger underneath it, pulling it lightly and giving her pussy a delightful wedgie.

She squirmed and moaned until I let go of the thong, releasing the pressure against her swollen pussy.

I dragged my lips down her neck and to her shoulder, then to her spine, where I stayed. I held her steady, breathing against her skin. "Spread those legs for me, babe."

She widened her stance and looked absolutely gorgeous hugging that tree. I lined myself at her heated pussy and thrust hard inside her. She let out a yelp, but she was ready and braced herself harder against the trunk as I took her from behind. We found a comfortable rhythm. My hands let go of her hips and snaked up her body where she'd teased her nipples into stones. I took over the right one and pushed harder. Her face pressed into the tree bark. She watched over her shoulder as my dick slid inside her, her eyes and lips begging for relief.

I pinched the nipple, and she screamed out, then froze.

"Don't worry. We're by the ocean. You can scream as much as you want. No one will hear us, and I'm sure Emma has the dogs on leash by now. The coyotes like to come out sometimes."

"Coyotes?"

"Hence the electric fence. Which they jump."

"I thought that was for burglars."

"That too."

"And what if your parents hear—"

"They'll probably celebrate and leave us alone. Trust me, Allie. We're safe."

I massaged her ass with my palms as my cock slid in and out, tantalizingly slow. She didn't object to my hand slipping from the front right between her belly and the tree and down to her swollen pussy. I slid my fingers underneath the lace and rubbed her clit while I fucked her from behind.

She let out small moans with each thrust, like a mystical siren, except she was singing right to my dick. Every single breath let out more sounds, and I was getting drunk on their melody.

"I'm gonna come," she finally breathed, bringing me to the breaking point. Allie shook in my hold, my balls zapped and contracted, and I spilled deep inside her. Thank God for IUDs. I was barely aware of my left arm shielding her from the tree. I held her against my body with my dick snuggled in her warmth and rubbed her with my right hand all the way through her longer settling orgasm. Seconds later, she spasmed in my grip for the second time, shaking. Just as she calmed, I flicked her tender flesh again. She trembled in my grip, pushing her hips into my hand, settling along one of my fingers until I could feel what I'd done to her pussy. I obliterated her. I lifted my hand and tilted her mouth to mine for a lingering kiss. She traced the seam of my lips with her devilish tongue.

"We can still go see the boathouse." I knew she wanted to. Tonight, having her at my family's home meant everything.

"Tristan? Is something wrong?"

"No. Nothing. Do you know how long it's been since a woman's been here? Keep in mind I'm turning forty in three years."

She shook her head, blinked, and waited. I fucking loved the vulnerability and trust. Life hadn't kicked her ass just yet, but if I played Hartley the right way, it wouldn't have to.

She smiled. "Forty's the new thirty. Thank you for bringing me here today. I love it, but we should return. Wilma's supposed to dye my hair."

"All right, but we're going to continue this at home, because I fucking can't get enough of you, Allie Green."

"Me neither, Mr. Silver."

I pulled out, oddly proud of my semen dripping out of her pussy. I removed her panties, which didn't add any coverage, and pocketed the fabric. Allie used the powder room in the boathouse to freshen up and then joined my mother in the basement studio.

We stayed in the upstairs family room. Julian sat on the couch with a glass of bourbon in his hand.

"I still can't believe I lost her." He sipped on his bourbon.

"You didn't. We're getting her back."

"Can you keep your dick in your pants long enough for us to do so?"

"What the hell is your problem?"

"Look, I'm sorry. I'm just stressed."

"Why don't you take a couple of days off? Allie will be ready, I promise you. And I know how much K means to you."

"She's barely a child. I should have never gotten her involved."

"She's a grown woman and knows what she wants."

"I could be her father."

"I think the experience is part of your appeal, brother. We've gone over this already. Stop denying what the rest of us know is true. You and Kendra are meant to be."

My phone rang, flashing my cousin's name. I slid my finger across the screen.

"James? We're at my parents'."

"I know. This is an emergency." I heard him breathe in through the receiver. "The auction's been moved to next weekend."

Tristan sat on the couch with his shirt open, tie undone, and a scotch in his hand. A whiff of the expensive alcohol floated in the air. The half-empty bottle reflected an orange light. We left the Silvers as soon as we washed my hair. Wilma wrapped my fresh cut into a towel, and I showered as soon as we arrived, but Tristan hadn't seen the haircut yet. Emma said a phone call had distracted him.

I walked three steps forward and unzipped the side of my red dress. I lowered it to the floor, slowly unveiling my new silky black lingerie that left little to the imagination. The scattered candlelight shone on my body, exposing the delicate areas where lace met skin. Tristan kept silent all the way home, and I could tell the call had bothered him. He breathed deep, controlled breaths while stripping me naked with his gaze. I removed my heels and strolled barefoot to the plush carpet at the foot of the couch. He tilted the half-empty glass to his lips and finished the scotch in one long and definitely painful swig. The glass echoed when he set it aside. I lifted to the couch, straddling him, and watched as he gripped my new hair into a fist and leaned into it for an inhalation.

"It doesn't smell like you. Not yet. It should smell like you."

I narrowed my brows. "It's freshly dyed. The smell will wear off in a couple of days. Tristan, what's the matter?"

Where was the uneasiness coming from?

"Nothing." He snaked his hands to around my back where he unclasped my bra, lowered the straps off my shoulders, and slid the cups off my breasts. His chest rumbled, and he brought me to his body, holding me skin to skin and breathing me in like I was his blend of drugs. I got lost in his scent and touch. The meandering fingers over my spine and needy eyes kept me in a fantasy land.

He kissed his way from my mouth to my breast and nipple. He drew his tongue around the hardened peak, gripped it between his teeth, and flicked it. Sharper pain shot through me, centering deep between my legs. The sensation quickly turned from a zap to a trickle intensifying in my panties. He pulled the nipple further out and released it again.

"Let me see you." His chest rumbled. "Stand up again."

I lifted off him and stood a foot away while he looked me over, shaking his head.

"You look amazing, Allie. I worry I'll have a tough time at the auction."

"Then it's a good thing we have time to get ready."

"That's the problem, though. We don't. The auction's next Sunday. It's why we left early. I'm sorry."

I released my breath slowly and calmed the sudden nerves. The last thing I wanted was for Tristan to panic and pull me from the job. Beyond Tristan's concern, the west side of Manhattan's skyline glittered in the night.

"What are you sorry about? This is what you've been waiting for, isn't it? Our chance to free Kendra is here."

"True."

"So embrace it. Do your best job, and if you want to forget about it beforehand, let me help you forget."

His eyes darted from the ground to mine. I dragged my

gaze to my hand and past my navel as I lowered my palm underneath my panties, touching myself between my legs. A clasp of desire tightened in my belly. The touch was painfully pleasing. Tristan's mouth opened. The set of candles he'd lit reflected in his eyes. My breaths shortened, their loudness seeming that of someone else. I cupped my left breast with my free hand and pinched the nipple the way he would have.

The sound of his buckle opening drew my attention to his crotch. He slipped his hand inside his shorts and removed his dick. Tristan leaned back against the couch, and while watching me, grasped himself and stroked up and down. The flesh swelled underneath his palm. I licked my lips, reached further down into my panties, and drew the heat with my playful fingertips to my clit.

Tristan's strokes quickened while my fingers circled faster and faster. As I watched him off himself, I flicked my bud, mimicking the slick movements of his tongue. I dug my feet steadily into the ground, parted enough for the breeze to sweep by my heated flesh. I followed his tantalizing strokes and cupped my left breast. The ache grew, and I masturbated to his rhythmic pumps... so close... and so fast...

"Stop," he ordered, and I froze, pulling my hand away from my pussy in slow motion. The ache of a denied orgasm passed through my body. My palm twitched with impatience, but I waited. The reward of having him finish me would trump the momentary torture. One lick and I'd be done, relishing in a mind-blowing orgasm.

Tristan let go of his dick, stood, and strode toward me. He cupped my ass and lowered himself to his knees and to my pussy. He inhaled near my panties, and I quivered.

"You smell fucking delicious." He pulled his tongue over the fabric, biting a little. He might as well have licked me up and down my slit. I pressed harder into him, wanting just one more touch, but he looked up at me from below.

I moaned with impatience, and just like that, his lips buzzed and pleasure spread from his teasing mouth like a promising current. His fingers traced my hip and drew up my inner thigh. I parted my legs and held my breath, waiting for him to finger me. By the time he tugged my panties aside, the room was spinning and I was panting.

Tristan's fingers slid inside me. I squeezed around the digits like I didn't want to let go, but it wasn't enough. I urged him to withdraw, and lowered my panties. He crawled up my body and kissed my slick hand.

Fucking hot.

I grasped the white shirt hanging over his shoulders and pushed it off his sculpted body. It crumpled to the floor. I reached up to his hair and raked my fingers along the scalp. He closed his eyes. We stood breasts to chest, or more like breasts to his torso. He supported my weight at the small of my back as he swayed his weight forward and lowered me to the plush carpet with ease. My back drowned in the soft fibers. It was only then that I noticed the soothing music over the speakers. It sounded like the eighties. Sexy and suave, like Tristan Silver. I'd never imagined the amount of sexiness an older man could exude.

He took his phone from the back pocket and thumbed the screen. A fireplace flicked on the wall. The crystal stones inside emanated a warm glow. He set the phone aside and lowered to his elbows, hovering above me. My need swirled in my belly as his lips grazed my earlobe, then ventured down to my jaw line and to a breath's distance away from my mouth.

I bent at the knees and lifted my feet to his hips, hooking his jeans. "Get these off. I need you inside me." I stretched my legs along his, and Tristan helped with the rest.

He brushed his hand over my cheek and thumb over my lower lip. The corner of his mouth lifted with a twist. Caged in his protective arms, I felt safer than anywhere I'd ever been in my life.

"I don't recognize you." His voice lowered to an intimate hush. His hazel eyes sparked with deep desire.

"I don't recognize me either. Wilma added permanent tint to my lips, and the brows and lashes are new as well."

"Gorgeous."

He positioned himself between my hips and moved forward in slow motion, hitting my depth. He stilled there and lowered his mouth to mine, taking my lips once more. He bit gently at the corner before he took my jawline's path towards the ear where he whispered, "You want me like this, inside you?"

I blinked and smiled, digging my fingers into his biceps and tilting my hips so I could take him deeper. His mouth returned to mine for a drawn-out kiss. He continued the sensual kissing journey over each brow and eye before settling on my mouth. His lips took control and comforted me at the same time.

He's hitting all the right buttons.

While his mouth fogged my senses, his experienced hands guided my body to yield to his. And I loved every minute of his touch. I loved letting go of the constant control my life had become. This man had everything planned. For the both of us.

With Tristan always at my side, it became more difficult to draw that line between home and work. And I hadn't even been to his offices a few blocks south yet. But it all blended into this need to spend all my time with this usually solitary and private man.

"After the auction, I want you to stay here. With me."

"Like move in?"

"Yeah, I love having you here. In my bed. I could really get used to this."

So could I.

Peaceful nights with no crying toddlers. Well, at least some peaceful nights because so far, each time I'd stayed at the penthouse, the night was never peaceful. Satisfying, yes, but I missed Laura and Foxy.

He pushed in all the way in, hitting me in that spot that brought me back to him. Tristan's tantalizing pace kept my attention on him and concentration on the swelling between my legs. I closed my eyes. His merciless pounding and the rhythmic rocking rubbed my clit in painful strokes.

"Look at me, baby. I want to see your face when you come."

I opened my eyes and arched my lower back. His tan glistened in the fireplace light. The pressure grew with his calculated thrusts. I grasped his biceps and dug my nails into his skin. Tristan gritted his teeth and lunged harder. I ground against him until just thinking about coming with Tristan inside me brought me undone. I shook in his hold as he stilled inside me, his gaze concentrating on my eyes and my lips, which I stupidly bit with silliness. He liked that. Somewhere in the back of my mind, I gloated as he marked my insides with his cum. How stupid was that? Yet I liked it. It felt possessive and submissive at the same time.

He pulled out slowly and lay on the rug beside me. He drew a blanket over us both, and I found a comfortable spot on my side and his arm pressed to his chest and heart where the white scar lifted the skin. I drew my finger over the mark, and he stilled as if I'd burned him.

"I'm sorry. I know this holds memories." The image of Tristan lying on the floor, bleeding from his heart, made my chest ache.

"It's not that. I actually believe the truth is a little embarrassing." He propped his body up on his elbow, facing me. "Your touch makes me horny, and I just want to take a moment to tell you—"

"Wait." I pressed my finger to his lips. I wasn't ready for this. Not that fast. "I don't think I'm ready to hear what you're going to say."

"That I'm very grateful for your help and for your company?"

"What?" I jerked away from his touch. One moment I was moving in, and the next I was his *company*?

"Tristan, what's really going on between us?" I asked.

"I thought we had this situation settled when I confirmed to Emma we're dating."

"So I'm dating my boss? That has to be against HR rules. You know, why haven't I even been to your office?"

"You'll come to the headquarters after the auction." He waited a moment. "I'd like you to stay on with us after the case. If you'd like, of course."

Of course I wanted that.

"Once we expose the group, we'll have a lot of work on our hands."

"Sounds… busy. You sure you'll find time for things like this?"

"You mean, for kissing you and fucking you?"

"Maybe."

"I'll always find time for you."

Tristan lifted his leg above me, straddling me. His cock rested at the side of his thigh, but I could already see it getting harder. "I love feeling your body. I love how the lace feels against your skin. I love watching you come and having you here, Allie. You become a different woman in my arms. My woman. You match my something, and I don't know what that something is, but it's… it's definitely something."

I laughed. "Something?"

"A vulnerable woman I love to please when in my arms, but a powerful woman in the daytime. Fearless and selfless."

"Powerful, you say?" I used all the muscles in my abs to pull myself up from underneath him and wrapped my arms around his neck.

Straddling him, I stared into his shrouded eyes, wondering

what secrets he had buried there. Kendra was a client Silver Securities had failed to protect. Everyone in the family was working on the case, and Tristan had gone to his office this week more than usual. To top it off, this Hartley family sounded like an elite organized crime group no one wanted to touch. Except for Tristan.

"That was an exceptional move. What's the matter?" He smoothed the back of his hand along my cheek.

"I need to see Laura."

"Your roommate?"

"Yes. I want to go home for a day or so. You know, before the auction. I need to burn off some energy and relax."

"I thought what we were doing was relaxing."

"I'm not saying it isn't."

"I'm not accusing."

"I'm sorry. I think I'm a little stressed, and sadly, no amount of orgasms will change that."

"All right, I'll do you a deal."

I lifted a single brow. "You have my attention."

"I'm going to carry you to my bed where I'll give you a massage."

I laughed. "I knew we'd end up in your bed."

He glanced outside, where the moon was shining across the river. "It's nighttime, and my bed is exactly where you should be. I'm serious, Allie. Let's go to bed."

He didn't wait for my reply and, in one swift move, scooped me into his arms.

I squealed in his tight grip, laughing.

"I promise you'll sleep like a baby afterward. I'm taking you out to burn off the stress in the morning, and I'll drop you off at the apartment around ten. You'll hang out with Laura and convince her to join us for dinner that evening."

Was he serious?

I physically turned his face to look at me. "Really?"

"Yeah. We said we'd do a double date, didn't we?"

"We did, but it's last minute, and she has a toddler. I asked earlier, but her sitter is busy and… oh, my God! Never mind. I think I just found her a sitter."

"Great!"

"Great! But you don't have to drive me to Long Island. I love taking the train."

He laughed. "Seriously, Allie. The quicker you get used to me driving you everywhere, the better. That's non-negotiable. So tomorrow is on?"

"Sounds like it's exactly what I need." I kissed him.

Tristan's promised massage over-delivered in every way. I fell asleep sometimes after he finished the full body run-down at my feet, pressing into my soles like they were the secret entrance to my heart. That night, I dreamed about him doing that same thing, except he was more than my boss. He was my husband.

Chapter 15

Tristan

I entered the graveled lot marked with two garbage containers and parked my Bentley by the metal building that screamed *please paint me*. Layers of colors were peeling off the walls. I surveyed the barren area in front. Rusted pipes and chains lay piled to the side. Remnants of shattered windows were propped against a stack of concrete blocks and wooden beams. Used paint cans had been left behind as well. It looked like Garry had work remaining. Further back, a pair of stray cats chased each other among the dried grasses and weeds.

"This neighborhood?"

"The outside renovations will be complete before Christmas. The inside is done, and this is where you'll be letting go of all that stress."

"I thought we did that last night." She didn't blush this time; she glowed.

"And the night before." I wiggled my brows and she giggled. "Sounds like we should continue with the tradition."

"I like that. Now, what is this place?"

"It looks rough on the outside, but you will love the inside."

"You've got me intrigued, Mr. Silver."

That familiar discomfort of my balls tightening in my boxer-briefs forced me to adjust myself before I opened the door and let her inside. The old hinges no longer squeaked, and the rubble and dust were gone. We had transformed the warehouse into a beautiful community gym ten years ago, and Garry oversaw renovations. The smell of leather and metal blended with a little bit of grease and paint as I examined the new equipment. Allie stood with her mouth wide open. I wasn't surprised—the Silver community gym was top of the line and every trainer's dream. She should have seen the kids' faces when we first opened.

"Wow. This is incredible. And definitely not what I expected." She pivoted on her heel to the end of the room. "Wait a minute? Are we boxing?"

"We can do whatever you want."

She stepped from one foot to another and bit her bottom lip. "I haven't boxed in years."

"You boxed before?"

"Oh, you didn't have that in my file?" She grinned with pride. "Yeah, I can hold my own."

Her confidence told me she likely did better than hold her own.

"That's one hell of a catch you have there, Silver!" I turned around at the sound of Garry's voice.

"Thanks, Garry. You're right. She's definitely special."

Allie scooted to my side and I leaned in. "Garry's a close friend of the family. Julian and I both trained with him as kids, along with our cousins. It was like a second home and I'm glad we made some updates."

"All this is free for the community?"

"Yes, that's always been the goal. Keeps the kids off the streets."

"Where are they now?"

"Likely at school."

She rolled her eyes at herself. "Right."

"The grand opening is next week." I secretly hoped we'd have more to celebrate by then, including Hartley's head and balls on a platter.

"Let me guess—Silver Securities sponsors this?"

"No." I laughed. "We bought it for Garry. He owns it. We just help."

She rolled her eyes again, but this time at me. Garry came right up to Allie and embraced her. I cleared my throat when the hold felt a little too long. The old man pulled away with a snicker.

"It's nice to meet you. Are you the one Tristan has been talking about?"

She glanced nervously at me and I gave her the nod. Of course she was the one I'd been talking about.

"I guess I am. It's a pleasure to meet you, Garry."

"She's a pretty one, Tristan." He looked Allie over the same way I had when I first met her. The petite frame did not match her true strength and ability.

"She's also taken."

"By who? You? I don't see a ring on that finger you fool and that makes a woman as free as a bird."

"A ring doesn't define a couple."

"You keep telling yourself that bullshit and you'll end up like me. Old and alone." He then turned to Allie. "Please tell me you're going to kick his ass today."

"I will do my best." She laughed.

Garry kissed her on the cheek and left.

"I like him."

"I don't know why I didn't connect the dots before, but you have something for older men. I feel like a baby beside Garry, yet you like him."

"Whoa, hold up. I'm not a panther. I like Garry but definitely not the way I like you."

Her cheeks tinted pink.

"Panther?"

"You know—women who like older men. Opposite of cougar."

I chuckled.

"I thought we've been over this, Tristan. Or are you just trying to get out of boxing me today because I will kick your ass?"

She made being around her so easy. Yet the primal vibe between us was off the charts.

"Challenge accepted." I felt my chest shake, and it appeared she liked that.

I lifted the medicine ball off the ground and threw it her way. She caught it with a grunt. The chest to ball impact appeared more like chest to stone. She bent at the knees, braced her feet into the ground, and extended her arms, pushing the ball with her entire weight to make it back to me.

"Not bad."

We passed the ball back and forth a dozen times until she finally said, "I don't think they'll be throwing medicine balls at the auction, Tristan."

I set the ball aside and picked up a pair of skipping ropes off the wall, handing one to her. "Let's warm up."

"Wuss," she coughed into her hand.

"You really want to do this?" I cocked my head sideways.

"Try me." She braced her hands on her hips.

"Fine," I removed the smaller sized boxing gloves off their hooks. "Take these and come inside the ring. The helmets are on the shelves. Take the one with the face guard."

She chuckled. "Okay."

"What's so funny?"

"You think you're actually going to make contact."

"You're full of yourself if you don't think I can." I followed her up through the ring ropes, then swept my finger over the phone screen. My favorite playlist blasted from overhead speakers.

"I gather you love the eighties."

"Best years of my life. You know, when you're a teenager and free. Sometimes I'm stuck in the decade for months."

She wiggled her nose. "We'll have to change that. I wouldn't mind giving your wardrobe an update either."

"What's wrong with my wardrobe?"

I shuffled my feet sideways and began a little jog to warm up while Allie stared at me inquisitively.

"When's the last time you shopped?"

"I have people for that."

"I'm not saying it's bad, it's just... well, I don't know many men who carry handkerchiefs in their pockets."

"How do you know I have one?"

"I was looking for a tissue and found a handkerchief instead."

"Did it serve its purpose?"

"Of course not. I would never put snot on something that had to be washed. Gross."

I laughed. "That's what they're for."

I helped her tape her fists and tie up the gloves before I slipped my hands into my own.

"Are we playing by the rules?"

Unfortunately, I gave her question too little thought.

"No rules, but you should probably avoid this area." I pointed to my crotch.

"If you think I'm aiming for your skilled cock, think again. Last thing I'd want is to damage you."

"You won't get a punch in."

She laughed. "Okay there, Silver."

"I'd never seen you this cheeky before."

"That's only because I know what I'm doing."

Did she? Was I underestimating her?

"All right. Let's do this."

"Wait." She stretched out her arm and stopped me. "I have a confession to make."

Was she stalling? Allie was never this talkative, which meant she was definitely nervous.

"I'm listening."

"I don't really go shopping often. I don't have the time to. Between the cop uniform and pajamas, I have no need for anything else."

"We'll have to change that."

She looked at me funny. I didn't know what I'd said, but I had no time to overthink it because Allie lifted her tiny hands in the gigantic gloves to protect her face and returned to her work mode.

"Are you ready to box or are we skipping all day, twinkle toes?"

Right, because *I* was the one delaying the fight. Although Allie was asking for it, I had the urge to fail just so I could hear her squeal in happiness.

"Ready if you are."

She took a protective position with a gloating smirk. "Try and hit me."

Her trot was cute and the circling technique even cuter, but all that cuteness disappeared the moment she lowered herself to the ground. All that cuteness also caught me off guard. She crouched to the floor and shot out an unexpected round kick and knocked my feet from underneath me. I had no time to react and fell backwards.

"Ouch," I groaned.

She leapt to her feet. "Oops, sorry. Did I hurt you?"

We both knew she hadn't.

I swore sometimes her fearlessness reminded me of Emma. When she focused, she held the ability to ignore the world and concentrate on the important stuff: everything that mattered. Her work and family.

"Hit me," she challenged again.

I stretched my shoulders and eased into a stance before throwing a straight punch, which she blocked.

"Try again. Harder."

She blocked my underhook as well.

"All right. I see a pattern here. How is it that I can't hit you but you can hit me?"

"Physics. There's a lot more of you to aim for and there's very little of me. Small size has its benefits. You may have strength on your side, but I have agility and instinct. Now, try to really hit me."

I shook my head. Maybe I had been going easy on her. My next hook came from the bottom up, but Allie stopped that one as well.

"What is it that boys call each other in these situations?" she taunted. "Pussy?"

I didn't want to hurt her. I… I couldn't.

"Come on, Silver. What if someone was coming after me? What would you do to him?"

I swung, but not quickly enough. Her responsive knockout came with a piercing ring in my ear, and I dropped to the floor. The room spun, and Allie's voice called my name from a distance.

"Tristan! Tristan!"

When I came around, my helmet and gloves were off.

"We should go to the hospital."

"There's no need."

"I knocked you out."

"I'm fine, Allie."

She grazed her palm along my swollen cheek. "I'm so sorry. That was very stupid of me."

I shut my eyes. My head pulsed. She pressed something cold to the spot, and I winced.

"On the bright side, I feel better about the auction now."

"I hit you. You fell down. And now your pretty face is… well, it's still pretty. The ice pack should reduce the bruising."

That's when I noticed she was holding an ice pack over the swelling.

"Thank you. I'll be okay, though."

Allie checked her watch. "It's noon. I should head home and change for tonight. Is it okay if I meet you at the Marina? My roomie has a late shift, and we'll be cutting it close with the sitter."

"Reservation is under—"

"Silver. I figured."

"Actually, it's under Flintstones."

"Oh, okay. I'll see you tonight."

I drove Allie home and returned to my office for the afternoon. I rarely showed up here, but somehow spending the next six or so hours at the penthouse, where Allie's scent would fuck with my dick and brain, didn't sound like optimal use of my time. I showered in my home office away from home and changed into a spare shirt and slacks.

Two hours before our meeting, James rushed through the door with Laila in his arms. His hair was disheveled, and his armpits were stained with sweat.

"The firkin babysitter's sick." He heaved air in.

"Firkin?" I laughed while he caught his breath. "Did you run up the stairs?"

"Quicker than elevator." Sweat dripped down his face.

"With Laila?" I looked at the giggling toddler.

"Yes. I told you. The babysitter's firkin sick."

That wasn't good news.

"We need this meeting." I removed Laila from his hold and placed her over my hip, the way I'd seen Emma do. Except I didn't have a hip, so I changed the hold to a more comfortable grip in my arms. "Go shower and change. Your office is still where it was before. How the fuck did you know where I was?"

"Fuck," Laila repeated.

I cringed, but it was still fucking cute.

James threw me a dirty look. "That's why I say firkin. Check the company app. Do you even own a phone?"

"Sorry." I turned my head to Laila. "Uncle Tristan's going to take you downstairs and buy you an ice cream while Daddy changes for his date."

"I can't firkin go. I told you—the babysitter's ill. I almost got marked at the coffee shop with that girl you asked me to check out, and well, let's just say you'll be more interested to hear about Marissa than you thought. Are you even listening to me?"

I'd asked James to follow up on the missing pregnant barista. Intel connected her to Wright.

"I always listen, and you need to relax. You're scaring my niece. Go shower. We'll stop by Mom's on the way to the Marina. Did you not call Emma? I'm sure she can handle two kids. Besides, Wilma will be thrilled."

"I didn't think." He pulled his fingers through his hair with annoyance. "The past few weeks have been… hard."

I saw the frustration of a fighting father in his eyes. Laila had been getting sicker more often. The doctors had run some tests, but had no clear answers. James changed Laila's dietary restrictions and kept a close eye on his girl while working from home. He balanced fatherhood as a single man better than most. In fact, he excelled.

"It's all right. I've got her. We'll be in the lobby."

Half an hour later we crossed the bridge to Long Island. We were lucky the roads were clear, because if we hit traffic, we'd be late. Laila ran to Emma across the driveway, nearly tripping over her feet. My sister picked up her little cousin in her arms while Wilma waved from the window with the other toddler Emma was sitting tonight.

"She can stay until the morning. Enjoy your night!"

I pressed my foot to the pedal and headed for the Marina.

I iced Tristan's swollen eye before he dropped me off at my apartment and returned to his office. We agreed to meet at the Marina early in the evening. I locked the door behind me, automatically stepping over a squeaky toy that wasn't there.

"Laura?"

Silence.

I checked the time. "She's not late yet."

I washed up before Laura returned with Foxy. She burst through the door with my godson screaming his head off. Vomit covered his shirt.

"If he's got what your babysitter has, I'm calling the evening off."

"Relax, Allie. It's just ice cream. I couldn't calm him down. I think he can sense he's going to be with new people for the evening. And Mrs. Brewer is not sick. She's just unavailable. Maybe it's better if I stay home?"

Laura's babysitter conveniently lived across the street, making shiftwork with a baby possible.

"Is that why you're so late? Because you've been moping all day? Who are you?"

"I'm not sure anymore." She sighed.

"Okay." I slowly removed Fox from her arms and brought him to my chest."

Laura slumped to the floor in the same spot where she had been standing. "I'm not ready to go on this date."

"You already have someone?"

"Technically, no. But I have seen him, and I've been thinking about him. A lot. And doing everything not to think about him. A lot."

Her desperate puppy face tugged at my heartstrings. She was lying to herself, and that was the truth. Laura needed stability, and someone who would understand her. This date couldn't come any sooner.

"I know exactly how to fix it," I said.

"You do?"

"Of course I do. And guess what? It doesn't involve tequila."

Her nose shriveled.

I reached for my godson. "Com on, Foxy. Auntie Allie is going to wash you while Mommy takes care of herself. Right, Mommy?" I stared Laura down. "Because lives depend on it. It's Auntie's only chance to go over a plan, and Mommy needs a night off."

"It's really that important?"

"I would change it if I could, but the guy has a young daughter with medical issues. He's as busy as you are, so you'll have a lot in common. When I say this is my only chance, I mean it. Besides, I think this will be good for you, and I already got the sitter. Go on. Hit the shower. I'll get Foxy ready for the night."

Laura dragged her feet and hugged us both, whispering in my ear, "Thank you. I'll go wash up."

While Laura took over the shower, I washed Foxy in the kitchen sink. He'd outgrown the space already, but wouldn't pass the opportunity to splash bubbles. I dried him and put on the pajamas Laura had laid out on a chair. I set Foxy down in a playpen and knocked on the bathroom door.

"Laura? Are you all right?"

"No."

"Can I come in?" I opened the door and found Laura sitting on the floor with the shower running.

"What's going on? Why aren't you getting ready?" I checked my watch again.

"This is a bad idea. I can feel it."

"It is not, and now we barely have time to make it. How about I drop him off at the sitter's and come back in time to get you? We can make it that way, but you have to shower. Please?"

She nodded and slowly peeled herself off the floor.

"Just shower and, well… start with a shower. Please. Come on Foxy, let's introduce you to your new best friend. I bet she has a room full of toys you've never seen before."

Laura froze. "Where exactly are you taking him? Oh my God! I'm a terrible mother. I don't even know where you're dropping off my son."

"It's Tristan's sister, and she's a verified babysitter with plenty of experience, two adult guardians, and the tightest security system I've ever seen. Trust me. I made the alarm go off with my ass. Foxy will never find a better sitter."

Laura's lips thinned and she wavered from one foot to another, as if deciding between the shower and Foxy.

"Laura, snap out of it, or I will snap it out of you."

She jumped up. "I'll be fine. I promise. I have a lot going on right now."

"I know. I'm sorry. We're running short on time, and you know how I feel about being late."

"I know, I know. I'll be ready when you return, but can we talk about this new hair? And are you wearing contacts?"

Her swift change of subject gave me the opportunity to set us on the right path to tonight's double date.

I wrapped a curl around my finger. "It's for work. Do you like it?"

"You look like a Lolita."

"That's sort of the point. Better than feeling like Tristan's wife."

"What are you talking about?"

"I dreamed we were married."

"Interesting."

"Not interesting! Too fast. Now go shower, so we can leave as soon as I get back. We can talk about work stuff on the way."

"Fine." She came in for another hug, kissing Foxy on his head. I grabbed the diaper bag and headed for the car, where I secured him in the car seat.

Although I'd met Tristan in Manhattan, I didn't live that far away from the Silvers on Long Island, except their residence was at the shore, and I was more inland. The Marina was walking distance from their house, but I had to return for Laura. I carefully backed out of the parking spot.

"We can do this, Foxy. Right?"

My godson loved car rides and spent the twenty-minute trip watching through the window. As I maneuvered up the winding driveway, thousands of fairy twinkle lights sparkled among the trees lining the path. It was beautiful, and Foxy squealed in happiness.

"Tinkle, tinkle."

"Yes, that's twinkle, twinkle."

I parked at the front, where Emma and Wilma were waiting on the porch. I unbuckled Fox from his seat and lifted him into my arms just as Bamm-Bamm and Pebbles ran up to sniff us both. Foxy squealed with happiness again.

"Don't worry. They're wonderful with kids," Emma said.

"This is Fox. I call him Foxy."

"Fox? Well, isn't that nice? We have a Fox in the family." She took him out of my arms just as he reached for the oversized necklace made of baby apples. "You like apples? You're just as cute as our Fox. Except he's much older." She kissed him on his forehead, the same way Laura usually did, and went inside, conversing with Foxy.

"Don't worry. He'll be fine," she called to me. "If you want, we can Facetime later."

"I'm sure Laura would like that." A video call would settle her nerves for the night. "We're meeting Tristan at the Marina, but we should have enough time to call you before then."

"Sounds good. Talk to you soon."

"Thank you, Emma." I handed her the diaper bag. "I owe you for this."

"Make me an aunt and we'll call it even."

I was beginning to understand the pressure Tristan faced from his sister and mother. This relationship with Tristan was fresh and complicated, but making babies was out of the question. Yet Tristan felt like the perfect best friend and partner, and for that simple reason, I had to help him before I worried about anything else. Once Kendra was safe, I'd move forward with work at Silver Securities and watch Wright get what he deserved, the way Tristan had promised. Life was falling into place.

I waved her goodbye and turned back around to drive home. Laura was waiting patiently by the curbside. Her black dress hugged her strong curves. Though the long sleeves covered her beautiful arms, they also complimented her figure. The low-cut neckline and bouncing boobs full of milk were definitely an asset on a night like tonight.

"You look gorgeous," I said as I pulled away.

"Thanks. I may have had a shot of tequila. You know, to ease the nerves. I'll pump that milk out. Was Foxy okay?"

"He was fine. We should have enough time to Facetime him from the Marina."

"Great! Have I told you how much I love you?"

"No, but you don't have to." I glanced at her. "I already know it."

We arrived at the Marina with fifteen minutes to spare. I connected Laura with Emma and Foxy near a quiet end of the patio and returned to the private table by the outdoor fireplace set for four. Tristan and James walked through the front door moments later. My breath stilled, and my memory flashed back to when I'd watched them stroll across the snow like they were parading down a fashion catwalk. Jesus, did they ever look confident and suave! I shut my eyes tight, trying to remember more from the trip to Colorado three years ago, when my vacation had been destroyed by food poisoning and an avalanche at the same time. By the time I opened my eyes, Tristan and his partner James were at the booth where I was sitting. Each was dressed in a light pullover with rolled-up sleeves and ripped jeans of different shades. They matched, yet each displayed a unique style.

"I'm sorry we're late." Tristan slid into the seat beside me while James sat across the table.

"You're not. We're early. My friend's just finishing a conversation around the corner."

"We stopped by Wilma and Fred's to drop off my niece."

Laura would love it when she heard Foxy would make a new friend.

"It's all right. I know all about kids. So…" I reached my hand over the table. "It's nice to see you again, James."

"Wait a minute. You two know each other?" Tristan asked.

"We met briefly in Colorado three years ago when James took me to the hospital. Food poisoning."

"In Colorado? At Silver's lodge?"

I nodded.

"Well, isn't this a small world?" Tristan relaxed in the seat.

I shook James's hand and met his kind eyes, those same eyes that had sparkled with silver when I opened the mountain lodge door as a nutcracker. The same eyes Laura couldn't stop talking about for weeks.

As recognition dawned on me in what seemed like slow motion, so did the consequent conclusion. "Oh, no, no, no…." I covered my mouth with one hand while reaching for something to grab. Tristan was the closest. I dug my fingers into his bare arm,

"What's the matter?" he asked.

"I think I made a mistake."

But I couldn't talk. The next thing I knew, I had tequila on my lips. Thank goodness for fancy Marina restaurants with everything on the menu. I had a feeling I'd made the right choice in ordering the starters. The liquor smoothed my throat, and I quickly organized my thoughts.

Stall.

"We should sit down," I said.

"We are sitting." Tristan wasn't buying my distraction. Was James?

Unlikely.

"Here, have my shot." Tristan slid the glass closer to me. "What mistake are you talking about?"

"No, one is enough. Thanks. I think I need to be the sober one tonight."

But my best friend may need a shot or two.

"Is your mother okay? Has something happened?"

Technically, not yet; but if I were to bet, someone was about to get murdered.

"No, it's not that. I just realized I ran into James again a few weeks ago. Briefly. Very briefly."

That's the truth. Stick to the truth.

"The morning Martinez was shot and fled the insurance office. I arrested Gabriel Silver by mistake."

"You made a mistake?" Tristan twisted in his seat, turning my way.

"Well, it wasn't my mistake. I did my job based on the information I had." I looked James dead in the eyes, which he rolled. "I was late, and shots were fired. It was a mess."

"I was buying Gabe time," James explained. "She's right, but I wouldn't call it a mess. More like… an interesting turn of events."

"Laura was there with me. Laura Young."

James stilled in his seat as the realization slowly hit.

"You know her?" Tristan turned in his seat, this time toward James.

James exhaled. "I do. Of course I remember Laura. How is she?"

As if on cue, Laura turned the corner and headed back to our table. Her head was down as she concentrated on her phone screen. She paused her pace as if she sensed something was off. Then froze, slowly moving her head from left to right in disbelief. The shock kept her still, as if she'd somehow disappear if she moved.

I excused myself from the table. "I'll be right back."

I slipped out of the seat and hurried to Laura, who was pointing towards the two men.

"Oh my God, is that who I think it is?"

I grabbed her by the elbow, turned her around, and we walked out of sight.

"You have some explaining to do."

Laura chewed on her fingernail.

"Please tell me that's not James Silver."

"It is. Why didn't you tell me?"

"I didn't know you were working with him. I saw him that morning we were called to the insurance company, and I was hoping not to run into him again."

"Why?"

"You know exactly why."

I did. The facts weren't difficult to put together. Laura had slept with James Silver, had his baby, and kept Foxy a secret. Obviously she'd lied about Foxy's daddy being an asshole because assholes don't drive sick women to hospitals in the middle of a snowstorm.

"Does he know about Foxy?"

"Are you crazy? He'd kill me, and I'm not sure how long I can hold onto this secret. How could you not have told me you were working with James Silver?"

"I didn't know! Maybe if you'd told me you slept with him, I could have helped."

"Well, you can't tell him now. At least not yet. Not until I'm ready, and I'm really not ready. It's girl code, sister code, and best friend code. Like a trifecta."

"Laura, I love you, but this is not a secret you want to hold onto for long. He deserves to know, and you deserve the help."

"Because he's a billionaire?"

"No, because he's Foxy's father."

"He's also involved and has a daughter."

"That doesn't change anything." I peeked from behind the corner. Tristan and James would notice if we didn't return soon. "It doesn't negate the fact he should know. I won't say anything for now, but you need to figure this out eventually. Tonight makes perfect sense."

"What? How?"

"I'm willing to cover for you for now, but you have to figure out how to tell that man he's Foxy's father. You can start by facing him tonight."

"What? You can't do that to me."

"Veto."

"You can't veto."

"I just did. If you want me to keep my mouth shut, you will have this dinner with us, so I can do my job. Now let's go."

I hooked her under my arm and nearly dragged her back to the table.

"Tristan, James. This is my roommate and my best friend Laura."

James turned in slow motion, stood up, lifted Laura's hand, and placed a shiver of a peck on the skin while she stood completely speechless. He didn't appear surprised to see her.

"*Y*ou said she has a kid?" James asked.

"A boy."

"And the father?"

"Not in the picture at the moment. Allie said they're figuring things out."

I sat in an armchair with a coffee in my hand while Laura helped Allie change inside a fitting room. After dinner, we'd requested an appointment at my aunt's private boutique for the final fitting, and Mary Wagner lived up to every promise she made. Every skimpy outfit Allie tried on fit too perfectly, so I sent her back to the changing room.

My mother's sister-in-law strolled into the room in true fashionista spirit. Dark curls spilled over her shoulders as she exuded Elvira Addams but in Madonna's style. The side-hustle boutique complemented her principal business, except she would never admit she owned one of the most elegant empires in the country. She hung a couple more outfits on the door and went back to the stockroom.

James kept his head lowered and attention focused on his phone, scrolling through birthday ideas for Laila. "Any kid who wants a clown for their birthday should watch *It*."

"If you project your fears onto Laila, you'll traumatize the kid."

"Laila is brave. Maybe that's why she likes clowns."

My first niece fought harder to live than most kids. James drove her from one doctor to another and hired the best nurses for her care, but no money could buy what Laila needed. At least, not legally.

"She likes clowns because she's almost three," I told him.

"Are you ready?" Laura stuck her head out from behind the curtain. We'd driven in separate cars from the Marina, so I'd had no chance to speak with Allie about the double date, which took a turn when we found out Laura and James already knew each other.

James set his phone on the table, and I straightened. Laura pulled the fabric aside, and Allie stepped out of the change room.

I shifted in my seat and immediately stuck a magazine in front of James' face. "Don't you dare fucking look."

The sheer fabric with embroidery sewn over the nipples and crotch revealed everything.

"What do you mean, don't look? I'm gonna be there with her."

I growled. "Fine. Put on a robe."

"You don't like it?" Allie adjusted the straps over her hips and shoulders.

"Better yet, change. Now."

A whistle blew from the second floor, where a woman was leaning over the floor barrier. Grace Wagner set her purse down and pointed at Allie's outfit.

"What's the matter with you? She looks amazing!"

"Gracie? What are you doing here?"

"Indulging. Aunt Mary was nice enough to give me a hand with, well… some stuff. Work stuff. For the salon. That outfit is hot." She pointed to Allie. "But it's not the innocent look you're going for. Sorry, I overheard earlier."

"What do you recommend?"

Grace pointed behind the glass wall. "Mary's sassy collection is what you're looking for. She can pull off any outfit with that body, I'm sure. Hey, James."

She waved, and Laura's head popped out of the change room again.

"What's up, Gracie?"

"I'm still looking for that date for the masquerade. You interested?" Grace winked and tilted her hip.

"I don't do tuxedos," James grunted.

"You're a Silver. You can do whatever and whomever you want."

Laura stepped out of the dressing room, and James grimaced. "If that were true, my baby brother would do you, Gracie."

"Don't speak the demon's name."

"Hunter's been asking about you."

She let out an exasperated "Argh…" and stomped down the stairs, just like my sister, Emma. Except Emma was fourteen, and Grace was… well, up there where most of her friends were having kids. Neither one was a beneficial influence on the other.

"It doesn't change the fact I'd like to skin him *Silence of the Lambs* style. Tell him I'll be ready to accept his apology when he matures, which is… ahem… never."

Grace and Hunter had been off and on since he was eighteen. Fast forward four years later, and the two of them still hadn't figured it out. Then again, who was I to judge? I was about to pawn the woman I was falling for to the scummiest of men.

James stood up and greeted Grace with a giant hug. "I

missed you. Sorry about my brother. I gotta go pick up Laila. Are you coming, Laura?"

Allie nudged her roommate forward. The awkward dinner date we'd started at the Marina wasn't over yet.

"I'll see you two in the morning." James shook my hand, kissed Grace on her cheek, and left with his very confused blind date.

"Sorry, I didn't mean to break up the party. You need a trim, Tristan." Grace messed my disheveled hair with her fingers, eyeing the lengthy strands. My cousin owned the most exclusive salon on Long Island. She was the master behind the cut that had inadvertently gotten me named Manhattan's most eligible bachelor. Allie called my messy look *sexy*, while I called it *too much attention*. "I haven't seen you at the salon in months."

"I'm keeping a low profile."

She chuckled. "Come over when you're ready. Emma can't be the only one who gets to play with that hair."

She winked and turned to Allie, who stood motionless, watching the exchange. My pawn had changed into the outfit Grace recommended and stood by the mirror like a flawless doll. I stared open-mouthed.

"Oh my God, Tristan, that's perfect. Look at her." Grace hopped closer to Allie and tied a loose string at her back.

"That's too sexy," I groaned.

"It's exactly what you need." Aunt Mary pinned Allie's hair on each side, exposing her long neck and drawing the eye to her chest.

"Allie, meet my cousin Grace Wagner. She's the one with the most style in the family."

My aunt cleared her throat.

"Sorry. Her and aunt Mary both have enough style for us all. Mary designs and approves all the suits for the Silvers."

My aunt's phone rang, and she excused herself.

Allie twirled on the spot. "You think this will work?"

She strolled to the couch, and my voice locked underneath my Adam's apple. The long legs supported her petite bell shape. Her freckles stood out over her beaming cheeks, and her eyes rounded as she transformed into an innocent target and my pawn.

"What's the matter?" I dragged my thumb over her pouty lip.

"Nothing. Just practicing for tomorrow."

I shook my head. "Don't. You look perfect. Too perfect. I'll break through the door if anything's off."

"Have some faith in tomorrow. James will be there, and no one's going to touch me. I've enjoyed working with you, Tristan. A lot."

Her voice cracked.

"You like being ogled by horny men?" I removed the sunglasses from my head and lowered them to the side table.

"I enjoy being ogled by one horny man." She spun in her skimpy black lace, which resembled a cheerleading outfit. "Do you like what you see, Mr. Silver?"

I loved seeing Allie in her element, but I didn't enjoy looking at her like she was a schoolgirl.

"You look… young. Too young." I coughed into my hand. "Aunt Mary?"

Aunt Mary examined the outfit, crouched to the ground ,and removed some fabric from underneath Allie's spiderweb corset. "It's not enough skin."

"Not enough?" My forehead creased. "It's too revealing and too sexy."

"That's the point." Allie examined herself in the mirror. "It has to catch the eye."

"Wrong." I stood up, removed a silky scarf from a mannequin and draped it over Allie's shoulders. "I don't want you catching any eyes. The fact you'll be there is hard enough."

My aunt yanked at the sheer fabric with a frown. "Tristan

Silver, this is what you asked for. It may not be for you, but it's perfect for your needs. Don't let emotions get in the way."

Emotions. Right. That little pesky problem hit me like a train. That distance I'd felt between us when we met narrowed with every hour, which made work a challenge.

"Your aunt is right, Tristan. Like it or not, this outfit fits the profile. She knows what she's talking about."

The black lace clung to her body, barely covering her.

"I've dressed men and women for decades. Speaking of which, I must run. I have a morning meeting, and this face needs her beauty sleep. It was a pleasure meeting you, Allie. And you know your way out, Tristan."

"Thank you, Aunt Mary."

My aunt left, and I remained in the dressing room with Allie. She wiggled her ass, looking over the outfit in the mirror.

"This is definitely a change from my uniform."

"Do you miss your work?"

"I do, but our work here is just as important."

"The fight won't be over once we get Kendra."

"Of course it won't. We're barely scratching the surface, Tristan. The girls I've seen on the street don't have a lot of choice. They need ways out."

"It's an underserved area Silver Securities hasn't explored. It's not the work we usually do, but it's definitely an area I'd like to expand into."

"So after the auction—"

"Why don't we worry about it then?" I told her. If my plans panned out, Allie would love working at Silver Securities. "You have enough on your mind, and this assignment will be difficult."

"If there's anyone who knows hard, it's me. It doesn't matter what they throw at me in there. I won't break."

"I'm glad to hear that. Both you and Laura are two strong women. I think James may have found his match."

"So, the date at the Marina tonight—"

"Was as uncomfortable as my grandmother's underwear. I tried them on when I was eight."

She laughed.

"Laura seemed stressed."

"She had every right to be."

I hadn't asked Allie about her friend's timid nature, but something was off. When Allie talked about Laura, she made her out to be a kick-ass woman.

"Why was Laura stressed?" I asked.

Allie sat on the seat beside me. "James never told you about Colorado?"

"No."

"Well, that's where he met Laura then his girlfriend showed up all pregnant, and Laura backed away? And then... well, there's more... but you know... sister code."

"Sister code?"

"I can't betray her trust."

"You realize I run a private investigation and securities company, don't you?"

"Yes...." She lengthened her reply. "But you're privy to the boyfriend code, which means you can't repeat what I tell you or not tell you privately."

"Who makes up these rules?"

"Everybody."

"Because if you're a very good private investigator, then it doesn't take a genius to figure it out."

"Figure what out?"

But Allie remained silent. I caught on after her third blink. "There's something you want to tell me I can't repeat to James."

"Correct."

"And if I promise not to tell anyone?"

Her mouth curved into a cautious smile. "Do you?"

I nodded, and she stepped up on her toes. My eyes grew wider with every word she whispered into my ear.

"You're kidding. I can't keep that secret from him."

"You no longer have a choice. You're bound by the boyfriend code."

It had been years since a woman had called me her boyfriend, and I still had a difficult time getting used to it. It didn't sound permanent enough.

"And if I break it?"

"Severe punishment will follow."

My chest rumbled. "I think I'm willing to gamble."

"You won't like it when you hear the punishment. Salt over open wounds isn't pleasant."

"Ouch."

"But more important, I don't want to lose a friend. Laura needs me and I need her, so you have to let them figure this out."

"And what about this? You and me?"

"What about it?" she asked. "You're my boss—"

"Partner. We already discussed this."

"Whatever. You're the partner I'm fucking."

Her blunt mouth turned me on, but she was wrong. "In my eyes, we're not just fucking."

"What exactly am I? You know… in your eyes?"

"You're the partner I'm falling for."

She gasped.

"I'm not sure I know how to figure this out, Allie, but I know you belong in my life, And there's something I need you to know before tomorrow night."

She pressed her finger to my lip. "Please, don't say it. Just don't say it before tomorrow because it will make it harder if you do. For the both of us. And from what I've seen, Kendra deserves more."

Kendra deserved nothing less than our full attention.

"I've never met anyone like you, Allie. I thought I had at one point—well, maybe I did—but you're... unexpectedly perfect."

Her lips thinned into a line, and freckles popped. "That's good, right?"

"Yeah. That's great. Move in with me."

"I already live in your penthouse."

"I mean permanently."

"You're crazy, Tristan. That's... unexpected, and we just met—"

"Yet I feel like I've known you for years. Is that even on the table for you?"

"What?"

"A relationship? A family?"

"Has your mother said something to you? Or Emma? Because you're acting like they drugged you."

"You're the one drugging me. I can't let anything happen to you at that auction. I was thinking you should go in late; you know, just before it closes. Give them a story—"

"We're not changing plans, and you're experiencing cold feet."

"I will not apologize for caring. I don't want to see any of my employees hurt, and that includes you. Remember the night we met?"

"At the burned club in the basement? Feels like ages ago."

"That was just our pit stop, Allie. Tomorrow will be another pit stop, and I'm making sure you're getting off that bus. At the right stop."

"We can't change plans now. Don't worry, Silver. I'm not a baby."

"No. You're not. But you're exactly what they're looking for."

The room smelled of mold and cigars. James steadied my stance before he let go of my elbow. I tried to peek through the cloth over my eyes, but I couldn't see anything. We'd trained for three straight days before the auction. I had memorized Kendra's and Martinez's faces, learned the sex-trafficking jargon, and practiced our rescue with James. We took the elevator to the fifth floor, where James affixed my blindfold and led me to the auction.

"The conference room should be half full, but the process shouldn't take long. If she's there, you know what to do. If she's not… well, I simply won't let you go."

"I trust you."

He stopped and gently grasped my arm.

"What's wrong?"

"You and Laura have been friends for a while, right?"

"Since police academy, but this isn't the right time, James. I… I can hear them." I filtered through the hum for familiar words, but couldn't make out any. James guided me forward, inside what I assumed was the conference room. A chill passed through my body, but I pushed the crawling fear aside. The cop in me listened to every crack, shuffle, cough, and whisper.

"Stand still. You'll be on your own in a sec," James whispered in my ear before he eased off my arm.

A door squeaked at the hinges. A short moment later, someone's shoulder brushed against mine. She smelled like a baby, but gasped with a desperate fear I hadn't heard before. I steadied my rushing pulse with a deeper breath and waited as the room settled and the hum turned into silence.

My body prickled with an odd sensation, as if thousands of eyes were staring at me, making me feel naked in my skimpy lingerie. I swallowed hard as shameful heat consumed me and took another deep breath. This one too helped a little.

"Remove your blindfolds."

The hairs on my nape stood tall. I lifted my arms to the back of my head and released the knot. My sight adjusted to the low lighting in a room that wasn't as shitty as I'd imagined. The tall columns and high chandeliers resembled a banquet hall. Plush furniture and velvet drapes, in varying red tones, pimped up the space. They'd set loungers with side tables and privacy booths up in front of us. In their seats were men with an appetite. I was wrong before—they were the shittiest thing in the room.

Where's James?

A waitress passed in front of me, clad only in an apron tied around her waist and nipple tassels. She set a man's drink on his table, and he grabbed her by her inner thigh. I cringed. Another girl in the long row of girls gasped, breaking the silence. The man laughed and brought the waitress to his lap, where she stayed with her legs lightly parted and his fingers up her pussy.

I looked away, but it was difficult not to find a disgusting pervert with a different obsession at every table. I searched through the faces, looking for Martinez, but I couldn't see him. My attention shifted to the row of girls beside me and their ghostly faces with shadowed eyes in search of Kendra. The girl on my right couldn't have been older than Emma. The longer I stared at her, the more I thought she could have passed for my younger sister. From her golden brown eyes to the auburn hair and high cheeks and freckles, the resemblance was astounding. Except… her stomach stuck out forward. She was pregnant.

I sucked in a sharp breath. It was Marissa, the same girl we'd been looking for. My stomach squeezed, and I wanted to throw up.

This room is messing with me.

As the reality of sex trafficking in a modern world hit me, I felt ill. My stomach turned inside out, but I pushed the pain away and concentrated on each hollow face again. None of them belonged to Kendra. Today would not be the day we saved her. I steadied my stance and squared my shoulders as everything else inside me shriveled into a ball of disappointment.

A middle-aged man in a suit clapped his hands, and the room of gents fell silent.

"You have thirty minutes. As you can see, our crop tonight is very youthful and special. Enjoy!"

It didn't take long for the first buyer to stand and cross the room. He walked up to a girl with a collar around her neck, clipped a leash he'd carried in his pocket to the fastening, and led her out the door. The MC marked the transaction on his phone and that was it. It was that easy.

Oh fuck.

My attention flew to the other side of the room, where a man lowered a girl's bra cups beneath her breasts. He fondled her nipple before he turned her around, slapped her ass, and forced her forward. She bent in half, exposing her backside, spread her legs on his command, and he jabbed a finger inside her. She cried out, but that only made the scumbag more excited, so he pushed harder.

"That's a good girl. If you don't like this, I'll make sure you do. You're tight enough for my boss's dick. You'll do." He then turned to the MC, nodded, took the girl under his arm and left.

Double fuck.

Someone lit a chocolate cigar, and the scent temporarily camouflaged the stench of unwelcome arousal. I followed its white puff as it floated across the room, settling above a man's head in the shadows. He stepped forward, and I froze. As my heart thumped in my chest, my nerves ceased responding. I urged my legs to head for the door, but I couldn't. Wright was staring at me from across the room. He lit a pipe and took a long drag before letting the smoke out of his lungs. He set it down and strolled across the room toward me. I bit the inside of my cheek until I broke through the skin and tasted blood.

James, where is James?

My vision blurred. I looked over my shoulder, but I couldn't find him. When I turned forward again, Wright was standing in front of the girl beside me. I froze. Not because I feared him, but because I'd made a promise to Tristan. My life wasn't the only one at stake. His predatory eyes took her in, making me nauseous. I kept my head turned slightly to the side to avoid direct eye contact, but my heart was hammering in my chest like it wanted to jump out. My insides twisted, and I held back the lurking bile. The inside of my cheek ached as I bit down harder. My molar cut through another spot and fresh blood filled my mouth. Wright removed a photo from his breast pocket. His gaze skidded from the picture in his hand to the girl beside me.

"You're expecting, sweetheart?"

The sound of his scruffy voice made me shudder. My knees wobbled underneath me, and my body flashed with heat and cold and heat again, raging through phases.

She must have nodded because he grinned, pleased. I wanted to puke.

"What's your name?"

"Marissa."

"You're a perfect distraction, and from now on, you're mine." He turned, nodded to the MC and left.

I let go of the longer breath I held and searched the room for James.

I have to get out of here.

"I want to see this one's pussy." A short man resembling a stump stood in front of me.

Where the hell did he come from?

He reached to touch me, but James blocked his way. At least, I thought it was James. The the prosthetic nose, cheeks, chin threw me off.

"She's not for sale."

"So why is she here?"

"It's none of your fucking business."

"The rules are—"

"Hey, buddy. I don't follow the rules. I break them. Now piss off!"

A bell dinged.

"Come on. Put this back on. We're done," James whispered, handing me a blindfold. He grabbed my arm like he owned me and guided me out the door.

"We're heading for the elevator."

I hurried to keep up with him, panting like a dog. Why was I so tired? The elevator chimed, and we stepped inside. James removed my blindfold, and I folded in half into his arms.

"Hey, hey. You're okay."

The small room spun as he pulled me up into a stronger hold.

"She wasn't there."

"I know."

"But Wright was there. Why the hell was he there?"

"Wright knows the congressman tied to Kendra's case. He's

also working for the Feds. If Karma knows what's right the Hartleys will figure out he snitched."

"Snitches get stitches."

"That's right. We need him for that case. The Feds need him alive and that's where we come in."

"You're working for the Feds?"

"With the Feds. With them, not for them. We do not discriminate between clients and you definitely didn't hear me say anything about any Silver clients. Got it?"

"Yeah, I got it. You have to keep Wright safe which makes him untouchable until...," I froze as it dawned on me and met his kind eyes. "Until we press charges for the crimes the Feds don't know about? And we can't do all that until Kendra's safe."

"That's right"

"Do the Feds know he just walked out with an underage girl?'

James blinked back with the answers I didn't want. "They need him for something bigger, Allie. Something that will save more than one girl."

"It won't save Marissa. Wait a minute—did you guys know he'd be there? Did Tristan know?"

"We thought there was a possibility."

My pulse raced, and my body flushed with anger. "He fucking put me in the same room with that fucking monster?"

Gravity yanked at my knees, and James scooped me into his arms again. "Come on, Allie. Stay with me."

The next thing I knew, I was on the floor with my legs up high and commotion around me. I was back in a hotel room but couldn't remember how I'd gotten there.

"Why? Why didn't you tell me?"

"She's in shock. Wright showed, Kendra didn't, and what the hell happened to you?" James held my feet in the air. I tilted my head to the right. Tristan's busted lip was bleeding at the scar.

"What happened?" I asked.

"It's nothing. A distraction."

Distraction. The word bounced in my mind, which couldn't settle on its meaning.

"I should have told you about Wright, Allie. I'm sorry."

"You shouldn't have punched him." Julian passed his brother an ice pack.

"Punched Wright?"

"I should have killed him."

"Who?" I asked in frustration. Why was everything so confusing? Why couldn't we just open that conference room door and free them all, today? Tristan remained silent.

"Donaldson didn't show." I turned at the sound of the new voice entering the room. "He had a mule. We don't have the pictures we need."

"That's Hunter, my brother." James motioned for him to come closer. They switched the hold, and James peeled off his prosthetic nose and chin.

"I think she'll be okay," Tristan said from above me. Hunter lowered my feet to the ground. "Find out where Wright went and get back to me. I'm taking her home."

"No!" I shot up. "No!"

"Allie, it's all right. You're safe." Tristan's hold tightened around my trembling body. The lightheadedness passed as he rocked me back and forth.

"Don't you get it? This isn't about me anymore!" I screamed and pointed my finger at his twitching palm as he reached for the syringe in his pocket. "And don't you dare sedate me. She wasn't there. Kendra wasn't there, and that bastard took Marissa and all those other girls and these fucking assholes." I tasted blood in my mouth for the third time and ran my tongue along the inside of my shredded cheek.

"I know, Allie." Tristan turned to James. "Sweep the building and go. We'll be fine here."

Tristan slowly wrapped himself around my body, taking me into his arms. "Are you okay?"

I didn't want his comfort, yet I needed him so badly. I lost the ability to control the whimpers. "Yes and no. It wasn't supposed to be this way. He wasn't supposed to be there. I thought you said—"

"I know what I said, Allie. I was afraid you'd back away, but I should have told you the truth. I'm so sorry. Please forgive me. I'll make sure justice comes his way."

"Justice? Is it justice for Wright to enslave an underage girl? For... for him to traffic her like she's just a piece of meat? Own her?" I sobbed, gripped Tristan's shirt and pulled until my fingers ached. He slowly uncoiled them and splayed my palm over his warm chest. His heart was beating in a calmer rhythm than mine. I closed my eyes and leaned my head over his chest.

"I'm so tired."

"Shhhhh," he cooed.

My body shook in his hold for several minutes before we moved to the couch in the corner. I sat in his lap, cradled in his arms like a child.

"All those helpless girls," I sobbed into his body.

"You don't have to do this again."

"What about Kendra?"

"We'll figure out a different way."

"No." I shook my head. "You said there will be another auction, so she has to be there. But what about the girls downstairs? Who's going to save them?"

"One at a time, Allie. One at a time. Even I don't have the power to save them all. Infiltrating this circle was tough enough, but I promise you, once we have Kendra, we'll do everything we can to save as many as we can."

I'd seen a lot on the street, but nothing as vulgar and brazen as I had tonight.

"Okay." I wiped my nose over his shirt and yawned.

He carried me to the bathroom, where he carefully washed me and the shower stream drowned my tears.

God, it hurt! It hurt so badly inside I wanted to tear my guts out. Tristan pulled a soaped scrubber over my arms and legs, washing away the clinging, tainted conference room air off my skin. I towel-dried my body, slipped into his oversized shirt, and climbed into bed. The lighting dimmed to a soothing glow as he spooned me from behind, uncoiling my body from the fetal position. I must have fallen asleep quickly because when I woke again it was after midnight, and Tristan wasn't there.

I slipped out of bed and sent him a quick text, but he didn't reply. I removed the towel from my dampened hair. The short dream in which I'd saved the girls wasn't real, but it could be. It only took one person to start the change. Why not me?

I need tequila.

I pulled on a pair of jeans and a tank top, took some cash, and headed downstairs. A handful of people were sitting along the counter and a couple in a corner, but none of them were Tristan. The bartender rested on his elbows and yawned.

I tapped the bar. "Tequila."

The troubled reflection in the mirror behind the bar gave me the goosebumps. I shuddered.

The barman's lids lifted lazily, but his eyes opened wide as soon as I left the crisp bills on the counter. Someone took a seat on my right. I turned on my stool and was surprised to see a familiar face.

"Are you alone?" he asked.

Where do I know him from?

The man was at least two decades or so older than Tristan, but clean cut, freshly shaved, and sporting what looked like a giant lime underneath his eye.

"For now. I'm waiting for someone."

"Too bad. I like younger women."

"And I like older men. My boyfriend would agree. You can

meet his fist when he finds you down here flirting with me. It will match that shiner under your eye."

Someone had busted his lip as well. It was swollen like a ball, matching the eye.

"Is that what you think I'm doing?"

"Isn't it?"

"I think I'll take my chance." He lifted a finger, and the barman poured him a clear liquor on ice. I was pretty sure it was vodka.

"My talent is running into fists."

Was he vying for my pity? Because I held no mercy for men who looked like this douche, like Wright, who abused and... and... did everything they shouldn't be doing. I had no patience to look at or to talk to another man.

I rolled my eyes and searched through my memory where I would have seen him. The cut over his upper cheek was fresh.

A low, sickened voice laughed from the corner booth. I turned in my seat in what felt like slow motion and startled. My stomach tightened with both nerves and hope.

She stood frozen like a porcelain doll on a window display. Bright red lipstick and blush brightened her powdered face. She turned in a circle before she took her spot, capturing the line of girls in the hidden camera embedded on her jewel. The pick in the room was younger than I expected; some were Emma's age.

I typed out the GO in a group message. We'd get every fucker in that room and every buyer attached to the transaction. I zoomed in the camera to the host with the tablet. Our guy was tracking every trade. James sat in the back row, watching Allie and waiting for the remaining girls to arrive. If luck was on our side, Kendra would show soon. The off-books operation buzzed with pedophiles and those with sexual tastes and fantasies more peculiar than average. We would coordinate the raids tomorrow night, but for now, my brother was waiting for my call in the bathroom by the main hall. Julian would grab Kendra the moment she showed.

Allie shifted, and the lens embedded in her jewels caught a familiar face. I zoomed the camera for a close-up. The scruffy beard, dark hair, and caterpillar eyebrows were unmistakable.

"Shit!"

What the fuck was Wright doing there?

I bolted through the door and down the stairs, but I couldn't get to the hall on the third floor fast enough. I cut across the skyway and across the back storage, then connected to the kitchen area, where I stopped behind a stack of vegetable crates. The smell of grease wafted from the deep fryer behind me as I found myself in a tight spot. I peered from behind the crates. The young Hartley brothers were sitting at a counter, focused on a basket of what smelled like buffalo chicken wings.

"The online sales show a seventy-five percent better performance than the auction. Less risk, as long as the legislation's on our side."

"We can buy all the legislation we need. What we're lacking are fresh bodies. Smart women with unpaid bills and willing bodies. Infinity's growing for a reason."

I couldn't distinguish between Chris's and Brad's voices, but it didn't take a genius to figure out Jeff's sons took after their father. Was Kendra even here tonight? Was she being sold online?

I removed my phone from my pocket and texted Ace Wagner what I'd heard. I lowered myself to the floor and was returning to the storage area when a woman with an oversized hat showed in the connecting hallway. She left through the back door, and I followed. A strong gust of wind pushed at my chest out in the parking lot. The woman's hat blew in the wind like a beach umbrella as she hurried. She caught it with her hand. Her dark curve-hugging outfit was barely visible in the night. Tires screeched, and an SUV turned the corner. I jumped up. A distant memory flashed through my mind, and I froze as the image of my skidding convertible played out. By the time my trance cleared, the jeep had pulled up to her side. She held onto her hat and jumped in.

The driver pumped the gas and the wheels screeched again, reviving my trauma.

I hurried after the vehicle and stopped where it had taken off with the woman. The smell of gasoline swirled around me. I bent to the ground where she'd dropped a white card. I flipped it over. A black infinity symbol was inked on the reverse.

Who the hell are you?

My phone beeped with a message from James. Kendra wasn't at the auction. I stood up and turned around, only to bump into the one person I didn't want to see.

"What the fuck are you doing here?" Jeff Hartley spat. His mouth tightened into a straight line. I followed his line of focus as he checked the entry door behind him.

"Business that's none of your business. Are you following me?" I went on the offense.

He scoffed. "You're not that important, Silver. But I believe you're the one following me."

"And what makes you think you're important enough?" I spat back. It wouldn't be long before the photographs James took at the auction surfaced, and it wouldn't be long before the trial started. If the scorned congressman went down, he'd take everyone along with him.

Hartley stepped forward, and his rotten breath assaulted my face. I held back a gag.

"You know what, I don't give a fuck what you're doing around here. You'll soon get exactly what you deserve. I'm completing my trade, and there's not a fucking thing you can do about it, Silver."

I grabbed his shirt, but he pushed my arms off him.

"What fucking trade?"

"Stop acting like you know nothing. You don't think I know you're on my ass? Tonight's just for show—to show my friends how behind the times you've fallen. Your girl doesn't attend auctions like these. From now on, she's mine. Kendra will get private meetings with her clients on my island, and that's where she'll fucking remain."

I swung with my left, surprising Hartley. He retaliated with a set of brass to my lip. It split at the scar. An iron tang filled my mouth as I fell backward. The contents of my pocket slipped out and crashed to the ground. My phone cracked in the corner. I stood up, intending to get him right back, but I refrained and wiped my mouth instead. He wasn't worth it. Obviously, Kendra wasn't here. The fucker gloated like a predator, and I couldn't wait to serve him.

"It won't be long before you go down, Hartley. You're going to regret it all when your sons can't give you grandchildren from behind bars and your mama loses that house you bought her with the laundered money. Your whole fucking family's going to pay."

He straightened his shirt. Hartley's face darkened to beet red as he sneered. "I already paid when my daughter got in that car with you. That ride down the hill was never meant for Simone, Silver. It was meant for you."

I grabbed my key chain and secured the car key between my fingers. The undercut came out on instinct.

"This is for Simone." I jammed my fist underneath his ribcage. The key broke through his white shirt between his ribs. He bent in half and yelped out in pain.

Two bodyguards stepped off the elevator, and I backed away.

"I won't forget this," Hartley groaned.

I disappeared before the bodyguards caught up. I ran around the hotel to an emergency side entrance, and I snuck through the rarely used door. I hurried upstairs before anyone could follow me. The auction would end within minutes, and I had to get Allie out of there.

I rushed back to the room, where James was sitting on the

floor beside an unconscious Allie while Julian held a compress to her head.

"What happened?"

"Fucking Wright was there, but she held up till the end. Donaldson must have invited him as a last-minute guest. I have no fucking clue, but did you see the girl he got?"

"The pregnant one? Yeah, we'll get on that."

"Is she okay?" I checked Allie's pulse.

"She's in shock. We need to get Donaldson out in the open. It's been too long. It's time." James grabbed a pair of socks and pulled them over Allie's feet.

"As soon as Kendra's back," my brother reminded him. "If they catch on who she really is, we'll never get her back."

I fanned my hand over Allie's face like it was some sort of magic wand. "Allie?"

She lay motionless and as vulnerable as I'd seen her. "Allie?" I tried again.

Her eyes opened wide, and she shot up, screaming. "No! No!"

My heart split in half. I grabbed her by her arms and held her steady. "Allie, it's all right. You're safe."

Over the next half hour, Allie lamented in my arms. She grieved for the girls we'd left behind and questioned Wright's presence along with the disgusting purchase. That man was the key to every fucked up mistake I couldn't repair at that moment. All I could do was promise her justice. It would come —because it had to. Although the damage his presence had done was significant, I'd repair it and make sure she'd never see the bastard again.

Allie collapsed in my arms soon after the shower. I wanted to take her home, but her tremors wouldn't stop. I lay down with her in bed, spooned her, and covered her with a blanket. My cousin and brother had left for their rooms. They'd wait there until it was safe to leave unnoticed in the morning. Allie woke several times before her body finally gave in to deeper sleep.

Exhausted, I picked up my phone around midnight. The screen had cracked, but it still worked, and I dialed Julian's number.

"I'm sorry we didn't get Kendra."

"I haven't given up on her in years, and I'm not about to start right now. They duped us. She wasn't meant to be here, but I'm not giving up. I'm going on the offense with this one, and I'm taking the plane to Jeff's island first thing in the morning."

The phone crackled in the background. My brother was in love with the troublemaker. He'd resisted her charm until all the passion she'd held for him since they met spilled over the rim and burned.

"You can't go alone. Surveillance shows radar and—"

"I know what surveillance shows. Gabe just landed. I've hunted and studied every piece of intel we have. I have a way in."

"This isn't only your fight. I'm going with you."

"I'm not going alone. Gabe's going with me and he wants dibs on Martinez, so you're staying here and taking care of the woman who risked her life tonight. No arguments. I'll call for backup if I need it."

I glanced over to where Allie was lying curled in a fetal position on the bed, her cheek squeezed into the flat pillow and her crooked duck lips shaped into a heart.

"She'll have questions when she wakes up, and you owe her some answers."

"Fucking Wright. I'm taking her home first thing in the morning. Let me know when you land. I'm gonna make sure we hunt down every single fucker from that auction. Wright won't see what's coming, and neither will Hartley."

"If we get the Hartleys, then we get them all."

I'd fantasized about the day it would be all over for years. I'd pictured his bloodied, lifeless face in that casket since the day the bastard hadn't let me inside Simone's hospital room. She'd lived a few days after the accident, but Hartley never gave me the chance to say goodbye.

"I swept the hotel before I left. The assholes scattered quicker than roaches." Julian's voice broke through the receiver.

"I think I busted my phone. Fly safe, Julian."

"Thanks."

The phone shut down before I hung up. I checked on Allie, covered her shoulder with a spare blanket, and dimmed the table lamp. She snuggled into the pillow, gripping the casing in her fists. I stretched my arms over my head. My muscles pulsed with pain and fatigue. I was just bending down to remove my shoes when a shadow passed by the hotel room door. Someone stopped on the other side and waited for what felt like forever. I held my breath and heard my heart beating in my eardrums. It was the only sound I heard before the shadows moved. I bolted for the door, ran out of the room, and followed the tall figure until the split in the hallway, where the woman disappeared inside one of the dozen doors. Before I could turn around, a sharp poke stabbed me in the back of my neck. I lifted my hand to the area and felt a dart poking out of my skin.

My vision blurred, and the hall faded in and out of focus. I turned around in slow motion, stumbling until I fell to my knees. A tall figure approached, but I couldn't make out the shadowed face, and I lost consciousness.

My common sense crawled into the dark corner where I'd hid all my life. I'd run all my life too, and look where that got me. I slung back my shot of tequila. The nerves eased as the liquor flew through my body like a bullet filled with adrenaline and confidence.

"Excuse me. I have unfinished business to take care of."

I left the man at the bar and strolled to the back booth. My cell phone burned in my jeans back pocket, but as much as I wanted to call Tristan, I couldn't. One wrong move and this chance would disappear. I pushed my shoulder blades together, lifting my boobs, and stopped by the secluded booth near the washroom entrance. Martinez was holding Kendra's leash. She trembled in her seat but made no eye contact. This was my chance.

"Do you have room for one more?" I asked.

He leaned sideways and looked past me to the bar before nodding to the seat across from him, beside Kendra. Behind us, a row of fake plants obstructed the street view. The secluded area provided concealment from the hotel lobby. Kendra lifted her head, and I clenched my fists under the table. I had refused to hope it could be her when I was at the bar, but now that I saw her up close, I knew it was. The night was not a waste after all.

Not if I could help it.

Her eyes were filled with emptiness, and red, like someone had drugged her. They probably had. The glimmer of hope I'd seen on her face in the photos Tristan had showed me was gone. In fact, in none of the photos had she looked so miserable. Kendra must have lost half her weight in the past few weeks. She lifted her hands onto the table. They'd tied her wrists with rope, which was fastened to the table's leg.

"Who's this?" I nodded her way.

"A bitch." He poured the tequila into the shot glasses.

"Why the ropes?"

"So she obeys. She's trouble. Drink." It wasn't a request.

I threw back the tequila like water. Judging by the way Martinez gripped the bottle, cutting shots wouldn't be easy.

"So you're like a zookeeper. She's your panther and I'm the puma." I growled.

"Sure. Something like that. I can find a cage for you as well."

Fucker.

"Would she come along?" I forced him a flirty, lustful look, like I really fucking liked him, while controlling the bubbling hate in my chest.

"No. She's waiting for her new owner." He checked his watch, frowned, and poured another round of shots. "We can leave once she's gone."

Martinez already sold her? Tristan's intelligence needed an update. Tonight could be the only chance I had to help Kendra. I couldn't really pull my phone out in front of Martinez right now, but as soon as the chance presented, I would text Tristan.

"Where would we go?"

"I already told you. To your cage, my puma."

He reached for my hand. His calloused fingers skimmed over my palm, and I pulled away on instinct. That forced me to cover up the mistake, and my hand went straight for the tequila shot. Except I knew I couldn't take it. I was at that tipping point, and I needed my wits.

"I don't enjoy drinking alone." I nodded to his glass. He grasped it between his fingers, and we lifted the shot to our lips. I used the moment he tilted his head back to empty the shot into the plant on the window behind me. Kendra sat motionless, with her head lowered.

I swept my hand across my mouth and set the glass down.

Martinez wasted no time pouring another one. The bastard intended to intoxicate me. The next three also ended up in the plant. I swayed from side to side and giggled like a happy drunk, fluttering my lashes, leaning forward, and earning the trust I needed for our break. He ate it all up. My plan was working… until I saw him slip a powdery substance into my glass.

Kendra's head flew up. She opened her eyes wide with a warning. But she didn't have to alert me. Martinez left his glass empty and watched me.

"What about you?" I pouted.

"I've had enough. This should be your last one too."

Fuck.

"Bathroom." Kendra's tiny voice barely made it across the table.

"Hold it. We're almost done."

"I can take your panther on a walk to the washroom. Unless you're afraid she'll bite?" I bit my lip and pushed my breasts forward. Martinez liked that.

"If she escapes, you're her replacement."

Wasn't the fucker planning to take me, anyway? Fucking prick.

"Grrr." I made a cat-like gesture of scratching the air with my nails.

He gripped my wrist before I stood up. "Drink first."

My poisoned tequila shot waited on the table, and Kendra's eyes bulged again.

Martinez let go of my hand with more caution than before. I picked up the glass and knew I couldn't get away with this one, so I looked at Kendra, saying, "Let's go pee-pee," and downed the shot.

He handed me Kendra's rope. "You have three minutes."

Once the bathroom door shut, I jumped into the first stall and shoved two fingers down my throat. The gag reflex was instant. My stomach pushed up the tequila along with every-thing in its acids. It tightened three times, emptying. I stood up, and the room spun. Whatever Martinez had given me was already in my bloodstream.

Kendra covered her mouth and heaved air in through her fingers. "Run. You should run while you can."

She shook like jello, and I shuffled my feet to the sink, grip-ping its sides. The room spun. I rinsed my mouth and braced myself on the porcelain. I took a deep breath and pressed my index to my lips. "Shh."

I removed my cell and typed: LOBBY BAR BATHROOM K MARTINEZ HURRY

I hit the send button and prayed Tristan's phone was on.

"Who are you?" Kendra asked.

"I'm Tristan's friend, and I'm not leaving without you. What did he slip me?" I worked my fingers on Kendra's rope, fighting the haze in my eyes.

"A tranquilizer. It was a lot. He'll kill us both for this."

I ignored the panic in her voice and focused on using the little time we had to our advantage. "If that's the case, we need to get rid of him. It's two against one. You seem strong enough,

Kendra. Please tell me you want out of this. I need you on my side. Are you with me?" I couldn't believe how much I craved my gun at this very moment.

The first rope strap unwound, but there was another one digging into her flesh. They'd glued together the last knot. My fingertips ached and my nails broke, but the rope finally gave way. Red strands of burned skin circled her wrists.

"I'm with you." She whispered.

The room faded in and out of focus.

I searched for another exit and focused on the small window in the last stall. If Tristan didn't pick up the message, we'd have to move. I hurried to the end of the room, stepped up onto the toilet, unlocked the latch, and lifted the window. Cold night air filled the bathroom.

"Do you know who he's waiting for? Who's your buyer?"

"Hartley… but I don't know which one."

Martinez knocked on the door. "Hurry."

"Almost done," I said in a half-drunk voice and checked my phone. No reply.

"Is he alone?" I asked.

"I don't think so. And they're always armed."

"I figured." I pulled out my phone and shoved it down her cleavage, right into her bra. "Julian and Tristan's numbers are there. They're in this hotel. Run and find them."

"What about you?" she asked.

"I'll be right behind you."

Martinez knocked again, this time harder, but I didn't answer. We had seconds left.

"Hop up." I locked my hands for a boost. She placed her foot in the scoop, and I helped her up to the window ledge. Jesus, was she ever light! She looked back down at me.

"Go! Jump. Now!"

I grabbed the ledge and pulled myself up as well, just as

Martinez pushed the bathroom door open. He rammed through with the guy I'd seen at the bar.

"Do not turn back," I called to her. She turned in a circle in the alley like she was getting her bearings.

The click of a gun sounded in my ears. I slid off the ledge in slow motion, but when I turned around, Martinez was no longer there. Instead, the guy from the bar pointed the gun into my neck.

"Pussy." I breathed. "Using guns to kidnap women. You're one of the biggest pussies I've seen in my life."

He lowered the gun and secured it in a holster behind him.

"Turn around, pretty face, and see what I do to girls like you."

I stood up despite the drugs that had already reached my bloodstream. The room fell in and out of focus.

"I'm not a girl, you fucker. I'm a woman."

"Working for Silver?" he asked. "Tristan Silver? Keep going and you'll end up like my daughter. Dead."

Hartley removed a switchblade from his pocket and didn't wait to attack. I moved out of his way without making contact. On his next approach, I lowered myself to the floor for the same roundhouse kick and knocked him off his feet. He grabbed my foot and pulled me down. I crashed to the floor. He slid the knife across my calf, cutting through my skin. I kicked his chin with my other foot, and the solid contact broke his jaw with a crunch. Brass knuckles slipped out of his pocket.

"You bitch. You just made the biggest mistake of your life." He aimed the switchblade at my chest, but I caught it between my hands and maneuvered the blade out of his grip. It slid across the bathroom floor. Hartley grabbed my foot and tried to twist it, but I kicked him in his face. He yelped in pain and curled into a fetal position. I stumbled to the bathroom door again, but stopped when I heard him next. "I'm going to find you, and you're going to pay."

Bloody, I turned on my heel and took three long steps towards him. I straddled him and started punching. One, two, three, four… a sharp stab slipped between my ribs. Hartley had struck me with another blade. I twisted his wrist and caught the knife he released. When he tried to grab it again, it slipped between us. The pressure of our joined hands reaching for it was enough to punch through.

He coughed. I pushed off his body, and the knife remained firmly in his gut.

"H… help me." He coughed blood from his mouth.

"Fuck you. You deserve much worse than this." I limped out the door to find Kendra and didn't look back.

My muscles gave way and my balance was off as I stumbled through the side door. The bartender was nowhere to be seen when I quietly left out the street door, all bloody and probably looking like I'd come off a set for *Carrie*. A pinch in my shoulder ached like a day-old bruise, and I lifted my fingers to the trickling blood. I hadn't even realized he'd jabbed me there.

Shit! Tristan, where are you?

I hurried down the street toward the end of the building, then checked each alley afterwards, but my knees buckled every few steps. The powdered substance I'd swallowed earlier cruised through my veins, and I slipped in and out of consciousness. The iron tang of blood filled my mouth. A faint memory of biting Hartley flashed in my mind: a finger, or perhaps a piece of flesh, off his forearm. My jaw definitely ached. If luck were on my side, he'd be dead.

The world blurred, but at some point I found the alley and froze: Kendra was kneeling on the pavement as Martinez pointed the gun at her head.

Blood trickled down my arm and fingers.

I'm so fucked.

And so I did the only thing I could. I screamed at the top of my lungs, grabbing the asshole's attention. He turned around in slow motion, aiming his gun my way. At least he wasn't aiming at Kendra. The gun went off.

One.

Two.

My tummy felt warm, my knees buckled, and the world went black.

Chapter 21

Tristan

My head throbbed with a pain unlike any I'd felt before. I lifted my hand to the back of my neck where the ache originated. The pea-sized bump underneath my fingertips pulsed and bled. The pressure between my eyes placed the room out of focus and brought up a memory of a woman walking away. I pushed myself off the stained hotel hall carpet, but I wasn't strong enough to stand. I dragged my lifeless limbs toward what I thought was my room. The more I moved, the quicker the contours came into shape and the more I remembered. The woman had been wearing Louboutin heels.

Who the fuck was she?

I grabbed at the flat wall, my palms pushing against the surface, and finally managed to get to my feet. My knees wobbled, but my legs held. I inched sideways along the wall to my closed hotel room. I slid the card across from the reader, and it opened.

"Allie?" I called out, but she wasn't in her bed.

Shit.

I checked the closet and the bathroom, but she wasn't there either. The worst of the worst flashed through my mind. Squeaking wheels; an ear-piercing scream I'd never forget; the rows of mourners wearing black. I shook off the memories, picked up my dead phone, and threw it against the wall. I hurried to the bathroom, opened the faucet, and waited until the stained water drained, then lowered my mouth to the flow.

I grabbed my gun from underneath the mattress and stumbled back to the hallway. The occupant next door walked out of his room, and I froze.

Wright stared at me open-mouthed; he had no clue the raging man in front of him was about to lose it. I removed the gun from the holster secured behind me and pointed it at his chest.

"Whoa, whoa! What are you doing?"

"Where is she?" I grunted.

"I don't know who you're talking about. I let the pregnant girl go."

"Where. Is. She?"

"I swear, I let her go. She's gone. You can put that gun away and check my room."

I stepped closer.

"Or keep the gun. Whatever. Go check."

"Lead the way and don't fucking try anything." I followed him inside the room and inspected every corner.

"What did you do with the girl?"

"I told you. I let her go."

"I don't believe the crap you're saying." I pointed the gun in his face.

"Listen, I… I know important people. You want that girl and the others, right? I'll testify in court against the Hartleys. I'll do anything you want."

Except Wright's priorities shifted with the wind. He held the power to put away some of the most influential and vile men in this country. While his testimony would clear Kendra's name, it would also put the Hartleys and the congressman behind bars.

"I'm not letting you out of my sight until you testify, you fuck. You're coming with me."

I twisted his arm behind his back, jutting the gun barrel in his spine.

"Let me go. I'll testify. I promise."

I ignored the lie floating on his maleficent tone. I'd wasted enough time with Wright and not looking for Allie. We couldn't wait another month to file the case, either, and I'd instruct Ace Wagner to proceed against Hartley in the morning.

"You blink the wrong way and I'll shoot. Do you understand?"

We took the staircase down to the lobby. He trembled like a coward. I concealed the gun between us as we walked past the half-sleeping concierge. We crossed the empty lobby to where low music carried from the bar. The barman wasn't in any better shape than the guy at the front desk.

I tapped the counter. "I'm looking for a girl with auburn hair, five four, brown eyes."

"Bathroom." He pointed. "But I don't think she's there anymore. Or she's been there a while."

I motioned for Wright to lead and followed him across the bar. I knocked hard on the women's bathroom door. "Anyone there?"

When no one replied, I pushed the door open. "I'm coming in."

The room stank of alcohol and antiseptic flush, but I hadn't expected a dead body in the middle of the floor.

"Holy fuck." Wright shimmied into a corner. "That's Hartley."

"Stay there," I warned, and stepped over the pool of blood. A blade was stuck in the middle of Hartley's gut, and blood trailed from his mouth.

"What the fuck happened here?"

He blinked, and I jumped up.

"Sss... Simone will fix things." He spat and choked on the pooling blood in his mouth.

"Where's Allie?" I screamed.

But he was already gone.

My heart raced and my ears buzzed. I scratched at my temple. The room was a bloody mess, with hand and footprints all over. Evidence of struggle was smeared across the mirror wall. Small hands and lots of blood, but Allie wasn't there. Had she been here? Was she injured?

I whipped my body around at Wright.

"What the hell was Hartley doing here?"

"I never met him. I just know Donaldson. That's all. I swear."

It didn't matter whether he was lying. Only Allie mattered.

I stepped up on the toilet near the window just as a double gunshot boomed from an alley further down the street. Wright remained in his corner, but there wasn't an ounce of me believing he'd stay there. I climbed through the broken window, jumped off onto the pavement, and followed a bloody trail to a second alley where I found them.

My cousin was standing there with his feet parted, pointing his gun into the darkness. I ran to his aid, but Gabe wasn't the one who needed help. Kendra came into view. My brother, Julian knelt at her side. Kendra lay curled into a ball by the garbage container. Her cheeks were sunken, and her hair stuck out of a sloppy bun.

Martinez lay dead on the ground. A dozen feet to his left, Allie was down near the wall. I ran to her side and checked her pulse. It weakened with every second. I inspected her body and found the bleeding wound in her abdomen. I lifted her side and examined her back. There was an exit wound near the kidney.

"Shit!"

"I didn't do this. He shot her." Kendra pointed to Martinez.

"I know, K. Come on, Gabe. Get a grip. Call an ambulance," I yelled out and ripped a sleeve off my shirt. I stuffed that in the back and ripped off my other sleeve for the front.

Gabe stood frozen with the gun resting at the side of his thigh, finally moved. He must have shot Martinez.

"Ambulance Gabe! Ambulance."

He jolted awake and removed the phone from his pocket.

"I was late." Julian looked up. "If it weren't for Gabe…"

"You're not late, Julian. Get a grip and help me."

My brother lifted Kendra's frail body into his arms, carried her to Allie's side, and set her close to us.

"Hold here." I took his hand and pressed it underneath Allie's ribs. "Don't let go."

I reached for the phone in his back pocket, hit the group emergency code, when Hunter pulled up to the curb. We brought her onto the sidewalk. James showed moments later. We patched up Allie and stopped the bleeding, but her pulse dropped so fast, I knew we couldn't wait for the ambulance. The boys helped us set Allie in the back seat. Julian's hand pressed over the wound. At one point, Allie cried out in pain.

"Shh, we're getting you to the hospital now."

She blinked three times, passed out again, and I refocused on the task.

"Let's go!"

Gabe set Kendra in the middle seat. He secured her and took over my hold on Allie. I crossed the middle compartment and slid into the driver's seat.

"Call Scar," I said to James. "He has a friend at the hospital, Julia Blakely. She'll be discreet."

I gripped the wheel, and for the first time in years felt the engine's strength like we were one.

Hold on.

The GPS pinged the hospital at fifteen minutes away. It'd be eleven if I broke every speed limit and ran every red light.

"You get the word out there to clear the way. We have a former cop fighting for her life."

I didn't want to be stopped, and I'd continue until I got her through that emergency door. It was the middle of the night and there was practically no traffic. I swerved on every turn, enough to keep the speed and not tip over. The wheels screeched. I fought to stay in the present, for Allie, for me and for the others. We'd gone through too much to lose another one of our own.

"She's losing blood again, Tristan!"

I startled on the highway, shook off the thoughts, and concentrated on the road. I pressed my foot harder on the gas. My back sank into the seat. This time, I heard nothing else except the engine's intimidating roar. Night lights passed, and it felt like moments later I pulled up to the hospital. Hunter was bent over Allie's chest, performing compressions. I could barely take the look in his eyes.

"How long?" I asked.

"Two minutes."

James waited at the door with two doctors. I lifted Allie's lifeless body out of the car and from then on, a team of nurses swarmed over her like ants.

"Code blue!" someone screamed and jumped off her body. They rolled a defibrillator out just past the entrance. Her pulse resumed, but the dripping blood along the floor left a grim promise.

I followed them inside until a nurse stopped me at the staff only entrance. It was hours before I let Emma take my bloody hands and guide me to the washroom. She washed them with my mom's help, and then we waited and waited.

A memory of walking hospital halls flashed through my mind. A doctor stood at the end of the hall, talking to Hartley. They argued, and though Hartley saw me, he wouldn't let me visit Simone. They didn't even allow me to say goodbye.

I must have dozed off because Emma's voice woke me sometimes after six in the morning. "Are they done yet?"

"Not yet, Ems," my father replied.

My little sister went to chat at the nurses' station, where she'd get another popsicle. I stood up and walked over to Laura. She had been pacing by the vending machine since arriving.

"Eighty-eight percent of gunshot victims without vascular injuries make it out." Laura chewed on her thumb.

"She's strong. She'll make it," I told her.

"Of course she'll make it and if she doesn't, I will hang you by your balls." Laura pointed her finger in my face. Statistic

"If she doesn't, I'll do the job myself, but she will. She has to."

"How did she slip out of your room?"

I pulled my hand through my hair. "I really don't need this right now, Laura. I know I fucked up."

"Big time."

"Well, I'm not the only one who fucks up, am I? How's my nephew?"

Her eyes grew wide, and I lowered my voice. "You should tell James."

"He'll find out when he needs to find out. I'm getting there. Today is obviously not the best time."

No, it wasn't.

She peeked over the frosted window, waiting for the doctor the same way everyone else in the room had. It had been four hours since they took her in to surgery. Emma hung out by the nurses' station. My mother was sitting with Peg, and my father was talked with Hunter and Ace Wagner in the corner.

Julian was elsewhere in the hospital with Kendra. The doctors had sedated her, but she had a long road to recovery.

Laura resumed her pacing. "What the fuck went wrong with that operation?"

"Everything."

"You boys can't keep up, and truthfully, you're getting old."

"I'm not even forty."

"You will be soon, and before you know it, you'll be chasing twenty-five-year-olds who don't come out of their mamma's basements because they're hacking every hour of the day. Now hire someone like that, and you've got yourselves an operation."

"Are you offering services?"

"Wait, what?"

"To work for Silver Securities. From what I've seen, you're good at your job."

"I said, hire computer geeks."

"Allie will need a trusted partner in our new sex-trafficking division."

"Wait, you're serious? I thought you were joking."

"Think about it, but you should know, James is the one who started the operation, so he'd be your boss."

"Oh, okay. I…I'll think about it."

"Don't take too long. It would be good for the both of you."

"Me and Allie?"

"No, you and James."

The staff-only door slid open, and my head whipped to the surgery entrance and two poker-faced doctors.

The sound of a pulse monitor beeped in my ears. The steady rhythm bounced from one end of the room to another: left to right, left to right. My nose tingled from the smell of antiseptic hand wash and flowers. I tried to move, but my head ached, so instead I reached up, stopping half way as something restrained my arm.

"Don't move."

Tristan's soothing voice came from my right, and I opened my eyes. His beautiful face slowly came into focus against a backdrop of bright warmth. Dark shadows underlined his smoky eyes, and a shade of worry was creased across his forehead. The scar on his upper lip lifted, bringing my attention to his mouth.

"What happened?" I didn't recognize my hoarse voice. "Where am I?"

I remembered Kendra on her knees, and Martinez pointing the gun at her head…

Tristan turned my way.

My hands flew underneath the sheets covering my body and to the bandage wrapped around my waist.

"He shot me!"

"Martinez is dead, and they found Hartley in the bathroom. I assume that was your blood on him."

Hartley is dead.

"I didn't make it out the window in time. He had a switchblade. We struggled, but I don't remember much after that."

"Maybe that's for the best." Tristan sat on the bed near my mid-section and took my hand into his. My mouth felt as if it had been stuffed with a hundred cotton balls. He passed me a cup with water like he sensed my thirst.

"Who shot Martinez?"

"Gabriel Silver. My cousin flew in from Austria. He's been waiting for the chance for years."

"I thought you guys needed Martinez for the case."

"His value declined when Hartley died."

"The Hartleys will come after me. His sons and brothers—"

"Don't worry. Your name is staying out of all this. I promise. But you had me worried for a while, Allie. You had us all worried."

The smooth end of a paper straw touched my lips. I sucked the water in, relieving my thirst.

"You're in the hospital. It's been five days." Tristan shifted on the bed.

I let go of the straw. "And Kendra?"

Please tell me she's safe.

"She's in the room next door. She has a long recovery ahead. Drink more."

The world suddenly felt brighter and warmer, and all that strength now absent from my body was worth the cost. I took a few more sips and relaxed into the mattress. Tristan set the cup aside.

"That makes me happy." The headache faded, but my eyelids felt heavy, and I could barely keep my eyes open.

"You're on morphine, but the doctors said you'll have a full recovery. The bullet flew right through you and missed all your organs. You were very lucky, Allie."

My stomach rumbled a little. Why was Tristan wearing a purple wig?

"You look funny. Did Emma color your hair?"

He tilted his head and took my hand in his again. It felt nice and warm. "No," he chuckled. "You've lived through what most don't survive, and you're medicated. It can all make you confused. Maybe you'd better sleep."

"Wilma saved us?"

Why was he chuckling so hard?

"No, you and Julian are the heroes. Gabe heard about the auction and flew in last minute. Thank God he did. He followed your blood trail from the lobby. It was half an hour before I woke up and got your text. I did nothing, Allie. This was all you."

Why was he so sad?

I shifted my head on the pillow. It was too comfortable and effective. "It's not your fault."

"What?"

"You're guilt-tripping yourself. I should have never left the room. That was my first mistake. I didn't recognize Hartley at the bar. Not until he stepped into that bathroom. He said something... something about you I can't remember. Crap." I snapped my fingers a few times as if that would bring the memory back.

"Don't worry about it, Allie. I'm just happy to see you safe. Both you and Kendra."

"When can I see Kendra?" The weight of my eyelids forced my eyes closed.

Someone knocked on the door, and my eyes flew open again. Emma's small head popped in.

"She awake yet?"

"For now." Tristan squeezed my hand into his warm palm,

and I wanted him to hold it like that forever. "Are you up for a few visitors?"

"Yes, please," I lied. But I couldn't say no to my favorite person in the world.

Emma rushed to my bedside before Tristan agreed. She carefully put both arms around me before setting the pink and blue daises on a table. Now that I had a good look around the room, I couldn't believe the copious amount of flowers.

"I'll let the rest of the clan know." Tristan crossed the room toward the window, pulled out his phone, and texted.

Emma took a deep breath, bringing my attention back to her. "We've been here every day, but Tristan kept shooing me away. I read in a book that you should talk to people who are unconscious to make them feel like they're still with us. He said you weren't unconscious—just sleeping—and I was saying too much nonsense that would make you confused, but I saw your eyes move and I knew you were listening."

I found Emma's presence comforting, as always. I closed my eyes, searching for the familiar sound of her voice as I slept.

I heard Tristan say he loves you.

My eyes flew open.

"You remember, don't you?" Her eyes bulged like two grapefruits, and her cheeks sprang upward.

"I was dreaming," I said hesitantly.

She leaned in closer. "Everything I said was true. Believe me." Her excitement was over the moon.

"What?"

She lowered to my ear and whispered, "I can't wait for you to live next door and finally be my aunt."

"No, no. I think you got that wrong."

She opened her mouth, but just then my mom and Mrs. Silver rushed into the room, pulled out chairs and sat beside Emma, who shut her mouth and pulled her fingers across her lips like she was fastening a zipper.

. . .

* * *

THAT EVENING, after everyone left, the doctor's news hit me like a brick wall.

"The baby is fine," Dr. Jaipers reassured me for the third time.

That's right. Tristan Silver had knocked me up.

"The bullet missed all the vital organs. I'm more concerned about your stress levels. From what I gather, you don't exactly work in Neverland."

"Does anyone else know? It's quite difficult keeping things from my family."

Had I just called Tristan family? Well, he would be in about nine months.

"Not yet. I've been waiting to tell you first, but these are the Silvers, so—"

"Yeah, I get it. Thank you. I'd like to keep this information private for now. But how is this possible? I have an IUD."

"You *had* an IUD. It must have gotten dislodged a few months back. It's possible you wouldn't even have noticed it while bleeding. We checked the ultrasound, and the device is no longer there."

Wonderful.

"Oh, my God!"

"What's the matter?"

"I think I killed my baby." I grabbed my stomach.

"Your baby is doing great, Ms. Green. You just need some rest and solid TLC. Please let me know if you need anything else."

"No, I mean, I think I may have harmed him... or her... a lot. I was drinking, and I had drugs slipped—"

"Ms. Green. The best thing you can do for you and your baby is to rest. A lot. And don't stress. Mr. Silver tells me you work for the company?" His brows lifted.

I guessed I did, so I nodded. At least, I was pretty sure I remembered doing so.

"It would be wise to remain off your feet for a few weeks, so I highly recommend a desk job."

"So the baby will be okay?"

"The blood work is strong, but it's too early to know everything. We'll be monitoring you closely. Don't stress. It's not good for either of the parents." He checked the chart and lifted his gaze to mine. "Is the dad in the picture?"

Oh, my God! Tristan! How would he react?

"Yes, he is." At least, I thought he would be. "But I need time to tell him. Can you please make sure my medical records are kept private? My family likes to be nosy." That was the understatement of the year. I'd be lucky if Tristan hadn't gone over my files already. I was certain I'd heard Wilma mention she was a nurse at some point.

My head throbbed, and I felt my blood pressure spike. The machine I was hooked to began beeped alarmingly.

"What's happening?"

"You need to relax, Ms. Green. If you want your baby to be well, learn how to control your breathing. Take a deep breath in. Hold it. Exhale. Good."

As I followed his motions, the monitors calmed, and the beeping sounds stabilized.

"Push the button if you need anything," he said before leaving.

"Thank you, Doctor."

Dr. Jaipers closed the door, and Emma's words from my dreams vibrated in my ears.

I can't wait for you to live next door and finally be my aunt.

Did Emma know? And if she knew, had she told Tristan?

Why hadn't he said anything? There was only one way to find out. I picked up the phone and called the best detective in town.

* * *

Emma peeked inside my room and I waved her in. She pulled a chair to my bedside and waited with her mouth shut tight.

"Hi," I said.

"How are you?" She beamed and resumed her unusually patient position.

"Anyone with you?" I asked.

"No. I came alone. I forged a note and cut school. If anyone finds out I'm gone, it won't be until this afternoon. And my parents will call my cell first. I have a back-up plan if they do."

Of course she did.

"Your brother is going to kill me when he finds out

"Something tells me you'll be the one calling the shots soon enough." She winked. "But he won't find out. I'm that good. I promise."

"All right. You're going to make a great PI one day."

"I know. Just have to make sure Tristan and Julian know as well. Why do you think I'm babysitting Laila? My cousin James is my backup option. So?" She grinned and tilted her head. "You called?"

Right. I did.

"How is Tristan? You know, when he's not here. Has he said anything to you about me?"

"Nothing. He's dealing with Kendra's case and new work stuff. He's reorganized departments and has been pulling fourteen-hour days. Then he visits you, and then he sleeps in his office, where he wakes up and does it all over again."

"How do you know he sleeps in his office?" I asked. And what in the world was going on? I was being released in three days and hoped Tristan would let me in on his work plans. *Our* work plans. I guessed now that I was pregnant, I had limited time to get going at Silver.

"I heard Mom saying he's stressed. Were you expecting him to say something to me?" Emma's knees bopped up and down. She bit her lip and drummed her fingers in silence over her leg.

"I think I remember you saying something when I was unconscious."

"Yes?" Emma beamed from ear to ear.

I took a deep breath in. "And I want to know whether you really said it, or whether it was my imagination—"

"It wasn't your imagination." She cut me off in a whisper. "I said it."

"So you really know?"

She looked over her shoulder to make sure the door was closed and leaned in. "You mean that you're pregnant?"

I gave her the eye with a little smile, and she squealed.

My eyes flew open. "Yes. Have you told Tristan?"

"He doesn't know, and this is the biggest secret I've had to keep in, like, forever. Well, almost the biggest. I have two pretty big secrets now. I thought you'd have told everyone by now, but you haven't, and Mom's been asking why I'm so quiet and whether I have boy troubles." She took a breath and rolled her eyes. "But honestly, who cares about boys when I'm going to be an aunt. Oh, my God, I'm so happy!" She rammed into me with her full weight. My ribcage ached.

"Ouch."

She eased her grip. "Sorry. Did I hurt you? Did I hurt the baby?"

"No, it's okay, but Emma—"

"I can't wait to be an aunt, and when Tristan finds out—"

"He can't find out." I grabbed her wrist and brought her attention to my face. The moment he found out he'd place me on leave. "At least not yet. I need you to keep this secret from him a little longer."

"You're asking a lot."

"I know, but I want to find the right time to tell him myself."

"That will not be easy. I've been keeping way too many secrets lately. First it's Laura, then it's you."

"You know about Laura?"

She cocked her head to the side. "I'm Foxy's babysitter. It's not that difficult to figure out."

"Easy for you."

"Anyway, all the secret keeping gets so confusing sometimes, you know. Whom I should tell what story or truth? I don't know, tsk, tsk." She shook her head. "This new secret may be too much—"

"I'll let you name the baby."

Her mouth dropped open and her eyes doubled in size. "Are you serious?"

Did I just say what I said?

I did, but I had no choice. Tristan had the right to find out about the baby from me. I simply had to find the right time.

"Yes, I am. Within reason, of course."

"Of course."

"But you need to ensure Tristan doesn't check my medical records."

"That's impossible. You know he will. I'm surprised he hasn't already. He really has a lot on his mind."

"Emma, you're the best investigator in this family, and we both know it."

Her head flew up.

"If anyone can make sure the papers don't say what we both know they say, it's you." I squeezed her hand and looked at her as if we were sorority sisters ready for a battle. "I believe in you, Emma, and if you want me to be your aunt, I can't tell you how important it is for Tristan to find out the right way and at the right time."

"I don't think you're giving him enough credit."

"Baby name, Emma," I reminded her. "Baby name."

"Okay, okay. I'll do it. I'll keep all your secrets and pray they don't tangle up into one big mess up there."

She wiggled her fingers around her head, making me laugh. I absolutely adored her.

"How did you find out?" I asked.

"The doctor was talking to the nurse when your blood work came in. You lost a lot of blood. People don't really notice when younger people are around. And after she asked about the baby, I double-checked the papers when they weren't looking, and the rest is history. You're not far along. A couple of weeks, I think. They said they hardly caught it themselves."

"Did anyone else hear?"

"No, I'm sure I'm the only one."

"Good. Are you up to the challenge of falsifying some medical records? Because you know Tristan will read the discharge papers."

"Peanuts. It'll be done before the end of the day."

I didn't know how she'd do it, and honestly; I had no strength to ask. I yawned.

"Thank you, Emma. You know, I thought of you as my little sister the moment I met you. Whatever happens, I'll always think of you that way."

She lowered herself to the bed for a gentler embrace, and for the first time in my life I felt that sisterly bond I'd wished for my entire life. Well, I had it with Laura. I was a lucky woman to have them both in my life.

"I'm thinking Betty," she said, still holding me. "For the baby. Or Barney, if it's a boy."

What had I gotten myself into?

artley's predatory reign had ended on top of urine-stained tiles. His brothers promised revenge, except they didn't know against whom. While his sons kept a lower profile, Chris and Brad Hartley were determined to finish what their father started. They'd carry out Hartley's private sex-island fantasy as soon as legislation cleared. Silver Securities was up to its elbows in work, and I couldn't have picked a better time to expand.

I turned the corner and stopped at a red light. An ambulance roared in the distance. Two weeks had passed since Allie had saved Kendra. A memory of driving Allie to the hospital that night flashed through my mind. Blood stained her clothes and skin. She fell in and out of consciousness halfway to the hospital, then completely passed out. road stretched into one of the longest rides of my life, and as I pictured life without Allie, I begged God to save her. I begged God to give me one last chance, and He did. They told me I'd almost lost her and called me a hero. I might have secured the belt around her leg and ripped off a shirt sleeve to pack her wounds, but I wasn't a hero. I was the bastard who'd pawned my woman and left her in a room with sick assholes.

The woman had sacrificed herself, and I couldn't love her any harder than I did. For fuck's sake, I could barely wait to tell her how much I loved her and regretted not saying so before. I used the time she spent recovering to organize the office, and to close an unexpected deal that fell into my lap.

Zaruch was sipping on his coffee as I walked up to his street-side table at a local café.

"Ah, perfect timing." He set his mug aside. "I ordered you a cappuccino."

"Anything else, Mr. Silver?" the barista asked.

"A plain croissant."

"Yes, Mr. Silver." The barista went to get the order.

"So? Please tell me you have good news this morning."

"The Jacobs accepted the offer. Congratulations, Tristan."

My longtime agent extended his hand. I shook his firm grip, smiling. That was one for one.

"You're serious?"

"I wouldn't joke about something like this."

"Holy crap. That's wonderful. Thank you. I appreciate your help. And the family doesn't know?"

"I believe Emma might have. I tried my best."

My brows furrowed.

The barista set my cappuccino and croissant on the table.

"I saw her by the shore when we were talking."

"That girl has business everywhere."

"Give the kid a break. She's loyal, and she'll keep her mouth shut."

I sighed. My little sister was following too closely in our footsteps, and she'd taken to Grace Wagner like the hairstylist was her new best friend. She had good people around her, just the wrong influences.

"Fine. I appreciate your discretion."

Zaruch removed an envelope from within his briefcase. "This is a copy. An original is already at your office. I hope the new home is everything your family's hoped for. May I ask if you're putting the penthouse on the market?"

"Not yet. But you'll be the first to know. Thanks for making this happen. It means a lot."

He shook his head and rolled his eyes. "You really don't know, do you?"

"What?"

His face wrinkled into weary folds. "A little bird told me Ms. Emma Silver has been telling the Jacobs she's seen a white figure in the attic window at night. They found it amusing."

"Let me guess—the home is not haunted."

"Well, who am I to argue against beliefs? Because if you believe in ghosts, that's what Emma claims lives in your future attic."

"Warning noted. And please apologize to the Jacobs for any harm my sister may have done. I will send over a bottle of their favorite."

"Already done, and all is well."

People like Zaruch made my life easier by a power of ten. He finished his coffee while I enjoyed mine. The morning was starting out just the way I liked my mornings: sunny, predictable, and successful.

"I'll call you when I'm ready with the penthouse."

The apartment was empty without Allie, but she'd insisted on staying at her home with Laura. She might have needed comfort, stability, and safety, but she sure went about getting it the hard way. Kendra was recovering in Julian's care. The withdrawal had torn through her like a hurricane. My brother had a tough road ahead with the trial, but Silver Securities would fulfill the contract it had made five years ago. Kendra would make it to two trials she didn't know awaited.

Wright had slipped from the bathroom and surveillance team. No one had seen him or Marissa since the auction. The young girl was the only one still missing from the raid.

Zaruch set a few bills on the table and nodded to something behind me. "I think you have a stalker."

I looked back over my shoulder. About forty feet away to the north, a woman was standing behind a corner flower store. Her oversized hat shadowed her face. She let go of the sunflowers and scurried down the road and into a grocery store.

"Has the media heard about the case yet?" I asked.

"Not that I know of, but I'm usually last to find out things."

Right, but my family would know.

"See you at the housewarming." My agent waved his cap and left.

Was housewarming even a thing?

I set my new house keys in my pocket and went to the meat market in search of lamb. Tonight, I'd feed Allie until a food coma hit, leaving her no choice but to celebrate the night in my bed. She was meeting me at the headquarters in less than two hours. Fresh mango, dragon fruit, and berries would go perfect with the coffee-flavored ice cream and champagne when she heard my news. Greg had already ordered pastries and cake and sent out the invitations. I checked my watch. By tonight, everything would change. And if all went well, Allie would be squirming underneath me.

I stopped by the flower shop on my way out of the market and my phone buzzed with a notification. I frowned as I picked out white roses for Allie and chrysanthemums for Simone. After an extensive autopsy, the Hartley brothers had laid their father to rest this morning. The brothers returned to hiding right after, but justice would be knocking on their door next. While their operations tightened and all investigations froze, it wouldn't be long before Wright and Donaldson publicly exposed them all.

I parked at the end of the cemetery and waited a good half hour before stepping out of the car. The wind blew, and clouds came in from the west, darkening the skies. Orange and red leaves littered the ground. On the next gust, the foliage spun into bursting tornadoes. The distinct smell of candle wax and grief filled the air. I removed the cap from my head and took the back path to the gravesite, where I lowered the chrysanthemums by Simone's headstone.

"Hey, it's been a while," I said.

Her father lay buried four feet to the right, under a fresh mound of soil topped with colorful wreaths piled one over another. I wanted to believe she'd be happier with him at her side, but that would be a lie. Him being this close to the daughter he'd killed was just another stab in the same wound he'd opened years ago. If Simone's soul was smart, she'd stay far away from him in the afterlife.

I prayed Jeffrey Hartley's damned soul wouldn't come near Simone's peace and would remain in the hell where he belonged.

"I hope he doesn't give you trouble." I removed the candle from the inside of my jacket pocket, set it by the flowers, and lit it. "He certainly won't be missed here."

The sound of leaves crunching behind me resonated in slow motion. It felt like hours passed before I turned around and faced a ghost from my past.

Emma kept both her promise and our secret. It had been two weeks since the auction. The hospital had released me the day before, and despite Tristan's pleading to stay at the penthouse, I'd returned to my apartment for a few days of peace and quiet. And still hadn't told him about our baby. Thankfully, my pregnancy felt like any other day—sickless and full of energy. Some days I wondered whether it was true, but the twenty-eighth pregnancy test plus another set of blood work confirmed it. Tristan was clueless. He was busy, helping with the arrests, so we barely saw each other. But today was different. Today he'd called me to his office to talk about work. And today I would tell him about the little secret I was carrying in my belly.

"Do you think Tristan will be happy?"

"He better be. You're gonna rock as a mother. Look at me." Laura winked.

"Right. I take it things are going well with James?"

"We're at that stage where I'm keeping him off my boobs, and he loves this prudish side of mine I don't really have. He thinks it's sexy and unexpected, and all I'm trying to do is keep him away from my milky titties."

"You mean Foxy's milky titties," I corrected.

"Whatever." She waved. "If you think about it for too long, life gets complicated."

"What does that even mean?"

"I think I'm going to wean Foxy off the milk."

"Cream. Your doctor said you produce cream. Like a cow."

"My OB was old and had dementia."

"He wasn't wrong. Foxy's going to be tall, just like his daddy."

"Right."

"Laura?"

"Soon. I'll tell him soon. I promise. Because I'm not sure Emma can keep the secrets much longer."

"She'll keep them. She's not a snitch."

Laura passed me my purse. "Good luck. I'm thrilled for you, and I'm happy you're going to be a mama."

"Thank you. I love you." I wrapped my arms tightly around my best friend and squeezed hard.

"Don't make the same mistake I did," she whispered. "Look at the shithole I've gotten myself into. Tell Tristan he's going to be a daddy and that he's a very lucky man."

"Thank you, Laura. I will."

The doorbell rang, and we let go of each other.

When I'd woken up this morning, I'd somewhat expected Tristan to pick me up in his Bentley, but he didn't. Charlie, his driver, showed up in a limo instead. I thought the move was more formal than usual for my first official day at the office, but then again, this was Silver. The driver took a wrong turn at some point, twice, and we made it with only ten minutes to spare. I thanked Charlie for the ride and tilted my head back. The building wasn't as tall as I'd imagined, but still very majestic, with a metallic luster which resembled silver. No logos, and just as enigmatic as its owners. I couldn't believe I was here.

The glass door to Silver Securities slid open.

I took a deep breath in, stepped inside, and crossed the granite lobby floor. The steady click of my heels echoed through the silent room. I checked in at the front desk and then took the exclusive Silver elevator to the top floor. The sleek decor and cleanliness of the place reminded me of a hotel.

My heart was beating hard in my chest. I couldn't wait to see him and tell him about our baby. My first ultrasound was coming up, and I hoped he'd come with me.

He will be happy. Thrilled. I know it.

The elevator dinged, and the doors slid open. I stepped inside and pressed the button for the top floor. Nervous prickles scattered over the back of my neck. I shook my shoulders free of the jitters.

Tristan had been busy, distant, and distracted since Kendra's rescue. She was at a rehab facility with Julian, awaiting a trial. I didn't know what kind of trial because I hadn't had enough time with Tristan to catch up. Either way, I owed Kendra my life.

Our lives.

I lowered my hand to my belly. In less than nine months, Emma would have another client. She'd been busy with Foxy and Laila, not to mention preoccupied with Laura's secret, enough to leave mine alone. She'd changed my medical records, as promised, and as of the last count, I owed her naming my next two children after this one.

I stepped out on the sleek top floor and walked to the front desk.

The clerk smiled. "You must be Allie Green. It's nice to finally meet you. I'm Greg Invega."

"Hi, Greg. It's nice to meet you as well."

"The pleasure's all mine. Would you like some water?"

"No, thank you."

"I hear you prefer tequila."

"What?"

"Sorry. That was a joke. Bad joke. I'm very good at making inappropriate jokes." His voice quaked.

"Don't worry about it. I do like tequila, but I'm definitely not drinking." I chuckled nervously. "You know, working here and all. I want to give it my best."

I doubted he bought my nervous grin and the fake double thumbs up, but at least his shoulders relaxed.

"Understood. Don't be nervous. You'll love it here. We're one big, happy family. Most of the time."

I laughed.

"Mr. Silver is waiting for you in his office. Come on in, I'll show you where that is."

I walked through the secure door Greg opened and met him on the other side of the glass wall. White leather couches and tables set with giant bouquets created semi-private seating areas. Soft music played overhead. The space felt cozier than I'd imagined, yet it was empty.

"That's his office." Greg pointed to the oversized door. "Go right on in."

"Thank you."

I took a deep breath, hugged my purse under my arm, and aimed a confident walk towards the door. I'd planned to leave a small box with tiny white booties on Tristan's desk and let him figure it out. The speech I'd practiced repeatedly jumbled in my mind. I might not have felt ready to tell Tristan I was pregnant, but it had to be done—because I wasn't about to pull a Laura.

I am going to tell the baby's father we are expecting.

The purse with the booties felt heavier as I approached his office. I stood in front of the frosted glass door with a sleek black logo for what felt like forever before I knocked.

The door swung open.

"Come in."

Tristan sat in his full suit and tie behind a mahogany desk. The polished wood glistened in the sunlight. The remaining space felt eerily professional and very white. He pressed a button on his phone, pausing a conversation. "I'm finishing up. Make yourself comfortable." He pointed to the cream leather couch.

I paced across the office and lowered to the cushioned seat, watching him from across the room. He pulled his fingers through his hair. I fanned my face. His broad, muscular shoulders and ripened arms stood out underneath the charcoal suit. He slid those fingers over the laptop the same way he slid them across my skin. I crossed my legs and licked my lips, suddenly wishing I'd taken Greg's offer for water. Those pesky pregnancy hormones were dancing between my legs, heating the party in my body.

He stood up and turned to face the window.

Okay, it's now or never.

I took a deep breath and tiptoed to his desk. I lowered the square package wrapped in white paper near a paperweight, then went back to the couch. He turned just as I sat down. His gaze caught the little gift.

His brows lifted, and he smiled, mouthing, "For me?"

I wiggled my brows at him.

He covered the phone and whispered, "Two minutes."

Okay, this was good. He was interested.

Tristan finally lowered the phone.

"Hello, Allie." The deep rumble from his chest reminded me how much I missed him. He hadn't touched me since the shooting, and this hormonal body was getting desperate.

"It should be me showering you with gifts. I can never thank you enough for saving Kendra. Actually, I got you roses, but I think I left them in the car. I've had a lot on my mind lately. Too much."

"I'm happy Kendra was at the hotel and that Julian got to us both in time."

"I know. That's why I wanted to talk to you. About what

happened. And Hartley… The work you did for us was dangerous, and you were hurt. I'm very sorry about that, Allie. If I could turn back the time—"

"Tristan, I know you're not one to cry over spilled milk."

Was he nervous? Why was he so nervous? He straightened his suit jacket, squared his shoulders, quickly checked his watch, and cleared his throat.

"You sustained severe injuries, and we both know you can't work in the field for a while. Not after everything you've been through. The doctors were clear it will be months before you're back to your full strength."

He finally connected his gaze with mine. "And for that reason, Allie, you're fired."

Tristan's words rang in my ears on a loop. "You're fired. You're fired. You're fired."

I rose from the couch in what felt like slow motion. The wrapped gift box with baby booties I'd set on my billionaire boyfriend boss's desk seemed completely inappropriate now. I'd timed that one like a bomb because he'd fired me before I could tell my boss I was carrying his child. How could he have fired me?

"What?"

"I said, you're fired."

Oh, my God. I can't tell him I'm pregnant now.

"Why? I don't understand. I thought—"

"Surprise!"

The office door flew open, and I jumped back. Laura, my mom, the Flintstones, and Emma walked through the doorway. What was Laura doing here? Behind the immediate family were more deliciously handsome men than I'd ever seen in one room in my life. I recognized the Silver brothers, but not the others. My mouth opened and closed and opened again. Someone popped a confetti wand. Laura glanced around as if looking for the same answers I was seeking, while Tristan's father popped a bottle of champagne. I turned in a circle, searching for Tristan's face, but just as I found him, Emma slammed into to my side. She threw her arms tight around my leg, looked up, and batted her lashes.

"What's going on Ems? What is this?" I asked her.

"This is one less secret I have to keep, that's what it is."

Shit. Secret.

Laura hugged me next while my eyes grew wider and wider.

"Grab. The box. Off. The desk."

My ventriloquist impression must have failed because Laura's nose scrunched and she looked at me like I was losing my mind.

"What?"

"If you love me, you'll get that box with baby booties on Tristan's desk and run. I didn't tell him I'm pregnant yet."

"Allie, that's crazy. He loves you, and you're having his baby. He should know."

"I don't disagree, but right now is not the right time. I want it to be special, not in a crowd."

"All right, all right. I'll get it as soon as he steps away. You should preoccupy him. I'm sure you can figure something out with those hormones."

As if on cue, Tristan's gaze lowered to the box. The corner of his mouth lifted as he squinted and removed the gift off the desk.

"Shit, shit, shit. You have to help me, right now! He's gonna open it!"

Heat and cold passed through my body. The golden streams of sunlight filtered between the blinds like ribbons of silk. The sounds in the room mixed into one, lifting in tone, and my legs gave into gravity. The temporary weightlessness changed into a strong hold as Tristan caught me in his arms before I hit the floor.

"Are you all right?" His lips moved, but I couldn't hear him. A hum of concern hovered around me as I focused of faces until I found Tristan's face again.

"Are you all right?" he repeated.

He fired me?

The room stopped spinning. "Yeah, I think so. What happened?"

"You fainted. Did you eat anything today?"

"I did. I think I'm just a little overwhelmed, that's all. Can someone explain what's happening?"

Laura peeked from behind Tristan with a thumbs up. She stuffed the box in her purse as Tristan covered my head with his palm.

"I'm so sorry, Allie."

"I… I don't have a fever."

Someone set a glass with orange juice beside my head, and I sipped through the bent straw. My heart was hammering in my chest. Tristan helped me to the couch while everyone stared. The low conversation resumed when I sat down.

"Just checking. You look flushed."

Flushed?

But he'd fired me. I was much more than flushed.

"Help me up," I said.

Tristan lifted me by the elbow, and we walked away from the crowd. The conversation resumed, and the family's attention finally dwindled.

"Champagne?" Greg passed me a flute, but Tristan stopped him before I could remove it from his hand. The single moment pressed a panic button inside me. Did he somehow know I couldn't drink?

"I think she needs another minute."

"No, I think we're done here." I turned away and headed for the door, but Tristan was quicker and blocked my way before I reached the closing frame. A wave of attention flowed our way.

"Whoa, Allie, I beg you. Please let me explain. I have to fire you."

"You're the boss. You don't have to do anything you don't want to." The air I sucked in tiny breaths wasn't helping. "You clearly don't want me a part of Silver Securities."

The deafening silence in the room made me unaware of Tristan's guests. They stood frozen, staring at me like I'd lost my mind.

"Allie, baby. You don't know what you're saying."

When he said 'baby,' I broke down even further. I sucked in the sobs on short inhalations. My phone buzzed with a text from Emma. I reached into my pocket to read:

Emma: Don't be sad. I'm calling my niece or nephew Baby-Puss for now ;)

I looked across the room to where she was standing by the window, smiling. I wanted to be part of this family so much that it hurt. Tristan's little sister had helped me keep my secret by forging my blood work at the hospital in exchange for choosing the baby's name. So far, all of them had been from the Flintstones. And I loved that too.

I broke in half, and Tristan took me into his arms, holding me tight. "Allie, I'm so sorry. Firing you is just a technicality, so I can hire you for a new position."

"Technicality?" I blubbered through tears and snot and repeated, "Technicality for what?"

"I'm sorry. I should have known it would be overdramatic. It's been a long day." He blinked the clouds away and his whiskey eyes brightened. "Maybe surprising you with a new job wasn't a good idea."

I pulled in a weep. "A new job?" Then: "Overdramatic?"

If overdramatic had a face, yes, it would be Tristan's right now. But could this be true? I wasn't fired? Were we really going to work together again?

"Really? I still work for Silver Securities?"

"Of course you do. Like it or not, you're a part of this family for the rest of your life."

My chest warmed a little. When I'd woken up this morning, I was so sure of my path that I'd never have predicted a bombshell like losing my job. The moment he'd told me I was fired, that I could possibly be pregnant and out of work planted a seed of doubt I couldn't easily weed. I let go of his hand.

"I think I'm okay now. What's the new job?"

He cleared his throat and stood up. "Settle down, everyone."

Another moment of panic passed through me. Jesus, was he about to propose? I wasn't ready for that, but then again, I didn't think I was ready for this baby, either.

"Allie's fine, but I haven't told her about the new job yet."

"She should get checked by a doctor." My mother's brows lifted. She was looking at me funny, like she could see right through me and my temporarily flat stomach.

"No, really. I'm fine, Mom. Job? What job?" I focused on Tristan.

Shit.

I was so off my game. These hormones were not only playing with my body but also with my instincts.

The conversation silenced. Tristan turned around to face me again and took my hands into his. "If you agree, you'll head the new division at Silver Securities along with a new partner." He pointed to Laura, and my best friend grinned from ear to ear.

"What?" I gaped and turned toward her. "You're working with me? For Silver Securities?"

"Woot, woot!" She lifted her flute of champagne in cheer. "Can't argue that you'll get a better partner, can you?"

"And you've been keeping this secret from me?"

I saw Emma roll her eyes at my comment. All right. I was a hypocrite.

"Sorry not sorry."

"Wait a minute—what exactly will we be doing?"

"Silver Securities partnered with a local safe house to form a rehab team. The Green Team, will investigate, gather evidence, provide security, and hopefully, catch the criminals. The Wagner brothers formed a team to help you with the legalities."

"The Green Team? After me?"

He nodded, and my eyes welled. Oh, these new hormones were a real treat.

"After one of the strongest women I know. Sorry, Wilma."

His mother bent down and kissed him on his head like he was still her young boy, and my heart squeezed at the sight. "As long as you're happy, I'll be elated."

She then leaned in to hug me and whispered in my ear, "You look wonderful, Allie."

"Thank you."

Maggie and John Silver took such a liking to my mother that they'd asked her to permanently move into the guesthouse, and she agreed. Tristan was right. I was part of this family, and I couldn't wait to tell them all the good news.

"Tristan, this is wonderful. I can't believe you did this."

"I know how hard the past couple of months have been. I'm sorry for everything, Allie. Once you're well, Silver Securities can't wait to have you here permanently."

Tristan's phone beeped, and he checked his message. He stiffened and stared down the long hallway, eyeing the exit.

"Grab something to drink and eat up. Mom made coconut sweet buns, and she won't leave until they're all gone. Excuse me."

He kissed me on the cheek and left. I followed his quick step out the door to where he disappeared down the hallway. The smell of sweet pastries and roast beef sandwiches brought my attention back to the room. My mouth watered and my stomach grumbled. The delicious aroma overpowered my resistance, and the next thing I knew, I was sitting behind Tristan's desk with a plate full of fruit, sandwiches, and pastries. I stuffed them in my mouth one after the other.

Emma sat on the mahogany desk, swinging her legs. "So? What do you think?" she asked.

"They're delicious." I bit into a cream-stuffed puff ball.

"No, silly. I mean about Baby Puss."

"I think you should keep trying. Tristan won't go for it."

"Let's ask him, then." She wiggled her brows.

"Let's not." I rammed the remaining cream puff into my mouth. "I'm gonna need you to hold onto that little secret for a while longer."

"But that's not fair. Do you know how many secrets I have to keep?"

"A lot?" I shrank my neck back like a turtle. "But that's what makes you so special."

"One day, when I work here, I'll make it a rule to have no secrets."

My stomach turned, and Emma whispered, "But don't worry. I won't say a word about Baby Puss."

"Shh."

Laura hopped up on the other side of the desk. "I think this is the only time Mr. Silver will let me sit here. But don't tell him I did."

Emma jumped off the table. "That's it. I'm full. This is too many secrets, and I have phone calls to make."

She strolled out of the office like she owned the place, and Laura frowned. "I don't think she likes me."

"It's not you. It's all the secrets she keeps. Besides, she adores babysitting Foxy," I said.

"Have you ever thought asking her for other secrets she might know? You know, like about James?"

"You think he's hiding something?"

"I don't know, but he goes to the doctor every month."

"Why don't you ask Emma to help? She loves investigating."

"Maybe."

I jabbed my finger into her arm. "I can't believe you kept this surprise from me. You knew I was going to the office this morning."

"And you know how good I am at keeping secrets. It had to be a surprise, so don't shoot the messenger. And I was sworn to secrecy with a mighty sword."

"Would that sword happen to be James's dick?'

She coughed into her hand and looked at me like I was the one losing my mind. James was the only decent guy she'd ever dated. Getting stuck together during an avalanche was the best thing that could have happened to them, they just couldn't see it yet.

"It's not his dick. Emma has a new obsession with sword collection. You should see them. I literally mean she swore me to secrecy about this job with the sword."

"Oh, sorry."

"No, things are good with James. Real good. He's a good father."

"So maybe it's time to tell him?"

"But things are good now," she whined. If it were up to Laura, she would keep Foxy's paternity a secret forever, just to avoid conflict. But the longer she waited, the larger her lie grew.

"You're not digging yourself a grave, my friend. You're already on the other side of the planet! What the fuck, Laura?"

"I'm trying to tell him, but now we'll be working together, and that comes with a lot of benefits I'm not ready to part with."

"What benefits?"

"His dick." She shrugged. "Or, at least, the potential of his dick."

"So you haven't slept with him yet?"

"Please, don't rub it in. I've rubbed it out enough. Don't get me wrong, I'd love to, but I can't get myself to do it because"—she curled her shoulders in and bent at the spine—"Because…"

"So what benefits are you taking about?"

Her mouth curved. "His arms, his smile, and I already know what's under those clothes even if I haven't seen it all for three years. But hell, it doesn't stop me from imagining all the naughty things we could be doing."

Yeah, I knew exactly what she meant, and so did my hormones. Before I'd arrived tonight, I'd had the silly image of Tristan grabbing me into his arms and spinning me high in the air. He'd be elated about becoming a father and would grin with that cute dimple. The scar on his upper lip would twist into one of those sexy daddy smiles. God, he would look good on a playground with his little one.

Guilt chewed at my patience. I'd have to tell him I was pregnant as soon as the opportunity presented itself. I glanced over to the window where he was standing, tall and wise, talking to one of the Wagner brothers. I still couldn't believe the man who walked into the auditorium was my man. When I weaseled my way inside the company for revenge, I'd had no clue he'd become a permanent part of my life. A life which had changed so quickly the past couple of months, it was difficult to predict the upcoming winter. Chills swept over my arms.

The dimple sank into his cheek and the scar on his upper lip twisted his smile into a sexy lopsided grin. Ah, how I wished I could touch that lip with my mouth and pussy. His whiskey eyes caught my stare, and my nipples hardened.

"You have to tell him." Laura urged. "You two are meant to be, no question about it."

"And you can't keep your secret forever. Foxy's growing up."

"That's not true. I didn't think I could introduce him to James, but it's worked so far. And Ems is keeping the secret."

"Until she blows."

"I may have not made the connection, Laura, but James would if you stopped dressing Foxy in costumes."

"Laila loves clowns. We went to a park to feed the ducks, and we even went to the aquarium. See? Quality time. Things are working out. Sort of."

"You put makeup on Foxy so his father wouldn't recognize him," I loud-whispered.

"Says the woman who hasn't told her boyfriend she's carrying."

"Shh." My mother side-eyed me from the corner. I'd visited with her yesterday to see how she was settling in, and she absolutely glowed. The move and safety the Silvers had given her was something I could never pay back. Nor did anyone make me feel like I had to. I would tell Tristan about our baby when the time was right, no sooner and no later. And that time wasn't right now.

"It's still early, but I'm telling him soon. There's no way I'm keeping this going for as long as you have."

She sank into her seat and reached for a marshmallow-topped brownie.

"That's what I used to say. Then I met James, and I really got to know him... and everything changed. He's an amazing father. And those eyes..."

She sighed like I'd never heard her sigh before. I wasn't sure whether she was talking about her son's eyes or James's, but it didn't matter—because they had the same eyes. The fact that James hadn't caught on boggled my mind. Then again, Laura had done a great job covering up her truth. Did she regret not telling James earlier? A good father had missed out on two years of his son's life.

I touched her arm. "Laura—"

"Did you see that beard? I mean, how many twenty-year-olds could pull off that growth?"

"I know exactly what you mean. The stamina, the experience, no bullshit. All the more reason you should tell him sooner than later."

"Look at us," she purred. "Perfect on the outside, full of secrets on the inside. One's hiding a son and the other a fetus. No twenty-year-old could handle our shit, so be grateful they're older."

Tristan would be happy once I told him I was pregnant, wouldn't he?

"I don't think they have a clue what's coming their way."

Laura laughed, and I slouched into the couch. I turned my head toward her. She reached to the side table beside her and passed me a chocolate praline truffle. I bit into the sweetness, and the chocolate melted on my tongue. The custom-ordered chocolates with a Silver Brothers logo stamped into the cut were always set in a bowl at Tristan's penthouse, and they were officially my favorite.

"Who's the redhead?" Laura asked.

"What?"

"Tall, thin, and territorial."

My back straightened. I scanned the room, but couldn't see the woman Laura had described.

"Territorial over what? Has Foxy kept you up at night?"

"No, but his daddy did." She winked. "Do you realize if we marry them, we'll have the same last name?"

"Marriage is not on the table."

"It's hypothetical, silly. It's not like I want that piece of fine man to wake up next to me every morning just so I can pick out a leftover crumb from his beard."

"Eww, gross. I'm glad Tristan's growth is not long enough to catch food."

"You'd disagree if you actually saw James in all his glory. They don't make boys in his shape. Those years of experience are hard-earned."

"Can we please stop talking about growth and men in

general, at least, until you actually sleep with him? I'm horny enough as it is. Now, what were you saying about a redhead?" I sipped my water. I was carrying the bottle everywhere with me because the doctor said hydration was important.

"I saw her earlier in the hall by the bathrooms. I thought she was Tristan's secretary because they were talking."

"Tristan's secretary is blond, and he's over there." I pointed to Greg, who was chatting with one of the Wagner brothers. The lawyers were sitting in the waiting area outside, enjoying what looked like a rare moment of peace. I took in the gathering. This company and all its employees blew my mind. The teamwork and diligence, brotherhood, friendships, close relatives, and trustworthy workforce worked for a reason, and I could see that reason playing out right in front of me. They trusted each other, and it was one of the many reasons I trusted Tristan.

"No, the redhead was definitely a woman," Laura said. "The oversized hat didn't catch your attention?"

"No, the chocolate croissants did."

She looked me over and smirked like she knew something I didn't. "I know they say you're eating for two, but the daily amount of calories required during a pregnancy is not that high."

"Shut up and don't judge. It's the only thing that will keep the hormones at bay for now. They don't tell you about this part in the books, but I googled it."

"You googled it? You could have asked me, you know. Seventy-three percent of pregnant women experience an increased sex drive."

"You were younger. I'm older."

She laughed. "I got pregnant three years ago, babe. Welcome to the knocked-up-in-her-early-twenties club."

"What happened three years ago?" James handed Laura a

glass of wine. The color drained from her face, and she took a quick sip.

"We were reminiscing about our Christmas in Colorado three years ago."

Laura took another sip, glaring at me to shut the fuck up.

The corner of his mouth lifted. "Yeah, that was a life-changing night, wasn't it? It's a miracle everyone came out alive."

"Hey, who was the redhead talking to Tristan earlier?" I asked him.

"Redhead?" His brows furrowed, and for a split second I thought he knew exactly who it was. "Not anyone I'm aware of."

"It must be his mistress." Laura lowered her voice, and I rolled my eyes.

"Tristan doesn't have another woman." I said.

"It was hypothetical."

"Well, he doesn't have a hypothetical woman either."

James shook his head. "You two crack me up."

"Why would he take her inside a conference room?" she asked.

James looked over his shoulder to the main hall. "Redhead, you say?"

"They went in the conference room together?" I mouthed.

The news dropped into the pit of my bottomless stomach, convincing me I needed another croissant.

"It's probably a client."

"On the weekend?"

"There are no weekends when you own a business."

"Laura's right. Our work is part of our lives, and business hours are all hours. With perks. Excuse me for a moment."

James left Tristan's office, and quickened his step down the hall.

"Is it normal for James to leave like that?" I asked.

"No, it's not, but I'm sure it's nothing."

"That's exactly what you say when it's something."

Tristan returned later that afternoon, but I didn't see James again. I drove home with Laura, and we picked Foxy up from the babysitter's on the way home. While my godson settled into his routine, I couldn't shake off the gnawing dread that had snuck up on me out of nowhere. The uneasiness only got worse, so I showered and decided to surprise Tristan. I changed into sexy lingerie that left nothing to the imagination, threw on a long coat, and left for Manhattan. Something had to give, and I prayed that something was my hormones.

Allie and Tristan's sizzling adventure continues in *Silver's Secret*, Book 4 in the *Silver Brothers Securities Family Saga*.

Silver's
SECRET
USA TODAY BESTSELLING AUTHOR
LACEY SILKS

ABOUT THE AUTHOR

USA Today Bestselling Author Lacey Silks crafts riveting romantic suspense filled with heat, spice, and pulse-pounding tension. Many of her endearing characters are inspired by her own life, and her loved ones often find themselves playfully woven into her tales. Her two children and her dog, Kygo, keep her days lively with homework queries and affectionate slobbery kisses (courtesy of Kygo, of course).

Outside of penning intense love stories, Lacey is an avid camper and skier. Naturally an early riser, she often finds herself reaching for coffee over water, crediting her billionaire heroes for her packed schedule.

Lacey's characters, replete with flaws and quirks, evoke laughter, sass, and emotion on every page. She cheekily measures men by their foot size, has a penchant for sultry lingerie, and harbors dreams of exploring the nation in a motorhome.

ACKNOWLEDGMENTS

Silver's Pawn is just the beginning of a very long family saga and I hope the intertwined stories will stay with you for a while. They've helped me escape those pesky life moments. These stories gave me hope for a happily ever after, which is not always as easy to find in real life as it is in books.

I couldn't have done the work without my reader support or the ever-inspiring indie author community filled with a wealth of knowledge. The continued encouragement and faith in my work, along with the outpouring of love, replenished my muse.

To my amazing editor who always finds the time for me, thank you for making my life easy and my writing understandable. I will chuckle over those 'silver eyes' for a while.

To my beta readers, thank you for your keen eyes! Once I read a story twenty times (or more), the details aren't easy to spot. Your feedback is invaluable and makes the novel what it should be. You make my words make sense.

To my family, the past few years have tested us in more ways than we would have liked, and I could not do what I love without you. Thank you for your support, faith and encouragement.

Maya, thank you for your artistic eye and cover design. I'm honoured to watch you grow and develop as an artist. Alex, your loving heart and sense of humour are a constant inspiration.

To my parents, this book would not have happened without you. Thank you for believing in my dreams.